STAR TREK®

STARFLEET
YEAR ONE

MICHAEL JAN FRIEDMAN

POCKET BOOKS

New York   London   Toronto   Sydney   Singapore

For Joan, One of Two

An *Original* Publication of POCKET BOOKS

 POCKET BOOKS, a division of Simon & Schuster, Inc.
1230 Avenue of the Americas, New York, NY 10020

Copyright © 2001 by Paramount Pictures. All Rights Reserved.

STAR TREK is a Registered Trademark of Paramount Pictures.

A VIACOM COMPANY

This book is published by Pocket Books, a division of Simon & Schuster, Inc., under exclusive license from Paramount Pictures.

All rights reserved, including the right to reproduce this book or portions thereof in any form whatsoever. For information address Pocket Books, 1230 Avenue of the Americas, New York, NY 10020

ISBN: 0-7434-3788-8

First Pocket Books printing March 2002

10 9 8 7 6 5 4 3 2 1

POCKET and colophon are registered trademarks of Simon & Schuster, Inc.

For information regarding special discounts for bulk purchases, please contact Simon & Schuster Special Sales at 1-800-456-6798 or business@simonandschuster.com

Printed in the U.S.A.

ACKNOWLEDGMENTS

Starfleet Year One is a special book in a lot of ways. First, it was the first in-depth look ever taken at that critical point in Star Trek time when the Romulan War ended and the Federation got under way.

That same year, you'll recall, also gave birth to the entity known as Starfleet. But it was a very different Starfleet, made up of captains without Academy training or any recognition of principles like the Prime Directive—because at this juncture, there was no Prime Directive and the Academy was just getting started.

The second element that set this project apart was its dearth of characters seen on the big or small screen. To my knowledge, every other Star Trek book has featured at least a cameo by someone we've met on TV or in the movies. In its original form, Starfleet had no such appearances. (In this expanded form I've added one screen-established character. However, she's more than a hundred years younger than when we saw her last, so I'm not sure that counts.)

Finally, this book is different because it was originally presented in a serialized format, the Star Trek publishing program's first attempt at such a stunt. That our twelve-month venture wasn't an unmitigated disaster is evidenced by the fact that Pocket was willing to go through that ringer all over again.

I was happy to blaze that trail, like the captains of my fledgling Starfleet going where no one (in his or her right mind) had ever gone before. But like any smart captain, I first made sure I was surrounded by the best and bravest of colleagues.

One was John Ordover, Pocket Books editor and Whiz

ACKNOWLEDGMENTS

Kid throwback to the days when science fiction made your heart pound. John liked the Year One idea from the beginning, tendered his usual invaluable contributions, and helped me turn the heat up a notch. He also functioned like a magazine editor, editing each monthly installment as it came in. I'm not sure which of us had more fun.

Then there's Scott Shannon, Pocket Books publisher. In this rather offbeat project, as in so many others, Scott has been quick to see the possibilities and steadfast in his support. If I say *Starfleet Year One* couldn't have been done without his vision and his resolve, it's the simple truth.

And where would I have been without Paula Block of Paramount Licensing? As usual, Paula was willing to go out on a long and shaky limb in the hope of giving our readers something new and satisfying, because at heart she's a fan herself. I've always been touched by the trust she's shown in me, and this time was no exception.

Finally, I want to mention Jessica McGiveny, who was a publishing assistant when this story began and has since received a well-deserved promotion. Jessica shepherded the serial through the publishing process, never missing a twist in the road—and there were many. On occasion, she even hand-delivered page proofs for my approval. (Really.)

And then there's Walter Emick, whose contribution shall remain mysterious but whose generosity was much appreciated.

And there you have it—the team that made *Starfleet Year One* a reality. On their behalf, I welcome you to the wonders and terrors of the twenty-second century, where the universe is a much bigger and more ominous place and the fascinating creature known as the Starfleet Captain is just a-bornin'.

Enjoy . . .

CHAPTER
1

COMMANDER BRYCE SHUMAR COULDN'T BELIEVE HIS turbolift had gotten stuck again.

For a moment, he just stood there, trying to remain calm—hopeful that it was just a temporary malfunction. Then his patience was rewarded as the narrow, dimly lit compartment jerked and labored and resumed its uncertain ascent.

The damned thing hadn't been running as smoothly as he would have liked for several months already. The cranky, all-too-familiar whine of the component that drove the compartment only underlined what the commander already knew—that the system was on its last legs.

Under normal circumstances, new turbolift parts would have appeared at the base in a matter of weeks— maybe less. But lift parts weren't exactly a tactical priority, so Shumar and his people were forced to make do with what they had.

After a few moments, the component cycled down and the commander's ascent was complete. Then the doors parted with a loud hiss and revealed a noisy, bustling operations center—Ops for short. It was packed with one sleek, black console after another—all of them manned, and all of them enclosed in a transparent dome that featured a breathtaking view of the stars.

The first day Shumar had set foot there, the place had impressed the hell out of him—almost enough to make him forget the value of what he had lost. But that was four long years ago. Now, he had learned to take it all for granted.

The big, convex viewer located in the center of the facility echoed the curve of the sprawling security console below it. Fixing his gaze on the screen, Shumar saw two ships making their way through the void on proximate parallel courses.

One was a splendid, splay-winged Rigelian transport vessel, its full-bellied hull the deep blue color of a mountain lake. The other was a black, needle-sharp Cochrane, capable of speeds as high as warp one point six, according to some reports.

It was hardly an unusual pairing, given the Cochrane's tactical advantages and the dangerous times in which they lived. Vessels carrying important cargo were almost always given escorts. Still, thought Shumar, it wouldn't hurt to make sure the ships were what they appeared to be.

"Run a scan," he told his redhaired security officer.

Morgan Kelly shot a glance at him over her shoulder.

"Might I remind the commander," she said, "that no Romulan has used subterfuge to approach an Earth base since the war began? Not even once?"

"Consider me reminded," Shumar told her, "and run the scan anyway."

"Way ahead of you," said Kelly, only half-suppressing a smile. She pointed to a monitor on her left, where the vessels' energy signatures were displayed. "According to our equipment, everything checks out. Those two are exactly what they're cracked up to be—a transport and its keeper."

Shumar frowned. "Tell them I'll meet them downstairs."

"Aye, sir," said the security officer. "And I'll be sure to tell them also what a lovely mood you're in."

The commander looked at her. "What kind of mood would *you* be in if you'd just learned your vessel had been destroyed?"

Kelly grunted. "Begging the commander's pardon, but it was nearly a month ago that you got that news."

Shumar's frown deepened. Had it really been that long since he learned what happened to the *John Burke?* "Time flies," he remarked drily, "when you're having fun."

Then he made his way back to the turbolift.

Though not a human himself, Alonis Cobaryn had seen his share of Earth bases floating in the void.

The one he saw on his primary monitor now was typical of the breed. It possessed a dark, boxlike body, four ribbed cargo globes that vaguely resembled the legs of a very slow quadruped on his homeworld, and a transparent bubble that served as the facility's brain.

3

There was also nothing unusual about the procedure he had been instructed to follow in his approach. And now that he was within a few kilometers of the base, Cobaryn was expected to begin that procedure.

But first, he pulled a toggle to switch one of his secondary monitors to a communications function. After all, he always liked to see in whose hands he was placing his molecular integrity.

The monitor screen fizzed over with static for a moment, then showed him the Earth base's security officer—a woman with high cheekbones, green eyes, and red hair pulled back into a somewhat unruly knot. What's more, she filled out her gold and black jumpsuit rather well.

All in all, Cobaryn mused, a rather attractive-looking individual. *For a human, that is.*

It took her about a second to take note of the visual link and look back at him. "If you were planning on cutting your engines," the woman told him, "this would be as good a time as any."

Cobaryn's mouth pulled up at the corners—as close as he could come to a human smile. "I could not agree more," he said. Tapping the requisite sequence into the touch pad of his helm-control console, he looked up again. "I have cut my engines."

"Acknowledged," said the security officer, checking her monitors with admirable efficiency to make sure all was as it should be.

Next, Cobaryn applied his braking thrusters until he had reduced his vessel's momentum to zero and assumed a position within half a kilometer of the base. The facility loomed larger than ever on his primary monitor, a dark blot on the stars.

"That'll be fine," the redhaired woman told him.

"I am pleased that you think so," he responded.

The officer's green eyes narrowed a bit, but she wasn't adverse to the banter. At least, that was how it seemed to Cobaryn.

"I suppose you'd like to beam over now," she said.

"If it is not too much trouble."

"And if it is?" the woman asked playfully.

Cobaryn shrugged. "Then I would be deprived of the opportunity to thank you for your assistance in person."

She chuckled. "You Rigelians don't lack confidence, do you?"

"I cannot speak for others," he remarked thoughtfully, "but as for myself...I do indeed believe that confidence is a virtue."

The officer considered him a moment longer. "Too bad your pal in the Cochrane doesn't have the same attitude."

Cobaryn tilted his head. "And why is that?" he inquired, at a loss as to the human's meaning.

A coy smile blossomed on the officer's face. "No offense, Captain, but the Cochrane jockey's a lot better-looking." Then she went on, almost in the same breath, "Get ready to beam over."

Cobaryn sat back in his chair, deflated by the woman's remark—if only for a moment. Then he recalled that humans often said the opposite of what they meant. Perhaps that was the case here.

"Ready," he replied.

"Good," said the security officer, embracing a lever in each hand. "Then here goes."

* * *

Commander Shumar stood in one of his base's smallest, darkest rooms and watched a faint shimmer of light appear like a will-o'-the-wisp over a raised transporter disc.

Gradually, the shimmer grew along its vertical axis. Then a ghostly image appeared in the same space—a vague impression of a muscular, silver-skinned humanoid dressed in loose-fitting black togs.

The transport captain, Shumar remarked inwardly. Obviously, he had been nicer to Kelly than the pilot of the Cochrane, or the security officer would have beamed the other man over first.

The base commander watched the shaft of illumination dim as the figure flickered, solidified, flickered again and solidified a bit more. Finally, after about forty-five seconds, the process was complete and the vertical blaze of light died altogether.

A moment later, a host of blue emergency globes activated themselves in a continuous line along the bulkheads. By their glare, Shumar could make out his guest's silvery features and ruby-red eyes, which gleamed beneath a flared brow ridge reminiscent of a triceratops' bony collar.

He was a Rigelian, the commander noted. More specifically, a denizen of Rigel IV, not to be confused with any of the other four inhabited planets in the Rigel star system. And he was smiling awkwardly.

Of course, smiling was a peculiarly Terran activity. It wasn't uncommon for aliens to look a little clumsy at it—which is why so few of them even made the attempt.

"Welcome to Earth Base Fourteen," said the human.

"Thank you," the Rigelian replied with what seemed

like studied politeness. He stepped down from the disc and extended a three-fingered hand. "Alonis Cobaryn at your service, Commander."

Shumar gripped the transport captain's offering. It felt much like a human appendage except for some variations in metacarpal structure and a complete lack of hair.

"You shake hands," the base commander observed.

"I do," Cobaryn confirmed.

Shumar studied him. "Most nonhumans don't, you know."

The Rigelian's ungainly smile widened, stretching an elaborate maze of tiny ridges that ran from his temples down to his jaw. "I have dealt with your people for a number of years now," he explained. "Sometimes I imagine I know as much about them as any human."

Shumar grunted. "I wish I could say the same about Rigelians. You're the first one I've seen in person in four years on this base."

"I am not surprised," said Cobaryn, his tone vaguely apologetic. "My people typically prefer the company of other Rigelians. In that I relish the opportunity to explore the intricacies of other cultures, I am considered something of a black sheep on my homeworld."

Suddenly, realization dawned. "Wait a minute," said the human. "Cobaryn...? Aren't you the fellow who charted Sector Two-seven-five?"

The alien lowered his hairless silver head ever so slightly. "I see that my reputation has preceded me."

Shumar found himself smiling. "I used your charts to navigate the Galendus Cluster on my way to—"

Before he could finish his sentence, the emergency illumination around them dimmed and another glimmer of light appeared over the transporter disc. Like the one before it, it lengthened little by little and gave rise to something clearly man-shaped.

This one was human, the base commander noted— the pilot of the Cochrane, no doubt. Shumar watched the shape flicker and take on substance by turns. In time, the new arrival became solid, the shaft of light fizzled out, and the emergency globes activated themselves again.

This time, they played on a tall, athletic-looking specimen with a lean face, close-cropped blond hair, and slate-blue eyes. His garb was civilian, like that of most escort pilots these days—a brown leather jacket over a rumpled, gray jumpsuit.

"Welcome to the base," said the commander. "My name's Shumar."

The other man looked at him for a second, but he didn't say a thing in return. Then he got down from the platform, walked past his fellow human, and left the transporter room by its only set of sliding doors.

As the titanium panels slid closed again, shutting out the marginally brighter light of the corridor outside, Shumar turned to Cobaryn. "What's the matter with your friend?" he asked, as puzzled as he was annoyed.

The Rigelian smiled without much enthusiasm. "Captain Dane is not very communicative. The one time we spoke, he described himself as a loner." He regarded the doors with his ruby-red orbs. "Frankly, given his attitude, I am surprised he takes part in the war effort at all."

"The *one* time?" Shumar echoed. He didn't get it. "But he was your escort, wasn't he?"

"He was," Cobaryn confirmed in a neutral tone. "Still,

as I noted, he was not a very loquacious one. He appeared to be troubled by something, though I cannot imagine what it might have been."

Shumar frowned. "It wouldn't hurt him to say a few words when he sets foot on someone else's base. I mean, I'm not exactly thrilled about my lot in life either right now, but I keep it to myself."

The Rigelian's eyes narrowed. "You would rather be somewhere else?"

"On a research vessel," Shumar told him unhesitatingly, "conducting planetary surveys. That's what I did before the war. Unfortunately, I'll have to get hold of a new ship if I want to pick up where I left off."

"The old one was commandeered, then?" asked Cobaryn.

Shumar nodded. "Four years ago, when I was given command of this place. Then, a little more than a month ago, it was blown to bits by the Romulans out near Gamma Llongo."

The Rigelian sighed. "You and I have much in common, then."

The commander looked at him askance. "Don't tell me they pressed *you* into service. You're not even human."

"Perhaps not," said Cobaryn. "But it is difficult to pursue a career as an explorer and stellar cartographer when the entire quadrant has become a war zone." His eyes crinkled at the corners. "Besides, it is foolish to pretend the Romulans are a threat to Earth alone."

"A number of species have done just that," Shumar noted, airing one of his pet peeves.

The Rigelian nodded wistfully. "Including my own, I

hesitate to admit. However, I cannot change my people's minds. All I can do is lend my own humble efforts to the cause and hope for the best."

The commander found the sentiment hard to argue with. "Come on," he said. "I'll arrange for some dinner. I'll bet you're dying for some fresh muttle pods after all those rations."

Cobaryn chuckled softly. "Indeed I am. And then, after dinner..."

Shumar glanced at him. "Yes?"

The Rigelian shrugged. "Perhaps you could introduce me to your security officer? The one with the splendid red hair?"

The request took the commander by surprise. "You mean Kelly?"

"Kelly," Cobaryn repeated, rolling the name a little awkwardly over his tongue. "A pleasing name. I would be most grateful."

The commander considered it. As far as he knew, his security officer wasn't attracted to nonhumans. But then, the Rigelian had asked for an introduction, not a weekend in Tahoe.

"If you like," Shumar suggested, "I can ask the lieutenant if she'd like to dine with us."

"Even better," said Cobaryn.

The Rigelian looked like a kid in a candy shop, thought the commander. He wasn't the least bit self-conscious about expressing his yen for Kelly—even to a man he had only just met.

Shumar found it hard not to like someone like that.

CHAPTER
2

AS CONNOR DANE ENTERED THE REC LOUNGE AT EARTH Base Fourteen, he didn't even consider parking himself at one of the small black tables the base's crew seemed so fond of. Instead, he made his way straight to the bar.

The bartender was tall, thin, and dour-faced, but he seemed to perk up a little at the sight of the newcomer. Of course, he probably didn't see too many new faces in his line of work.

"Get you something?" he asked.

Dane nodded. "Tequila, neat. And a beer to chase it with."

"We've got a *dozen* beers," said the bartender.

The Cochrane jockey slid himself onto a stool. "Your choice."

The bartender smiled as if his customer had made a joke. "You sure you wouldn't want to hear our list?"

"Life's too short," said Dane. "Just close your eyes and reach into the freezer. I promise I won't send it back, whatever it is."

The bartender's brow knit. "You're not kidding, are you?"

"I'm not kidding," the captain assured him.

The bartender shrugged. "Whatever you say."

A moment later, he produced a shot glass full of pale gold liquor. And a moment after that, he plunked a bottle of amber beer down beside it, a wisp of frosty vapor trailing from its open mouth.

"There you go," he said. He leaned back against the shelf behind him and folded his arms across his chest. "I guess you'd be the Cochrane jock who checked in a couple of minutes ago."

Dane didn't answer, hoping the man would get the message. As luck would have it, he didn't.

"You know," said the bartender, "my brother flew one of those needlenoses back before the war." He looked at the ceiling as if he were trying to remember something. "Must have been ten, eleven—"

"Listen, pal," Dane snapped, his voice taut and preemptive.

It got the bartender's attention. "What?"

"I know a lot of people come to places like this for conversation. Maybe your commander does that, or that foxy redheaded number behind the security console. But I'm not looking for anything like that. All I want is to kick back a little and pretend I'm somewhere besides a hunk of titanium in the middle of—"

Suddenly, a high-pitched ringing sound filled the place. Scowling at the interruption, Dane turned to the emergency monitor above the bar—one of hundreds located all around the base.

A moment later, the screen came alive, showing him the swarthy, dark-browed visage of the man in charge of the place. What was the commander's name again? he asked himself. Shumac? No…Shu*mar.* He didn't often pay attention to things like that, but this time the name seemed to have stuck.

"Attention," said the base commander, the muscles working in his temples. "All hands to battle stations. Our long-range scanners have detected a Romulan attack force at a distance of twenty-six million kilometers."

The Cochrane jockey bit his lip. At full impulse, the Romulans would arrive in something under eleven minutes. That didn't leave him much time.

As the lounge's contingent of uniformed officers bolted for the door, Dane raised his glass of tequila and downed it at a gulp. Then he took a long swig of his beer and wiped his mouth with the back of his hand.

The bartender looked at him as if he'd grown another head. "Didn't you hear what the commander said?" he asked.

The captain nodded. "I heard." Ignoring the man's concern, he held his beer up to the light, admiring its consistency. Then he raised the bottle's mouth to his lips and took another long pull at its contents.

"But…" the bartender sputtered, "if you heard, what the devil are you still *doing* here?"

Dane smiled grimly at him. "The Romulans may rip this base in half, pal. They may even kill me. But I'll be damned if they're going to keep me from enjoying a re-freshing beverage."

Finally, he finished off his beer and placed the bottle on the bar. Then he got up from his stool, pulled down on the front of his jacket, and headed back to the base's only transporter room.

His message to his staff delivered, Commander Shumar turned from the two-way viewscreen set into the Ops center's comm console and eyed the officer seated beside him.

"Have you got the *Nimitz* yet?" he asked.

Ibañez, who had been Shumar's communications officer for the last two and a half years, looked more perturbed than the commander had ever seen him. "Not yet," the man replied, making adjustments to his control settings.

"What's wrong?" Shumar asked.

"They're just not responding," Ibañez told him.

The commander cursed under his breath. "How can that be? They're supposed to be listening twenty-four hours a day."

The comm officer shook his head from side to side. "I don't know what the trouble is, sir."

Shumar glared at the console's main screen, where he could see Ibañez's hail running over and over again on all Earth Command frequencies. Then he gazed at the stars that blazed above him. Why in hell didn't the *Nimitz* answer? he wondered.

According to the last intelligence Shumar had received from Command, the Christopher-class vessel was within ninety million kilometers of Base Fourteen.

At that distance, one might expect a communications delay of several seconds, but no more. And yet, Ibañez had been trying to raise the *Nimitz* for nearly a minute without success.

Without the warship's clout, the commander reflected, they wouldn't be able to withstand a Romulan attack for very long. No Earth base could. Clearly, they had a problem on their hands.

Of course, there was still a chance the *Nimitz* would respond. Shumar fervently hoped that that would be the case.

"Keep trying them," he told Ibañez.

"Aye, sir," came the reply.

Crossing the room, the commander passed by the engineering and life support consoles on his way to the security station. When he reached Kelly, he saw her look up at him. She seemed to sense his concern.

"What's the matter?" the redhead asked.

Shumar suppressed a curse. "We're having trouble raising the *Nimitz*."

Kelly's eyes widened. "Tell me you're kidding."

"I'm not the kidding type," he reminded her.

She swallowed. "That's right. You're not."

The commander leaned a little closer to her. "This could be a mess, Kelly. I'm going to need your help."

She took a breath, then let it out. It seemed to steady her. "I'm with you," the security officer assured him.

That settled, Shumar took a look at the monitors on Kelly's console. The Romulan warships, represented by four red blips on the long-range scanner screen, were bearing down on them. They had less than ten minutes to go before visual contact.

The commander turned his attention to the transporter monitor, where he could see that someone was being beamed off the station. "That Cochrane pilot had better be good," he said.

Kelly tapped a fingernail on the transporter screen. "That's not the Cochrane pilot. That's Cobaryn."

Shumar looked at her. "What . . . ?"

The woman shrugged. "The Rigelian showed up in the transporter room and the Cochrane jock didn't. Who was I to argue?"

The commander's teeth ground together. True, Cobaryn had a valuable cargo to protect—medicines and foodstuffs that might be of help to some other Earth base—and technically, this wasn't his fight.

But the Rigelian had seemed so engaging—so *human* in many respects. And by human standards, it seemed like a slimy thing to abandon a base at the first sign of trouble.

"Transport complete," said Kelly, reading the results off the pertinent screen. "Cobaryn is out of here."

Shumar forced himself to wish the Rigelian luck. "What about the Cochrane pilot? He's got to be around the base—"

His officer held her hand up. "Hang on a second, Commander. I think our friend has finally arrived." Her fingers flying over her controls, she opened a channel to the transporter room. "This is security. Nothing like taking your sweet time, Captain."

"Better late than never," came the casual response.

Obviously, Shumar observed, Dane wasn't easily flustered. But then, that might be a good thing. After all, the Cochrane might be all the help they would get.

"Get on the platform," said Kelly.

"I'm on it," Dane answered.

The security officer took that as a signal to manipulate her controls. Pulling back slowly on a series of levers, she tracked the dematerialization and emission processes on her transporter screen. Then she glanced meaningfully at the commander.

"He's on his way," said Kelly.

Shumar nodded soberly. "I sincerely hope the man's a better pilot than he is a human being."

The first thing Connor Dane noticed as he materialized in his cockpit was the flashing proximity alarm on his control panel.

He swore volubly, thinking that the base's scanners had been off a few light-years and that the Romulans had arrived earlier than expected. But as he checked his external scan monitor, the captain realized it wasn't the Romulans who had set off the alarm.

It was the Rigelian transport.

Craning his neck to look out of his cockpit's transparent hood, Dane confirmed the scan reading. For some reason, that idiot Cobaryn hadn't taken off yet. He was still floating in space beside the Cochrane.

Shaking his head, Dane punched a stud in his panel and activated his vessel's communications function. "Cobaryn," he said, "this is Dane. You've got to move your blasted ship!"

He expected to hear a response taut with urgency. However, the Rigelian didn't sound the least bit distressed.

"I assure you," said Cobaryn, "I *intend* to move it."

The human didn't understand. "For Earthsakes, when?"

"When the enemy arrives," the transport captain replied calmly.

"But it'll be too late by then," Dane argued, fighting the feeling that he was swimming upstream against a serious flood of reality.

"Too late to escape," Cobaryn allowed. "But not too late to take part in the battle."

The human didn't get it. Maybe the tequila had affected him more than he'd imagined. "You've got no weapons," he reminded the Rigelian. "How are you planning to slug it out in a space battle?"

"I would be perfectly happy to discuss tactics with you," Cobaryn told him reasonably, "but I think the time for discussion is past. It appears the Romulans have arrived."

Spurred by the remark, Dane checked his scan monitor. Sure enough, there were four Romulan warships nearing visual range.

Bringing his engines online, he raised his shields and powered up his weapons batteries. Then he put the question of the transport captain aside and braced himself for combat.

Shumar eyed the Romulan vessels on Kelly's screen. At high mag, each one showed up as a sleek, silver cylinder with a cigar-shaped plasma nacelle on either side of it and a blue-green winged predator painted on its underbelly.

No question about it, the base commander mused grimly. The enemy had a flair for the dramatic.

"Shields up," he said. "Stand by, all weapons stations."

Kelly leaned forward and pulled down on a series of toggles. "Shields up," she confirmed. She checked a couple of readouts. "Weapons stations standing by, awaiting your orders."

Shumar's stomach had never felt so tight. But then, in the past, Romulan assault forces had been deflected from the base by the *Nimitz* or some other Terran vessel. In four years as commander, he had never had to mount a lone defense against an enemy attack.

Until *now*.

"Fifty kilometers," said Kelly. "Forty. Thirty. Twenty . . ." Suddenly, she looked up at the transparent dome and pointed at a swarm of silver dots. "There they are!"

CHAPTER
3

His heart pounding at the sight of the Romulans, Shumar was tempted to give the order to fire. However, he held the impulse in check, knowing his weapons would pack a bigger wallop at close range.

On the other hand, so would the enemy's.

"Ten kilometers," Kelly announced. "They're firing missiles!"

Even as the words escaped the security officer's lips, a swarm of blunt silver missiles rained down on the Earth base. Shumar felt the deck shudder beneath him as they exploded against the shields, sending up gouts of white fire that blotted out the stars.

"Deflectors down twenty-five percent," Kelly reported. "No casualties, no structural damage."

So far, the commander thought.

As the atomic fires faded and the Romulans peeled off for another pass, Shumar leaned over the security console's intercom grid. "All stations," he barked, "target and fire!"

Suddenly, a pack of black and gold projectiles erupted from the Earth base's four separate launchers. The barrage caught up with the enemy vessels before they could climb out of range, detonating with the same atomic fury the Romulans had unleashed moments earlier.

Unlike the Earth base, however, the invaders' ships were moving targets—and they had put that advantage to good use. Even without the benefit of his scanners, the commander could tell that he hadn't scored any direct hits. At best, he had shaken the Romulans up a bit.

Then he saw something dart through the blossoms of white fire like a streamlined black wasp, stabbing at one of the invaders with a stinger of splendid blue energy. At such close quarters, the Romulan's shields couldn't stand up against the laser attack. All the enemy could do was attempt to shake its tormentor.

But the Cochrane pilot wouldn't veer off. Despite the danger that one of the other intruders would draw a bead on him, he twisted and turned against the reemerging stars and stung his prey again and again.

Finally, Dane's tenacity paid off. His laser beams penetrated the Romulan ship's deflector shields and pierced its hull in the right place. There was an immense, silent burst of white light—and when it receded, the invader vessel was gone.

One down, Shumar thought. But there were still three to go. And the Cochrane, which had been their best weapon by far, was under heavy pressure from the remaining assault ships.

Maneuvering smartly in close quarters, the Romulans had abandoned the use of missiles and were using the laser strategy that had worked for their adversary. The Cochrane was harried on every side by lethal, blue lances of coherent electromagnetic radiation.

But despite the odds, Dane managed to weave his way through the enemy's gauntlet. And before the Romulans could surround him again, he ducked for cover behind the Earth base.

Until then, Shumar hadn't dared to fire his atomics again for fear of hitting the Cochrane. But when he recognized his ally drop out of the fray for the moment, he saw a chance to do some damage.

"Target," he snapped into the intercom grid, "and fire!"

Before the commander could draw another breath, another flock of black and gold missiles took wing in the direction of the Romulans. Left in disarray by their pursuit of the Cochrane, the enemy vessels had a harder time avoiding the base's barrage.

One of them took an explosion broadside. Another absorbed two hits—one to its belly and another to one of its nacelles.

At first, it seemed to Shumar that the Romulans had survived the volley. Then the damaged nacelle blew apart in a flash of white energy, setting off a series of smaller explosions along the length of the enemy ship. Finally, there was an enormous flare that encompassed the entire vessel—and just like that, the assault force had been cut in half.

But there was no time for the defenders to cheer their good fortune. After all, the two remaining Romulans hadn't been spectators all this time.

Knowing that it would take the base a few precious seconds to reload its missile launchers, the enemy commanders brought their ships even nearer to their target than before—so near, in fact, that Shumar thought he could see the scratches on their hulls. Then each of the vessels released a frightening wave of atomics.

At such close range, there was no possibility of their missing, no chance that the Earth base's shields would spare it more than a portion of the impact. There was only the sense of impending doom.

Suddenly, the Ops center was engulfed in a blinding blaze of light and the commander felt the deck jerk out from under his feet. It seemed to him for a brief moment that he was flying, sailing through the air as if the artificial gravity had cut out.

Then something hit him in the chest with bone-rattling force, pounding the breath out of him. Opening his eyes, he saw that he was draped over a console, a warm, metallic taste in his mouth.

The taste of blood, Shumar realized.

Pushing himself off the console, he winced at a red-hot pain in his side. Broken rib, he thought. Maybe more than one. But even if that was so, it was the least of his problems.

Ops was littered with the bodies of his officers, some of them dead or unconscious—and the rest perhaps wishing for the same result. As those capable of moving groaned and pulled themselves to their feet, the commander happened to look up—and saw the erratic, red crackle of energy above the crazed surface of their dome.

He knew what it meant. Their shields had been battered down, or very nearly so—and the next missile that detonated anywhere near the base would vaporize it from top to bottom.

Worse, the two surviving Romulans were wheeling, coming back for another pass. The insignia on their undersides loomed like gargantuan birds of prey, eager to tear their victims apart.

Unfortunately, Shumar didn't know if any of his weapons officers were still in one piece—and there was no time to find out. All he could do was establish a link between his controls and the base's tactical array and try to stave off the enemy by himself.

Cursing, ignoring the agony in his side, he attacked the toggle switches on his console. A moment later, one of his monitors showed him a green and black schematic of the base's weapons systems. One of the missile launchers was still operational, it seemed—though it was incapable of being loaded again. It would only accommodate the missile already inside it.

His fingers stabbing the keys like manic insects, the commander slaved the launcher to his controls. Then he tried to target the Romulans before they scattered his atoms across space.

All the while, he knew in his heart that he would be too late. The base's launch system simply wasn't fast enough to respond in time. But he couldn't just stand there and wait for the inevitable, could he? He had to try to beat the odds.

Then something happened—something Shumar didn't

know quite what to make of at first. There was a flash of something big and blue in the heavens above him, something that seemed vaguely shiplike in form and structure.

It reminded him of a Rigelian transport vessel. But that was impossible, the commander told himself. Cobaryn had left already, entire minutes before the Romulans arrived.

Before he could get a better look at the thing, before he could tell if his initial impression had been at all correct, the object slammed into one of the Romulan warships.

For a moment, the two vessels slid sideways, locked in a hateful embrace. Then an explosion ripped through both of them like heat lightning. Shumar couldn't tell where the chaos had begun, but by the time it was over both ships had been reduced to atoms.

Cobaryn, he thought, his heart sinking. The Rigelian hadn't left them after all. He had only gone far enough to keep the enemy from noticing him—then sacrificed himself and his vessel to save the Earth base.

But for all the transport captain had done, the battle was far from over. The last of the Romulans, diverted from its target by Cobaryn's timely intervention, was looping around to make another run.

Gritting his teeth, the commander did his best to place the enemy in his sights. Unfortunately, he wasn't a soldier by trade. He was a scientist who had never imagined he would be shooting at anyone, much less doing so with a hundred lives hanging in the balance.

The Romulan completed its loop and headed directly for the shieldless operations center. His heart slamming against his ribs, Shumar worked his controls until he had drawn a bead on the vessel. Then he reached for the square red stud that would serve as his trigger.

But just as he was about to release his single missile, he saw a slender black shape come hurtling overhead. Only then did he realize that the Romulan wasn't headed for Ops at all—it was closing with Dane's Cochrane.

But this time, the enemy didn't have to worry about hitting its sister ships. It could fire at the Cochrane all day. And eventually, it would impale the smaller vessel on a laser beam.

Then it would finish off the defenseless base.

It didn't seem fair, the commander told himself. Not after what Cobaryn had done. Not after Dane's valiant maneuvers. Not after some of his people had manned this place for the last five years, taking a chunk out of their lives to help Earth win its war of survival.

He would be damned if he was going to let all that courage and sacrifice go to waste. Glaring at the monitor he had assigned to the weapons function, Shumar fought to reacquire his target.

Meanwhile, the Romulan's lasers found the Cochrane, shivering it with a direct hit to its shields. And before it could twist out of the way, it took a second solid blow to its underbelly.

Dane couldn't take much more of that, Shumar noted. If he was going to help the Cochrane pilot, if he was going to make any difference at all, he was going to have to do it quickly.

Come on, he told himself, perspiration pouring down

both sides of his face. Stay with it, for godsakes. If Kelly can do this, so can you.

Then, all of a sudden, there it was. The Romulan was right there in his crosshairs. The commander was so surprised, he almost forgot to press the square red stud.

Almost.

As Shumar watched, fascinated by the event he had himself set in motion, the base's lone remaining missile cut a path through starry space and detonated near the Romulan's bow.

It wasn't enough to destroy the enemy vessel. It wasn't even enough to punch a hole in her shields. But it was more than enough to buy the Cochrane some time.

Taking advantage of the opportunity, Dane brought his needle-thin ship about in what must have been a gut-wrenching U-turn. Then he hit the Romulan with all the laser power at his disposal.

His electric-blue beams raked mercilessly at the enemy's deflectors, sending tendrils and shoots of energy radiating from each point of contact. The Romulan tried to shake its pursuer but the Cochrane hung on, matching the larger vessel tack for tack and spin for spin.

Then the improbable happened. The enemy's plasma trail...vanished.

The vessel didn't lose velocity—not there in space, where there was no friction to slow it down. But the Romulan was proceeding along a straight line, making no effort to evade the Cochrane.

Because it couldn't, Shumar realized. Because its engines had gone offline, leaving it dead and powerless. It had become a sitting duck for its adversary, not unlike the Earth base.

The Cochrane's attack hadn't hit the Romulan's propulsion system hard enough to blow it up. It hadn't started a chain reaction. It had simply knocked something loose, making the system useless for the moment.

But as unlikely as that seemed, what happened next was even harder to believe. As the commander tried to activate his console's comm function so he could speak with the Cochrane, he caught the opening of the lift doors out of the corner of his eye.

He turned to see who was there. As fortune would have it, he found himself staring at Alonis Cobaryn.

"Commander," said the transport captain, his voice taut with urgency, "you cannot let Dane destroy that ship!"

Shumar looked at him. "How did you... ?"

And then it came to him. *The transporter.*

Cobaryn must have set his vessel's controls on heat-seek and beamed himself off sometime prior to impact. And he had been on the base ever since, making his way up to Ops.

"Tell him not to fire again!" the Rigelian demanded, joining the commander at his console. "He must not destroy it!"

Shumar shook his head in confusion, his throbbing ribs a distraction he couldn't ignore anymore. "Why not?" he asked.

Cobaryn's crimson eyes opened wide beneath his brow ridge. "Because none of us have ever seen the inside of a Romulan ship, much less one of the Romulans themselves. This is our chance to learn something about them—probably the only chance we will ever get!"

It took a moment for the import of the Rigelian's statement to sink in. He was right, the human realized. This *was* an unheard-of opportunity.

"Give me a laser pistol," Cobaryn suggested. "I can beam aboard, look around—take some scan readings. The data will be invaluable."

Shumar had a feeling the transport captain wasn't talking about strategic data. Nonetheless, a little reconaissance might go a long way toward furthering their understanding of Romulan technologies. Earth Command would be salivating if it knew what kind of treasure they held in their hands.

He flipped the toggle that would make his communications function operational. "This is Commander Shumar," he said into the grid. "Come in, Captain Dane. Repeat—"

But before he could finish his sentence, the Romulan began to come alive again. Its nacelles started glowing with scarlet plasma fire, indicating that the problem it had experienced was only temporary.

My God, the commander thought.

But luckily for them, Dane hadn't relaxed his guard. Before the invader could bring its shields up all the way, the Cochrane speared it amidships with a devastating burst of laser fire.

It took a moment for the electromagnetic beams to pierce the Romulan vessel to its heart—but only a moment. Then the enemy exploded in a dazzling display of prismatic light.

"No," said Cobaryn, real pain in his voice. "We were so close…"

Shumar turned to him. The scientist in him couldn't

help sympathizing with the Rigelian. "Their engines were coming back online. There was nothing else we could have done."

Cobaryn looked at him, the skin around his eyes pinched with distress. "To get a look at the Romulans, to see how they lived . . . I tell you, I would have given a great deal for that."

"But not your life," the commander assumed.

The transport captain didn't answer. He just sighed and looked away, dealing with his disappointment as best he could.

"Sir?" said a feminine voice.

Shumar turned in the other direction and saw Kelly standing there. There was an angry red swelling at the point of the woman's brow that cried out for medical attention.

"I'm sorry I blacked out," she said in an emotion-laden voice. I—" Her voice caught and she looked down at the floor, embarrassed. "I wish I could've been more helpful."

The commander looked at his security officer. "For godsakes, Kelly...you did all you could. Like anyone else."

But he could see she wasn't satisfied with that. Kelly was a fighter, after all. In her mind, she had let him down.

"Have someone see to that injury," he told her.

Kelly nodded. "Aye, sir. After I help some of the others."

"I will help, too," Cobaryn suggested.

The security officer looked at him. "Suit yourself," she said.

As the two of them retreated, Shumar looked around his battered operations center. In the aftermath of the battle, most of his people were still rising to their feet or helping others to do the same thing.

But a few were still lying on the deck, unmoving, their heads lying at angles no living being could tolerate. The commander felt a lump in his throat and swallowed it back.

So much death, he thought numbly. In all the years Shumar had spent on the base, he had never seen its like. Not with the *Nimitz* and other ships like it patrolling Earth's perimeter.

What the hell had *happened?* he asked himself. Where *was* the *Nimitz?* Why hadn't it answered his calls for help?

Suddenly, a voice cut through the miasma of shock and suffering. "This is Dane," it said.

Cobaryn looked at the console. He had forgotten about the Cochrane pilot. "Dane," he echoed. "Are you all right?"

"Not a scratch," the man shot back. "Now, somebody want to beam me back to that godforsaken base of yours...or am I going to have to crack open my victory bottle right here on the ship?"

CHAPTER
4

CAPTAIN DANIEL HAGEDORN STUDIED THE STARS STREAMing by on his forward viewscreen, wondering how many Romulan warships he was bypassing in his passage through subspace.

Thanks to the people at research and development, this was the longest faster-than-light jump he had ever made. In fact, it was the longest faster-than-light jump *any* Earthman had ever made.

And it couldn't have come at a better time. They had finally pushed the Romulans back far enough to get some sense of their military infrastructure, some idea of how to cripple their war effort.

Hence, this mission to take out the enemy's number one command center—the nexus for all strategic communications between the Romulan fleet and the Romulan homeworlds. Without it, the Romulans would quickly find their forces in disarray. They would have no rational choice but to withdraw instantly from Terran space.

Hagedorn frowned ever so slightly at his eagerness. He didn't like to let himself think too far ahead. Captains got into trouble that way. It was better to focus on the objective at hand and let the results take care of themselves.

He turned to his navigator, positioned at a free-standing console to his right. "How much longer, Mr. Tavarez?"

The man checked the monitors on his shiny black control panel. "A little more than a minute, sir."

"Thank you," Hagedorn told Tavarez. Then he looked to his helmsman, who was situated at the same kind of console to his left. "Ready to drop out of warp, Mr. St. Claire?"

The helmsman tapped a couple of studs to fine-tune their course. "Ready when you are, sir."

Finally, the captain addressed his weapons officer, a petite Asian woman who was seated directly ahead of him, between helm and navigation. "Power to all batteries, Lt. Hosokawa."

Hosokawa's fingers crawled deftly over her instruments. "Power to lasers and launchers," she confirmed.

Hagedorn took a breath and sat back in his padded leather center seat. Since his Christopher 2000 was still tearing through subspace, there was no point in trying to contact the captains of the half-dozen other starships who had been assigned this mission under his command. Still, like any good wing commander preparing for an engagement, he reeled off their names and his impressions of them in the privacy of his mind.

Andre Beschta. A rock; a tough, relentless warrior—willing to put his life on the line for any one of his friends. Seeing him in combat, one would never suspect what a clown the man could be when he was off-duty...or how well-loved he was by his crew and colleagues alike.

Uri Reulbach, quiet and studious by nature but utterly ruthless in battle. Reulbach was their point man, their risk-taker, the one who took the heat off all the rest of them.

The Stiles brothers, Jake and Aaron, both of them fiery and determined. No Earthmen had shown as much courage against the Romulans as the Stiles family—or gotten themselves killed quite as often. All in all, three cousins and an uncle had perished at the hands of the invader. It had gotten to be a grim joke between Jake and Aaron as to who was going to die next.

Amanda McTigue, thoughtful and compassionate, who by her own admission felt every blow she struck against the enemy. Fortunately, it didn't stop her from demonstrating a predatorlike ferocity that none of her wingmates could ever hope to match.

Finally, there was Hiro Matsura—the newcomer in their ranks. The youngster had joined them only a couple of months earlier, but he had earned the respect of his wingmates right from the start. Matsura seemed to do best when paired with Beschta, who had taken the tyro under his wing.

And how did Hagedorn see *himself?* As the glue that held them all together, of course. He wasn't the toughest of them or the fiercest or even the most effective—nor did he have to be. His job was a simple one—to make his wingmates work as a single unit, tight, efficient, and economical in achieving their goal.

If they succeeded, it was because they had been strong and deft and courageous. If they failed, it was because *he* had failed *them*. It might not have been fair, but that was the way Hagedorn's superiors looked at it— and as a result, the way he had come to look at it, too.

"Permission to leave subspace, sir," said St. Claire.

The captain nodded. "Permission granted, Lieutenant."

As they dropped out of warp, Hagedorn saw the starry streaks on the viewscreen shorten abruptly into points of light. Of course, he observed silently, a few of those points were actually nearby planets reflecting their sun's illumination.

And unless they had badly miscalculated, one of those planets was Cheron, the barren world deep in Romulan territory about which their objective spun in blissful orbit. But not for long, if Hagedorn and the others had anything to say about it.

"Confirm our position," he told his navigator.

"Confirmed," said Tavarez. "We're on the outskirts of the target system. Cheron is dead ahead."

Before the man could finish his advisory, Hagedorn saw one of the other Christophers become visible off his port bow. A second later, one of her wingmates joined her.

Then the subspace radio checks began coming in. As Hagedorn knew, they were more of a ritual than a necessity—like a pregame cheer before an ancient football game—but that didn't make them any less important.

"Beschta here. You can't get rid of me so easily."

"Stiles, Jake…present and accounted for."

"Stiles, Aaron…right behind you, sir."

"McTigue, on your starboard flank."

"Matsura here."

Hagedorn waited a moment. "Captain Reulbach?"

No answer.

He bit his lip. "Uri?"

Suddenly, the last of the Christophers rippled into sight above and slightly forward of Hagedorn's vessel. He breathed a sigh of relief.

"This is the *Achilles*," said Reulbach. "Sorry about the delay. We had a little trouble with our port nacelle. Fortunately, it won't be an issue until we reenter subspace."

Hagedorn frowned. He didn't like the idea that his comrade might be hobbling home. After all, they didn't know how many enemy ships might be guarding the command center. Even if they were successful in their mission, they might wind up with half the Romulan fleet on their tails.

But he couldn't call off the mission because of one crotchety nacelle. "Acknowledged," he told Reulbach.

Then he set his sights on the viewscreen again, and in particular on the pale blue star in the center of it—which wasn't really a star at all. He didn't have to consult Tavarez to know that it would take them nearly eight hours to reach it at impulse speeds.

Eight hours, Hagedorn thought. For the first seven and three quarters of them, he and his wing would likely not be detected by the Romulans. After all, the enemy didn't have any reason to expect them there.

But once they came in scan range of the command center...

That, he knew, would be a different story entirely.

As he sped toward the blue world fixed at maximum magnification on his viewscreen, Jake Stiles used the controls embedded in his armrest to establish a comm link with his brother.

"Stiles here," said Aaron, his voice clear and free of static.

"Stiles here, too," Jake responded.

His brother chuckled over the link. "I was wondering when I'd hear from you, *Anaconda*. Feeling lonely?"

"Only for the moment," said Jake. "Before long, I bet, we'll have a few Romulans for company."

"I know what you're going to ask," Aaron told him. "And don't worry. I'll take down twice my share of birdies. That way they won't have to dig a hole for you back home."

"Funny," Jake responded. "I was just going to tell *you* the same thing. I guess they're right about great minds thinking alike."

"I guess so," said his brother. "Except no one ever told me I had a great mind. And now that I think about it, I doubt they ever told you that either."

"All right," Jake conceded. "So maybe mediocre minds think alike, too. And this one is thinking what a shame it'd be to go home alone."

Aaron grunted. "I hear you. Especially with the war effectively over, if this little gambit works the way it's supposed to. So I guess we'll just have to keep on bucking the family curse."

"I guess so," Jake agreed.

Silence for a moment. "Stiles out," said his brother.

"That makes two of us," Jake told him.

"Captain Stiles," said his navigator, a sturdy blond woman named Rasmussen. "Scanners are picking up an enemy squadron." She pressed a series of buttons to extract more data. "Looks like eleven ships. Heading three-one-four mark six."

Eleven of them, Stiles reflected. They had hoped not to encounter so many, especially this far out. And there were likely to be a lot more of them hanging back closer to the command center.

But this was Earth Command's best wing. One way or another, the captain told himself, they would get the job done.

He looked back over his shoulder at Lavagetto, his communications officer. "Transmit our readings to the other ships, Lieutenant. Then request orders from Captain Hagedorn."

"Aye, sir," said the comm officer.

Stiles eyed the viewscreen. "When can we get a visual?"

"In about thirty seconds, sir," Rasmussen replied.

"This is Hagedorn," their wing commander broke in, his voice ringing from one end of the Christopher's bridge to the other. "Assume bull's-eye formation and go to full impulse."

Stiles pressed his comm stud. "Acknowledged," he told Hagedorn. He turned to Myerson, his helmsman. "You heard the man, Lieutenant."

"Full impulse, sir," said Myerson.

"The Romulans have picked us up," Rasmussen reported crisply. "They're heading right for us, sir."

The captain's teeth ground together. He always felt much better when he could actually *see* the enemy. "How about that visual?" he asked his navigator, trying to mask his discomfort.

Rasmussen worked at her controls. "Coming right up, sir."

A moment later, the ghostly blue disc of Cheron gave way to a squadron of eleven Romulan warships. They were traveling in a honeycomb formation, a typical birdie approach.

But they wouldn't be flying that formation for long, Jake Stiles mused. Not after he and his pals had blown a hole through it.

"Laser range in three minutes and twenty seconds," reported Chang, the *Anaconda*'s veteran weapons officer.

Stiles eyed the enemy warships. "Raise shields."

"Aye, sir," came Chang's reply.

The Romulans seemed to loom larger with each passing moment. The captain felt his mouth go dry as dust. But then, he thought, it always seemed to do that before a battle.

"Two minutes," the weapons officer announced.

Stiles nodded. "Target lasers."

"Targeting," said Chang.

In his brother's ship, the captain told himself, Aaron would be doing the same things—receiving the same information and giving the same orders to his crew. And in a dark, secluded part of his mind, he would be thinking about the family curse.

It was hard not to.

"One minute," the weapons officer reported.

Hagedorn's voice came crackling over their comm link.

"Maintain formation," he told them, so there wouldn't be any mistake.

"We're with you," Jake Stiles assured him.

"Forty-five seconds," Chang announced. "All systems operating at maximum efficiency, sir."

The captain considered the viewscreen again. There was no break in the Romulans' formation. Obviously, they still didn't believe the Earthmen were planning to barrel right through them.

"Thirty seconds," said the weapons officer.

The captain felt a bead of perspiration tracing a trail down the side of his face. "Fire on my mark," he told Chang.

"Aye, sir," came the reply. "Twenty seconds..."

Good luck, he told his brother silently.

"Fifteen," said the weapons officer. "Ten. Five..."

On the viewscreen, the Romulans' weapons ports belched beams of cold blue flame. Stiles's ship shuddered and bucked under the impact of the assault. But her shields held.

Then it was the Earthman's turn. Glaring at the swiftly approaching enemy, he yelled, "Fire!"

The Romulans were rocked by a dozen direct laser hits. However, none of them was forced out of line.

A second time, Stiles's vessel took the brunt of the enemy's barrage. And a second time, he returned it with equal fury. Then they were on top of the Romulans. It looked as if they would have to rotate to find a gap in the birdies' wall, if they were to survive.

But at the last possible second, the Romulans lost

their nerve. Breaking formation, they peeled off in half a dozen different directions. Inwardly, Stiles cheered Hagedorn's resolve. A less confident commander would have blinked and made easy targets of them.

As it was, he had made easy targets of the enemy.

"Target and fire!" the captain barked.

With Chang working his controls, the *Anaconda* stabbed a Romulan's bird-bedecked belly with a pair of sizzling blue laser beams. And before the enemy could come out of her loop, the Earth vessel skewered her again.

"Their shields are buckling, sir!" Rasmussen called out.

"Stay with her!" Stiles insisted.

Myerson clung fiercely to the Romulan's tail; Chang ripped at her hindquarters with blue bursts of laser fire. Before long, one of the birdie's nacelles fizzled and went dark, and a moment later the other nacelle lost power as well.

The Romulan was dead in space, unable to move. But the captain knew she could still be dangerous. Once before, he had seen a crippled birdie reach out with her lasers and rake an unsuspecting Christopher.

But not this time. Stiles leaned forward in his seat. "Target and launch!" he snapped.

The weapons officer bent to his work again with grim efficiency. But instead of another laser barrage, he unleashed a black-and-gold missile at the enemy ship.

As the Earth captain looked on, the projectile penetrated one of the Romulan's empty nacelles. For a heartbeat, nothing happened. Then the enemy vessel shook itself to pieces in a blaze of atomic fire.

"Romulan off the starboard bow!" Rasmussen called out.

"Get it on the screen!" Stiles ordered.

The navigator had barely accomplished her task when the Romulan rolled under a spectacular laser volley. A moment later, Stiles saw the source of it, as McTigue's *Christopher* came twisting into view.

The captain made a mental note to thank the woman when he got the chance. But in the meantime, he could best express his gratitude by adding some firepower to McTigue's attack.

"Mr. Chang!" he cried out. "Target and fire!"

Stiles's lasers sent the Romulan rolling even harder, creating a web of destructive energy that spread outward from the point of impact. Then McTigue hit the enemy again, showing no mercy.

The Romulan tried to get off some shots of her own, but she was too beleaguered to target properly. Finally, with her shields torn up, she was easy prey for Stiles.

"Mr. Chang," he said, "target and launch!"

The *Christopher's* missile sped through space like a well-thrown dart. When it reached its objective, the enemy spasmed and came apart in a blinding white rush of energy.

But Stiles and his crew weren't done yet. There were still as many as nine Romulans carving up the void, their laser sights trained on the *Anaconda* or one of her wingmates.

"Romulan to port!" Rasmussen shouted suddenly.

"Evade!" the captain told his helmsman.

Under the navigator's expert guidance, the enemy vessel slid into sight on their forward viewscreen. Stiles almost wished it hadn't. The Romulan was right on top of them, ready to release a close-range laser barrage—and he knew there wasn't anything they could do about it.

"Brace yourselves!" he roared.

The viewscreen blanched suddenly, causing him to blink and turn away. Then came the impact—a bone-rattling blow that tore Stiles halfway out of his seat and made a geyser of sparks out of an unoccupied aft console. But when it was over, the *Anaconda* was still in one piece.

Someone moved to the damaged console with a fire extinguisher while the captain glowered at the forward screen. Fortunately, it still afforded him a good view of their adversary.

"Shields down seventy-five percent!" Rasmussen told him.

"Mr. Myerson," Stiles growled, "get that birdie off our tail! Mr. Chang—target and fire at will!"

But before they could obey either of those orders, the Romulan veered to starboard and began to put distance between herself and the Earth ship. For the merest fraction of a second, the captain was caught off-balance. Then he turned to his officers.

"Belay that last set of orders!" he told them. "Effect pursuit, Mr. Myerson! Don't let that Romulan get away!"

"Aye, sir!" the helmsman responded, moving to tax the ship's impulse engines to their fullest.

Suddenly, the enemy tacked sharply to port—and a moment later, Stiles saw why. Two of the other Christophers were approaching from the opposite direction, one of them less than a kilometer ahead of the other.

He recognized the vessels by their markings. Reulbach's ship was the one in front, of course. And the one behind it, looking as good as it had ever looked in its life, was his brother Aaron's.

The captain didn't know how the rest of the battle was going, but he liked the signs he was getting. After all, he had seen a Romulan turn tail in the middle of an engagement. And though her retreat had become a three-on-one, none of the other birdies were coming to her rescue.

Best of all, his brother was still alive and well. Good portents indeed, Jake Stiles told himself.

But he had barely completed the thought when he saw something that wasn't good at all. As Reulbach and Aaron homed in on the enemy, Reulbach's ship began to rotate for no apparent reason.

What the devil's going on? Stiles wondered, a chill cooling the small of his back.

Then Reulbach's port nacelle exploded in a flare of white-hot plasma. And before the captain knew it, before he could even contemplate a rescue, the rest of the ship blew up as well.

"My God," Stiles muttered. And it wasn't just Uri Reulbach whose death had emblazoned itself on his eyes.

Because Aaron's vessel was right behind Reulbach's—so close to it that the younger Stiles couldn't avoid the Christopher's explosion. So close that Aaron couldn't help running into the expanding plasma cloud, which could do to deflectors and titanium hulls what acid did to tissue paper.

Unable to take his eyes from the viewscreen, Jake Stiles shook his head. No, he thought numbly, it can't be. Not my brother. Not this way, caught in the blast from a lousy nacelle.

Then he saw something emerge from the burgeoning

plasma cloud—something that looked a lot like the nose of Aaron's ship. As Stiles leaned forward in his seat, spellbound, he saw the rest of his brother's vessel slide out of the cloud as well.

He studied the Christopher with eyes that didn't dare believe. But as hard as he looked, as intensely as he scrutinized her, he couldn't find anything wrong with her. Against all odds, Aaron's ship had come through hell unscathed.

"Sir!" Rasmussen called out. "Romulan behind us!"

Stiles stiffened at the news. When no one came to the other birdie's rescue, he had allowed himself to relax—to imagine the enemy was falling back. Obviously, he had jumped to the wrong conclusion.

The Romulan in question slid onto his viewscreen. It was close—even closer than the other birdie had been. So nerve-shatteringly close that Stiles could barely see anything else.

"Helm," he thundered, "evasive maneuvers! Weapons—target and fire!"

The enemy fell off his screen again as Myerson pulled them into a gut-wrenching loop. The captain felt his jaw clench as he waited for information from his navigator.

"They're hanging with us!" Rasmussen exclaimed. "Range—half a kilometer! Bearing two-four-two—"

But before she could finish her report, Stiles felt his head snap back like a whip. As he fell forward again, he realized that something had slammed them from behind—and slammed them *hard*.

Chang turned in his seat. He didn't look happy. "Sir," he said, "the shields are gone."

There was a silence afterward that seemed to drag on for hours, but couldn't really have lasted even a second. It was a silence that absorbed all hope, all possibility of survival.

Then the Romulans bludgeoned them again.

Stiles felt the deck jerk savagely beneath his feet—once, twice, and a third time, touching off explosion after explosion all around him. Somehow he managed to hold on to his seat. But his bridge gradually became the substance of nightmare—a field of fire and sparking consoles and thick, black plumes of smoke.

As they cleared for a moment, he saw Myerson. The man was slumped in his chair, his control panel aflame.

The captain started forward, imagining he could help Myerson—until the crewman slithered to the deck and his head lolled in Stiles's direction. Then he saw Myerson's blackened husk of a face and the sickeningly liquid eyes that stared out of it and he knew his helmsman was beyond help.

The captain looked around with smoke-stung eyes. He couldn't find any sign of Chang or Rasmussen...or Lavagetto either, for that matter. He didn't know where they had gone or if they were dead or alive.

But he knew *one* thing. He had to get them out of this mess—at least until the other Christophers could free themselves and come to his aid. And if Myerson's controls were slagged, he would have to reroute helm control to Rasmussen's navigation console.

Making his way through the smoky miasma, Stiles found the right console and slid in behind it. Fortunately, it hadn't suffered any serious damage—only a few scorchmarks on its left side. He pulled on the switches that would establish a link to the *Anaconda*'s helm.

Nothing happened.

The captain cursed, his voice cutting through the sputter and sizzle of his dying ship. The console was all right, it seemed, but the ship's helm function had been thrown offline. He wouldn't be able to take control of it from the bridge or anywhere else until repairs were made.

And there was no time for that. No time at all, he thought.

As if to confirm his conclusion, something exploded in his face and sent him flying. He had a vague impression of coming down again, but he wasn't sure how or where or even why. He only knew that he was in the grip of a terrible, searing pain.

Fighting it, Stiles managed to lift his head and open his eyes. He couldn't see anything except thick, dark waves of smoke. They were moving slowly but certainly, reaching out to claim him like some infernal surf.

And there was nothing he could do about it.

Nothing.

As the pain throbbed deeper within him, his head fell back to the deck. And unexpectedly, despite his torment, he began to laugh.

All this time, he had been worried that the family curse would strike his brother. And in the end, whom had it claimed? Which Stiles had it added to the funeral pyre?

Him.

* * *

Hiro Matsura eyed his forward viewscreen, where a Romulan vessel was pounding the daylights out of one of his disabled wingmates.

"Target and fire!" he told his weapons officer—for what seemed like the hundredth time that day.

Twin laser beams shot through space and sent the Romulan reeling. But still she maintained her attack on the Christopher.

"Their shields are down fifty-five percent!" his navigator announced.

"Fire again!" the captain ordered.

His lasers dealt the Romulan another blow—but it didn't stop her from blasting away at the Earth ship, burning away even her serial number. Matsura felt his teeth grind together.

"Their shields are down *eighty* percent!" his navigator amended.

Matsura knew his atomics would get the enemy's attention faster than another laser barrage. However, he had only half the eight missiles with which he had started out from Earth—and with even a portion of the Romulan's deflectors up, an explosion wouldn't destroy her anyway.

As a result, he picked the only other option left to him—the one Captain Beschta had chosen a month earlier when it was Matsura's vessel hanging in space, waiting for a grisly end. "Lieutenant Barker," he said, "put us in front of that Christopher."

"Aye, sir," came the helmsman's reply.

A moment later, the Romulan seemed to swing around on the captain's viewscreen. But in reality, it was an Earth ship that was moving, interposing herself between the enemy and her battered wingmate.

It was a maneuver that came with a price—and Matsura paid it. His vessel shuddered violently as she absorbed a close-quarters barrage. Still, he was in a better position to weather the storm than the other Earth vessel.

And then it was *his* turn.

"Fire!" Matsura told his weapons officer.

As before, twin laser beams speared the Romulan. But this time, without its shields to protect it, it didn't just lurch under the impact.

It crumpled like a metal can under an especially heavy boot. And it kept on crumpling.

Finally, the enemy vanished in a rage of pure, white light. And when the light was gone, there was nothing left but debris.

But Matsura didn't have time to celebrate the Romulan's destruction. Turning to his navigator, a woman named Williams, he called for a scan report on the damaged Christopher.

The navigator's face told the story even before she spoke. "No sign of survivors, sir—and her warp core is approaching critical. It's a wonder the damned thing didn't blow some time ago."

No sooner had the woman spoken than the Christopher went up in a blaze of plasma. Captain Matsura swallowed and accepted the loss as best he could—though at this point, he still had no idea whose ship it was.

Not Beschta's, he thought. It had better *not* be Beschta's. The big man had been his mentor, his friend.

"Bring us about," Matsura told his helmsman, "and find me a Romulan with whom I can work out my anger."

"Aye, sir," came the response.

But as the image on the viewscreen expanded to a wider view, Matsura began to wonder if there were any Romulans left. As far as he could tell, the only vessels around him were Christophers.

His navigator confirmed his observation. "There's no trace of the enemy, sir. Either they've fled or they've been destroyed."

The captain breathed a sigh of relief. "And the good guys?" he asked, steeling himself for the verdict.

The bridge was silent for a moment. Then his navigator said, "Two down, sir. I make them out to be Captain Reulbach and Captain Stiles. That is . . . Captain *Jake* Stiles."

Matsura winced. They had both been brave men. He wished he had gotten the chance to know them better.

"May they rest in peace," he said awkwardly, never good with such things.

Suddenly, Captain Hagedorn's voice surrounded him. "You can stand down—the battle's over. Transmit reports."

Matsura did as he was told. After a minute or so, he heard the wing commander's voice again.

"It could have been worse," Hagedorn told them, his voice slow and heavy despite his appraisal. "On the minus side, we lost two of our wingmates. On the plus side, all enemy ships have been accounted for—and the vessels we've got left are viable enough to press ahead."

Matsura took a deep breath and let it out. He knew what the commander would say next.

"Let's go," Hagedorn told them, never one to disappoint.

Seeing one of the Christophers come about and head

for Cheron, Matsura turned to his helmsman. "Follow that ship," he said.

"Aye, Captain," responded Barker.

And they resumed their progress toward the command center.

Aaron Stiles knew he had two choices.

He could die by degrees, wasting away inside under the crushing weight of his sorrow. Or he could try to put his brother's death behind him and make the Romulans pay for what they had done.

In the end, he chose the latter.

Aaron Stiles followed his wing commander eighty million kilometers deeper into enemy territory, to the very brink of the command center orbiting serenely around the blue planet Cheron. And there, he did what he had set out to do. He made the Romulans pay with every ship they threw against him.

Not just for his brother, he told himself, but for all the members of the Stiles family who had died to keep their homeworld free. For Uri Reulbach and a dozen others who had perished serving alongside him. For all the Earthborn heroes whose names he had never known.

After all, he had enough hate and anger inside him to go around.

It didn't matter to him that he and his comrades were outnumbered two to one. Aaron Stiles plunged through the enemy's ranks like an angel of death, absorbing hit after hit, wishing he could see the Romulans' faces as they painted the void with the brilliance of their destruction.

And when he looked around and saw that the enemy's

vessels had all been annihilated, he went after the command center itself. Of course, it wasn't without its defenses—but none of them fazed Aaron Stiles. He hammered at the center with his lasers and his warheads and his rage, and eventually it yielded because he wouldn't accept any other outcome.

And when it was all over, when the Romulan command center was cracked and broken and spiraling down to the planet's surface, when all his fury was spent and his adversaries smashed to atoms, Aaron Stiles did one thing more.

He wept.

CHAPTER
5

PRESIDENT LYDIA LITTLEJOHN SAT ON HER WINDOWSILL and watched the sun melt into the mists over San Francisco Bay. She rubbed her tired eyes. Littlejohn had always believed that if Earth could win her war with the Romulans, everything after that would come easy.

As it turned out, she had been wrong.

"They should have responded by now," said Admiral Walker, a bushy-browed lion of a man in his early sixties. As usual, he was pacing the length of the president's office. "The bastards are having second thoughts."

Clarisse Dumont, a diminutive, pinch-faced woman a bit older than the admiral, shook her head. "As usual, you're jumping to conclusions. If you knew the Romulans better," she said, brushing lint off the sleeve of her woolen sweater, "you would understand they're just taking their time. They *like* to take their time."

Walker shot her an incredulous look. "*I* don't know the Romulans?" he harrumphed. "I've only been directing our forces against them for the last four and a half years."

"As I've pointed out several times before," Dumont told him with undisguised contempt, "fighting the Romulans and *knowing* the Romulans are two vastly different things."

"And how would you know that," asked the admiral, "considering you've never knocked heads with them? Never traded laser shots? Hell, you've never even seen one of their birdships."

"I've never seen a quark either," the woman countered sharply, "but I have no doubt that it exists."

Walker grunted. "You don't have to remind me about your credentials, Ms. Dumont. But a Nobel prize in particle physics doesn't make you an expert on alien behavior."

"That's true," said Littlejohn, interceding in her colleagues' discussion for perhaps the tenth time in the last few hours. "But in addition to being one of Earth's foremost scientists, Admiral, Clarisse is also one of our foremost linguists. And without her help, we would never have gotten this far in our negotiations."

Walker's nostrils flared. "I don't dispute the value of her contribution, Madame President. I just don't see why she feels compelled to dispute the value of *mine*."

Littlejohn sighed. "We're all on edge, Ed. We haven't slept much in the last two days and we're afraid that if we say the wrong thing, these talks are going to fall apart. So if Clarisse seems a little cranky, I think we can find it in our heart to forgive her."

Dumont shot a look at her. "Cranky, Madame President? Why, I've never been cranky in my entire—"

"President Littlejohn?" said a voice.

Littlejohn recognized it as that of Stuckey, one of the communications specialists who had been coordinating their dialogue with the Romulans from an office lower in the building. The president licked her lips. "Have we received a response?" she asked hopefully.

"We have indeed," said Stuckey. "Shall I put it through, ma'am?"

"By all means," the president told him.

A moment later, her office was filled with the fluid, strangely melodious voice of a high-ranking Romulan official—not the individual actually in charge of Romulan society, but someone empowered to speak for him.

Littlejohn was able to recognize a word of the alien's speech here or there. After all, they had been negotiating the same items for days. But for the most part, it was gibberish to her.

The message went on for what seemed like a long time—longer than usual, certainly. Also, she thought, the words were expressed in an emotional context she didn't believe she had heard before. It sounded more contentious to her, more belligerent.

Oh no, the president told herself. Not another step backward. Not when it seemed as if we were getting somewhere.

Then the message was over. Dumont plunked herself down in a chair and massaged the bridge of her bony nose.

"What did they say?" the admiral demanded. "For the love of sanity, woman, don't leave us hanging here!"

Dumont looked up at him. Then she turned to Little-john. "What they said," she began, "was they accept our terms. The neutral zone, the termination of their claim to the Algeron system...the whole ball of wax."

The president didn't believe it. "If they were going to give in across the board, why didn't they concede anything before this? Why did they seem so bloody uncoopcrative?"

The older woman smiled knowingly. "As I said," she explained, "the Romulans like to take their time."

Commander Bryce Shumar stood outside the turbolift doors and surveyed his base's operations center.

The place looked a lot better than it had a couple of weeks earlier. Shumar and his staff had patched up the various systems and corresponding consoles and brought them back online. Even the weapons launchers were working again, though he didn't expect to have to use them.

Not with the war over...

Of course, the commander reflected, it had been easier to repair their machines than their people. He had lost eight good men and women to the Romulans, and four more of his officers might never be the same.

But they had won the war. They had beaten back the alien aggressor.

Shumar understood now where the *Nimitz* had been while his base was under attack. The ship, like half a dozen others, had quickly and secretly been moved up to the front—all so the enemy wouldn't notice that a flight wing had slipped away and made the jump into Romulan space.

The commander couldn't help applauding what that wing had accomplished. But at the same time, he resented having been left so vulnerable. He resented the deaths of the eight people who had given their lives for him.

"Sir?" said Kelly, who was again ensconced at her security console.

He glanced at her. "Yes?"

"Commander Applegate has beamed aboard and is on his way up," the security officer reported.

Shumar nodded. "Thanks."

He would have met the man in the transporter room, but Applegate insisted that they rendezvous at Ops. Apparently, the new base commander got a little queasy when he transported.

Abruptly, Shumar heard the lift beep and saw its doors slide open. A tall, fair-haired fellow in an Earth Command uniform stepped out of the compartment and nodded to him.

"Good to meet you in person," Applegate said, extending his hand.

Shumar shook it. "Same here." He indicated Ops with a gesture. "As you can see, we cleaned up the place for you."

Applegate nodded appraisingly. "If not for the burn marks," he observed, "one would never be able to tell that this facility was the focus of a pitched space battle."

Shumar winced. People who used the pronoun "one" had always bothered him. However, he wouldn't have to get along with Applegate for more than a half hour or so. That was when the *Manticore* was scheduled to leave...with the *former* commander of Earth Base Fourteen securely aboard.

"I shouldn't have too much trouble here," said the new man. He smiled thinly. "Running a peacetime base shouldn't be nearly as difficult as running it during wartime."

"For your sake," Shumar told him, "I hope that's true."

"Well," said Applegate, "you probably have a few things to take care of before you go. Don't let me keep you."

Shumar nodded, though he had already packed and said his good-byes. "Thanks. I'll check in with you before I take off...to see if you have any last-minute questions, that sort of thing."

"Outstanding," responded his successor.

The commander winced again. He didn't care much for people who used the word "outstanding" either.

Making his way to Kelly, he leaned over and pretended to check her monitors. "He's not half as bad in person as he was onscreen."

"You're lying," she replied. "I know you."

"You'll be all right," Shumar assured her.

"I won't," she insisted. She looked at him. "Promise me something."

He shrugged. "What?"

"That when you get your hands on another ship, you'll take me along."

The commander chuckled softly. "What would I do with a security officer on a research vessel?"

Kelly scowled at him. "I can do a lot more than run a

security console and you know it. In fact, I was third in my high school class in biogenetics. So what do you say?"

Shumar sighed. "It doesn't pay very well."

"Neither does Earth Command, in case you haven't noticed." She glanced at Applegate. "Tell you what, I'll work for free. Just promise me."

"You would do better to hook up with Captain Cobaryn," he said. "Mapping expeditions can be a lot more exciting."

Kelly rolled her eyes. "Let's make a deal. You won't mention Captain Cobaryn and I won't mention Captain Dane."

The commander's stomach churned at the mere mention of the man's name. In his opinion, the galaxy wouldn't have lost anything if Dane had perished in the battle for the base.

"I agree," he said.

"Now promise," Kelly told him. "Say you'll take me with you first chance you get."

Shumar nodded. "All right. I promise."

"Thanks," said the security officer. "Now get out of here. Some of us still have work to do."

He smiled. "Take care, Kelly."

Patting her on the shoulder, he started for the turbo-lift. But he wasn't halfway there before he heard Ibañez calling him back.

"Commander?" said the communications officer.

"Yes?" responded Applegate, who had wandered in among the consoles.

Shumar looked at him and their eyes met. Then, as one, they turned to Ibañez for clarification.

"Sorry," the comm officer told Applegate. "I meant Commander Shumar."

The blond man smiled politely. "Of course." And he resumed his tour of the operations center.

Shumar made his way over to Ibañez. "What is it?" he asked.

"Commander," the man told him, "there's a subspace message from Earth. It looks like you've got new orders."

The commander felt his brow furrow. "That's not possible. My resignation was approved. After today, I'm no longer in the service."

Ibañez shrugged helplessly. "There's no mistake, sir. You're to report to the president's office."

Shumar looked at him. "The president...of *Earth?*"

"That's right," said the comm officer. He pointed to his screen. "When you get there, you're to meet with someone named Clarisse Dumont. Unfortunately, this doesn't say what she wants with you."

The commander knew Clarisse Dumont. For a short while, they had served on the same university faculty. Of course, that was before she had won the Nobel prize for particle physics.

But what did she have to do with Earth Command? And why was she summoning him to the president's office, of all places?

"Do me a favor," Ibañez told him. "The suspense is killing me. When you get to Earth and you meet with this woman, give us a call and let us know what it's all about?"

Shumar nodded. "I'll do that," he said numbly, making another promise he wasn't sure he could keep.

* * *

Ambassador Doreen Barstowe shaded her eyes.

To the east, under a thin, ocher-colored sky that ran to a dark, mountainous horizon, a cleverly designed configuration of variously colored shrubs moved restlessly with the wind. With its twists and turns and sheer variety, it was the most impressive example of a Vulcan maze garden that the ambassador had ever seen.

Barstowe turned back to the thin, elderly Vulcan who had shown her to this part of Sammak's estate, and stood with her now on the landing behind his house. "Are you certain he's out there?" she wondered.

The attendant, who had identified himself as Sonadh, regarded the woman as if he had better things to do than escort an alien around his master's grounds.

"Sammak told me that he would be working in his garden," Sonadh assured her. "As for certainty . . . it is said that such a state can only be achieved through investigation." He lifted his wrinkled chin. "Would you like me to conduct one for you?"

Barstowe smiled at the hint of sarcasm in the suggestion. "No. Thank you anyway. I'll take a look around myself, if that's all right."

"It is indeed," the Vulcan told her. Then he turned and walked back into the embrace of his master's domicile, a sprawling, white structure whose size alone was evidence of Sammak's prominence.

The ambassador gazed at the profusion of color again. If Sammak was out there, she told herself, she would find him soon enough—and no doubt derive pleasure from the finding. She descended several white stone steps to the level of the ground and began her search at the only place possible—the maze's remarkably unobtrusive entrance.

The shrubs that bordered the initial passageway were a majestic golden orange, lighter than the sky above them. But soon they gave way to an ethereal silver, a sprightly green, and a soft, pale yellow. It was immediately after that, in a corridor of deep, startling crimson, that Barstowe caught sight of a humanoid figure in white garb.

Sammak, she thought. No question about it. She could tell by the curling gray of his hair. The Vulcan was kneeling, pruning back a branch that had grown out too far.

He didn't turn to acknowledge his guest. Instead, he spoke a single word of recognition: "Ambassador."

Barstowe responded with the same economy. "Sammak."

Finally, he glanced at her. "I trust you are in good health."

"I am," she told him. "And you?"

"I have no complaints," the Vulcan responded.

The human touched the crimson shrubbery, which was made up of slim, pointed leaves. "I don't recall seeing this color the last time I was out here," she said. "Is it a seasonal effect?"

Sammak looked pleased. "It is," he confirmed. "In the colder months, these tuula leaves turn pink with small brown spots." He assessed them for a moment, brushing the underside of one with his forefinger. "But I have come to prefer them this way."

"So do I," Barstowe told him.

The Vulcan regarded her. "It has been a long time since last we saw each other. More than three years."

"Travel has been limited," the ambassador noted. "None of us in the diplomatic corps get around as much as we would like."

Sammak's brow creased ever so slightly. "But I do not imagine you have come to Vulcan simply to compliment me on my tuula bushes."

Barstowe smiled. "That's true. In fact, I came to give you some news. It seems the Romulans are suing for peace."

Sammak was known to be a great believer in the teachings of Surak, an individual who prided himself on his ability to master his emotions. Yet even he couldn't conceal a look of surprise...and approval as well, she thought.

"Peace," said the Vulcan, savoring the word.

"That's right. The Romulans were staggered by their defeat at Cheron," the ambassador explained. "If the war goes on much longer, their homeworlds will be threatened."

Sammak looked at her. "Poetic justice?"

Barstowe shrugged. "One might say that."

A few years earlier, the Romulans had pushed their offensive all the way into Earth's solar system. If not for the courage and determination of Earth's forces, the war might have ended then and there.

For a moment, the Vulcan seemed to mull over the information she had given him. "I am pleased, of course," he said at last. "As you know, Ambassador, I spoke against my world's decision to remain neutral in the conflict."

Barstowe nodded. "I recall your speech. It was quite stirring."

"For all the good it did. Clearly, neutrality was an illogical stance. If the Romulans had succeeded against Earth, they would have come after Vulcan in time as well."

"We of Earth always believed so," said the ambassador. "Together, my people and yours might have pushed the Romulans back in three years instead of five or six. And if we could have secured the aid of some of the other neutral worlds, it might only have been a matter of months."

The Vulcan sighed. "It is useless to engage in conjecture. The past is the past. Surak taught us to look to the future."

Barstowe saw her chance. She took it.

"I'm glad you hold that conviction," she told Sammak. "You see, my superiors have a revolutionary idea—one that can radically change the face of this quadrant for the better."

The Vulcan returned his attention to her, his dark eyes narrowing. "And the nature of this idea...?"

The human met his gaze. "I'm talking about a union of worlds. A federation designed to offer its members mutual protection against aggressor species like the Romulans...and maybe even facilitate an exchange of ideas into the bargain."

Sammak took some time to ponder the notion. "A federation," he repeated. He shrugged. "It is, as you say, a revolutionary concept."

"But one whose time has come," said Barstowe. "As we speak, similar conversations are taking place between Earth's ambassadors and people of vision on a dozen worlds from Sol to Rigel—worlds like Andor, Dopterius, Arbaza, Dedderai, and Vobilin."

The Vulcan cocked an eyebrow. "I am impressed."

Barstowe smiled again. "That's a start. But what I really want—what I *need*—is your support, my friend. You see, I would like very much to present this idea to T'pau...and I'm sure my arguments would be more persuasive if I didn't have to present them alone."

Sammak considered the proposition for a moment. Then he nodded. "I will accompany you to T'pau's court, Ambassador. And as you suggest, we will plead your case together."

The human inclined her head. "Thank you, my friend."

Her host shook his head. "No, Ambassador. For giving me an opportunity to improve my people's lot, it is I who should thank you."

"Have it your way," Barstowe told him. "Who am I to argue with someone as eloquent as Sammak of Vulcan?"

CHAPTER
6

WHEN ADMIRAL WALKER ENTERED THE ROOM, FORTY-SIX faces turned in his direction and forty-six hands came up to salute him.

He knew every one of them by name. Redfern, Hagedorn, McTigue, Santorini . . . Beschta, Barrios, Jones, Woo . . .

"At ease," the admiral said, advancing with echoing footfalls to the exact center of the soaring gold and black conference facility.

Earth Command's surviving captains relaxed, but not much. After all, they were men and women who had learned to thrive on discipline. That was why they were still alive when so many of their comrades were dead.

All around Walker, curved observation ports conformed to the shape of Command Base's titanium-reinforced outer hull, each one displaying bits and pieces of the visible galaxy. Only a couple of weeks ago, Earth's forces had seen the enemy abandon the last of the closer pieces.

As for those that were farther away . . . well, the admiral thought, that was the subject of this blasted meeting, now wasn't it?

"I know you've all got people you want to see and no one deserves to see them more than you do," he told the assemblage, his voice bounding from bulkhead to bulkhead. "With that in mind, I'll try to make this brief."

Forty-six pairs of eyes attended him, waiting for him to begin. Walker took a breath and did what his duty demanded of him.

"I have just come from a meeting with President Littlejohn—a very important meeting, I might add." The admiral scanned his officers' faces. "She tells me there's a change on the horizon—one that may keep us from being caught with our pants down the next time an invader comes knocking."

The prospect met with nods and grunts of approval. No surprise there, Walker mused. These were the men and women who had borne the brunt of Earth's miserable lack of readiness for five long, hard war years. No one could be happier to see some improvements made.

That is, if they were the *right* improvements.

"This change," he told them, "is manifesting itself as something called The United Federation of Planets. It's an organization that's going to include Earth and her allies. So far, we've got eight official takers. Several more are expected to follow over the course of the next few weeks."

The captains exchanged glances. They seemed impressed but also a little skeptical. The admiral didn't blame them. Nothing of this magnitude had ever been seriously contemplated.

"And that's not all," he said. "This Federation will enjoy the services of something tentatively called a 'star fleet'—an entity that draws on the resources of not just Earth, but all member worlds."

"You mean we'll be flying alongside Tellarites?" asked Stiles.

"And Dopterians?" added Beschta, obviously finding the notion a little difficult to swallow.

"Right now," Walker declared, cutting through the buzz, "the plan is for all fleet vessels to include mixed crews. In other words, we'll be working shoulder to shoulder with all Federation species."

The officers' skepticism seemed to increase. Hagedorn raised his hand and the admiral pointed to him. "Yes, Captain?"

"These fleet vessels, sir . . . where will they come from?"

"A good question," said Walker. "For the time being, we'll be pressing our Christophers into service. However, I expect we'll start building a new breed of ships before too long."

Hagedorn nodded thoughtfully. "And will our crews simply be expanded, sir? Or will we be losing some of our human crewmen to make room for the aliens who'll be joining us?"

The admiral cleared his throat. "Actually," he told his officers with unconcealed distaste, "it hasn't been decided yet who will be asked to command these vessels."

The skepticism he had seen in his audience escalated into outright disbelief. But then, Walker himself hadn't believed it when the president apprised him of the situation.

"Sir," Beschta rumbled, "this is an outrage! We are the only ones with experience in such matters. How can an alien be expected to come out of nowhere and take command of a military vessel?"

The admiral scowled. This was the part of his presidential briefing that he had liked the least. "I truly regret having to impart this information," he told the men and women standing around him, "but there's some opposition to the idea of a purely *military*-style fleet..."

Bryce Shumar gazed at the small, wrinkled woman standing on the other side of the briefing room. "A star fleet," he repeated.

"That's right," said Clarisse Dumont. "An entity that will draw on the talents of each and every Federation member world...and eventually, over a period of several years, replace Earth Command and every other indigenous military organization."

"That's very interesting," the commander told her. And it was, of course   especially the notion of a united federation of worlds. "But what has it got to do with me?"

Dumont frowned, accentuating the lines in her face. "There's a lot about this star fleet that's not settled yet, Mr. Shumar...a lot of contention over what kind of fleet it's going to be."

The commander folded his arms across his chest, his interest piqued. "What kind of contention?"

The woman shrugged. "If people like Admiral Ed

Walker have their way, the fleet will be a strictly military organization, dedicated to patrolling our part of the galaxy and defending member planets against real or perceived aggression. But to my mind, that would be a waste of an unprecedented scientific opportunity."

Her eyes lit up. "Think of it, Mr. Shumar. Think of the possibilities with regard to research and exploration. We could seek out undiscovered life-forms, unearth previously unknown civilizations. We could go where no Earthman has ever gone before."

It was unprecedented, all right. "I'm listening."

"If we're going to make that point," Dumont told him, "if we're going to establish the vision of a research fleet as something worth pursuing, we're going to need scientists in the center seats of our vessels. Scientists like you, Mr. Shumar."

He looked at her. "You're asking me to apply for a captaincy? After I spent years on a remote Earth base, watching out for Romulans and longing for the day I could return to my work?"

"I'm sure your work is important," the woman conceded. "But this is more important. This may be the most important thing you ever do."

Shumar wished he could tell her she was crazy. But he couldn't. He saw the same possibilities she did, heaven help him.

Dumont fixed him on the spit of her gaze. "Will you do it? Will you help me mold the future?"

He frowned, hating the idea of putting off his research yet again. But, really, what choice did he have?

"Yes," said Shumar. "I'll do it."

Dumont nodded. "Good. And keep in mind, you'll be

receiving the support of some of the most powerful people on Earth—men and women who see this opportunity the same way we do. With even a little luck, we'll turn this star fleet into the kind of organization we can all be proud of."

Shumar figured that it was worth the sacrifice. He just wished it were someone else who had been called on to make it.

Hiro Matsura stared out a curved observation port and longed to get back among the stars.

The last two days on Command Base had been increasingly tedious for him—and he wasn't the only one who felt that way. The other Christopher captains were antsy as well. He could tell by the way they stood, the way they ate, the way they talked. They wanted out of this place.

"Touch of cabin fever?" asked a feminine voice.

Matsura turned and saw Amanda McTigue joining him at the observation port. "More than a touch," he admitted.

McTigue frowned a bit beneath her crown of plaited blond hair. "We'll be out of here before you know it," she told him. "That is, most of us. The ones they end up picking for this new fleet of theirs...who knows what'll happen to *them*."

"Yeah," said Matsura. "Who knows."

He knew there wasn't a chance in hell that he had been selected by the Fleet Commission. After all, he'd heard there were only six spots open, and three of them had reportedly been earmarked for nonmilitary personnel.

Hagedorn was dead certain to get one spot, and Stiles

and Beschta were the front runners for the other two. There were a couple of space jockeys deserving of the honor in Eagle and Viper squadrons as well, but Matsura's money was on his wingmates.

After all, they were the best. They had proven that over and over again. And Hagedorn, Stiles, and Beschta were the best of the best.

Suddenly, the door slid open and Admiral Walker entered the room. Matsura and McTigue and everyone else in the place faced Walker and straightened, one hand raised in a salute. As always, Beschta thrust his rounded, stubbly chin out with an air of invincibility.

"Good morning, Admiral," said a dozen captains at once, their voices echoing in the chamber.

"Morning," Walker replied flatly, as if the word left a sour taste in his mouth. "At ease, people."

As Matsura relaxed, he noticed that the admiral didn't look happy. But then, when had Big Ed Walker *ever* looked happy?

"I've received a list of the Star Fleet Commission's selections," the admiral announced. He took in everyone present with a glance. "As I expected, three of you have been chosen to command vessels."

Here it comes, Matsura thought. He turned to Beschta, Hagedorn, and Stiles, who were standing together in the front rank of the group, and prepared to congratulate them on their appointments.

Walker turned to Hagedorn. "Congratulations, Captain. You've been appointed a captain in Star Fleet."

Matsura's wing leader nodded, expressionless as always. He seemed to accept the assignment like any other.

"Sir," was his only response.

Next, the admiral turned his gaze on Stiles. "Congratulations," he remarked. "You've been selected as well."

Stiles's smile said he had only gotten what he deserved. "Thank you, sir," he told Admiral Walker.

"You're quite welcome," the admiral replied.

Beschta, Matsura thought, rooting silently for his friend and mentor. *Say the word. Beschta.*

For a moment, Walker's gaze fell on the big man and Matsura believed he had gotten his wish. Then the admiral turned away from Beschta and searched the crowd for someone else.

Damn, thought Matsura. It's not fair.

He was still thinking that when Walker's gaze fell on him—and stayed there. "Congratulations," said the admiral, staring at the young man across what seemed like an impossible distance. "You're our third and final representative. Do us proud, Captain."

Matsura felt his heart start to pound against his ribs. Had he heard Walker right? No…it was impossible, he told himself.

"Me, sir?" he blurted.

The admiral nodded, his blue eyes piercingly sharp beneath his bushy white brows. "That's right, Captain Matsura. *You.*"

Matsura tried to absorb the implications of what he had just heard. "I…I don't…I mean, thank you, sir."

"Don't mention it," said the admiral.

The other captains in the room looked at one another, confused and maybe even a little angry. No doubt, they were asking themselves the same question Matsura was: why *him?* Why, out of all of the brave men and women standing in that room, had Hiro Matsura been tapped for the Federation's new fleet?

Out of the corner of his eye, he saw Beschta's reaction. The big man looked embarrassed, as if he had suddenly realized he had come to the meeting without his pants. Then he turned to Matsura.

His expression didn't change. But without warning, he brought his hands together with explosive results. The report echoed throughout the chamber. Then Beschta did it a second time. And a third.

By then, some of the other captains had joined in. With each successive clap, their number grew, encompassing the disappointed as well as the admiring. Before long, everyone but Admiral Walker was applauding, making a thunderous sound that Matsura could feel as well as hear.

The admiral nodded approvingly. Then, as the noise began to die down, he said, "Dismissed." And with that, he turned and left the chamber.

Matsura was dazed. He couldn't bring himself to believe what had happened. However, the sadness in Beschta's eyes told him it was true.

The younger man made his way through the crowd until he stood in front of his hulking mentor. For a moment, neither of them spoke. Then Beschta shrugged his massive shoulders.

"It's no big deal," he growled. But the bitterness in his voice belied his dismissal of the matter.

Matsura shook his head. "It isn't right," he said.

Anger flared in Beschta's eyes. "It doesn't have to be right. It is what it is. Make the most of it, Hiro—or I'll be the first to tear you out of the center seat and pound you into the deck. You hear me?"

Matsura could see the pain through the big man's act. "It should have been you," he insisted.

Beschta lowered his face closer to his protégé's. "Don't ever let me hear you say that again," he grated. *"Ever."*

The younger man swallowed, afraid of what his friend might do. "Okay," he conceded. Suddenly, an idea came to him. "Why don't you sign on with me as my exec? That way, I know I'll come back in one piece."

The big man's eyes narrowed in thought for a moment. Then he waved away the idea. "I've got better things to do than be your first officer," he rumbled proudly. "There's still an Earth Command, isn't there? There are still ships that need flying?"

"Of course," Matsura assured him.

"Then that's what I'll do," said Beschta. He managed a lopsided smile. "If your fancy Star Fleet gives you a day off sometime, come look for me. I'll be the one flying circles around all the others."

Matsura grinned. "I'll do that."

But he knew as well as the big man did that Earth Command wouldn't be what it had been in the past. After all, there weren't any more Romulans for them to fight. And whenever a threat reared its head, Star Fleet would be the first wave of defense against it.

Beschta nodded his big, jowly face. "Good. And as the admiral told you...make us proud."

Matsura sighed. "I'll do that, too," he said.

CHAPTER
7

AS CONNOR DANE SLIPPED INTO AN ORBIT AROUND COMmand Base, he saw on his primary monitor that there were still a handful of Christophers hanging around the place. He glanced at the warships, observing their powerful if awkward-looking lines.

"Can't hold a candle to you, baby," Dane whispered to his ship, patting his console with genuine affection.

Then he punched in a comm link to the base's security console. After a second or two, a round-faced woman with pretty eyes and long dark hair appeared on the monitor screen.

"Something I can do for you?" she asked.

"I believe I'm expected," he said. "Connor Dane."

The woman tapped a pad and checked one of her

monitors. "So you are," she noted. "I'll tell the transporter officer. Morales out."

With that, her image vanished and Dane's view of the base was restored. Swiveling in his seat, he got up and walked to the rear of his bridge, where he could stand apart from his instruments. The last thing he wanted was to materialize with a toggle switch in his belly button.

Before long, the Cochrane jockey saw the air around him begin to shimmer, warning him that he was about to be whisked away. The next thing he knew, he was standing on a raised platform in the base's transporter chamber.

Of course, this chamber was a lot bigger and better lit than the ones he was used to. But then, this was Command Base, the key to Earth's resounding victory over the Romulans. It didn't surprise him that it might rate a few extra perks.

The transporter operator was a stocky man with a tawny crew cut. He eyed Dane with a certain amount of curiosity.

"Something wrong?" the captain asked.

The man shrugged. "Honestly?"

"Honestly," Dane insisted.

The operator shot him a look of disdain. "I was wondering," he said, "what kind of man could see a bunch of birdies invade his system and not want to put on a uniform."

The captain stroked his chin. "Let's see now...I'd say it was the kind that was too busy popping Romulans out of space to worry about it." He stepped down from the platform. "Satisfied?"

The man's eyes widened. "You drove an escort ship? Geez, I didn't—"

"You didn't think," Dane said, finishing the man's remark his own way. "But then, guys like you never do."

Leaving the operator red-faced, he exited from the chamber through its single set of sliding doors. Then he looked around for the nearest turbolift.

As it turned out, it was just a few meters away, on the opposite side of a rotunda. Crossing to it, Dane went inside and punched in his destination. As the doors closed and the compartment began to move, he took a deep breath.

He would get this over as soon as he could, he assured himself. He would satisfy his curiosity. Then he would get back in his Cochrane and put as much distance between himself and Command Base as he possibly could.

The lift's titanium panels slid apart sooner than he had expected, revealing a short corridor shared by five black doors. Dane knew enough about Command protocol to figure out which one he wanted.

Advancing to the farthest of the doors, he touched the pad set into the bulkhead beside it. Inside, where he couldn't hear it, a chime was sounding, alerting the officer within that he had company.

With a rush of air, the door moved aside. Beyond it stood a broad-shouldered man in a black and gold admiral's uniform, his hair whiter than Dane remembered it.

Big Ed Walker's eyes narrowed beneath bushy brows. "Connor," he said. He indicated a chair in his anteroom. "Come on in."

Dane took the seat. Then he eyed the admiral. "I'm

glad you recognize me, Uncle Ed. For a moment there, I thought you were confusing me with someone who had some ambition to be a Starfleet captain."

Walker chuckled drily as he pulled up a chair across from his nephew. "Funny, son. But then, you always did have a lively sense of humor."

"I'm glad I amuse you," said Dane. "But I didn't come here to crack jokes, Uncle Ed. I came to find out how my hat got thrown in the ring. I mean, you and I haven't exactly been close for a good many years now, so I know it wasn't a case of nepotism."

The admiral nodded reasonably. "That's true, Connor. But then, you can't call that my fault, can you? You were the one who chose to leave the service and strike out on your own."

"I had no desire to be a military man," Dane tossed back. "No one seemed to believe that."

Walker smiled grimly. "I still don't. What you accomplished during the war, the reputation you earned yourself...that just proves you had it in you all along. You're a born officer, son, a natural leader—"

"So are dozens of other space jockeys," Dane pointed out, "guys who'd give their right arms to join your Starfleet. But you picked me instead." He leaned forward in his chair, deadly serious. "So tell me...what's the deal, Uncle Ed?"

The older man scowled, accentuating the lines in his face. "There's a war going on, son—a war for the future of Starfleet. And I find myself in the position of having to command the good guys."

Dane shook his head. "I don't get it."

Walker heaved a sigh. "The fleet is being put together

by a commission of twelve people, humans as well as aliens—each of them a bigwig in his or her own way."

"I've heard that much already," Dane told him.

"What you may not have heard," the admiral said, "is that some of those commissioners would like to turn their new fleet into a big butterfly-catching expedition—an organization of scientists and mapmakers and precious little else."

"And that's not to your liking," his nephew noted.

"I'm all for the advancement of science," his uncle told him. "Anyone will tell you that. But I haven't forgotten how it felt to have the Romulans breathing down our necks at the beginning of the war. I haven't forgotten how close they came to conquering us. And I'm determined not to let it happen again—not here on Earth or on any other peaceful planet."

Dane looked at him. "That doesn't explain—"

"Why we submitted your name to the commission?" Walker said, finishing the question for his nephew. He shrugged. "The truth is you're a compromise—a civilian who nonetheless has the qualifications to command a ship. To the opposition, you're as acceptable a candidate as they come." He smiled again. "But then, they don't know you the way I do."

Dane tilted his head. "Meaning?"

"Meaning I know that, deep down inside, you regret leaving the military. And I'm confident that when push comes to shove, you'll come down on the side of the good guys."

And redeem yourself in your family's eyes, the younger man thought. His uncle hadn't said it out loud, of course. But then, he didn't have to.

Walker regarded him. "I don't hear you joking, son. Does that mean I might not have been entirely wrong in my assessment?"

Dane shook his head. "Let me give you some advice, Uncle Ed. If you think I'm going to become some kind of stooge for you, don't hold your breath. The only reason I came here was to find out how the commission had gotten my name." He stood up. "And now that I've done that, I'm going to bid you a real fond adieu."

But as he headed for the door, his uncle spoke up again. "You can help me or not help me," he said. "That's up to you. But don't deprive the Federation of a good captain on my account."

Dane turned and looked back at him. "What?"

"You're still one of the best men for the job," Walker told him. "Regardless of whether you plan to become my 'stooge' or not."

The Cochrane jockey stared at him a moment longer, wary of giving any credence to the man. Then he left his uncle's quarters and headed back to his ship...with a bit more on his mind than he had planned.

Bryce Shumar had already entered the stately blue-gray building that housed Earth Command headquarters and was presenting his credentials to the woman at the security desk when an all too familiar face showed up beside him.

The other man glanced in Shumar's direction. There was a flicker of recognition in his slate-blue eyes, a hint of a sneer. Then he looked away again, without a civil word.

But then, in Shumar's experience, Connor Dane had

never been civil. From the moment he set foot on Earth Base Fourteen, the Cochrane pilot had been devoid of charity and compassion and respect for anyone but himself.

After their desperate battle with the Romulans, Shumar would have expected anyone else to lend a hand with the dead and the injured. But Dane had spent most of his time in the lounge tossing back shots of tequila. And when the tequila supply was exhausted, the pilot had retreated to his ship—whcrc hc was still dozing off a hangover when the *Nimitz* arrived.

As far as Shumar was concerned, Dane lacked a piece of what made people human. He was and probably always would be something lower on the evolutionary scale, no matter how good he was at the helm of a spacecraft.

He wondered what the Cochrane pilot was doing there at Earth Command—but he didn't wonder for long. It wasn't any of his business, he told himself, as he returned his attention to the security guard.

"Everything's in order," the woman said, returning the commander's identification card to him. "You may proceed through the doors to the right, then make a left at the first intersection. When you reach a dead end, you've found the briefing room."

Shumar nodded to her. "Thank you."

Making his way through a pair of dark sliding doors, he negotiated a long, high-ceilinged corridor with a gray stone floor and textured white walls. Every few meters, the commander passed a large bronze representation of the Earth Command insignia—a north-pole view of Earth supported by a pair of laurel wreaths.

Before too long, he came to the intersection of which the guard had spoken. Before he could make his turn, he heard the sound of footsteps and instinctively looked back down the corridor to see who had made them.

As it turned out, it was Dane.

Frowning, Shumar went left and followed a hallway that ran perpendicular to the first. It was decorated the same way, with the Command insignia placed at intervals along the walls. But here, there were dark sets of sliding doors between the insignias.

The commander ignored them. The only item of interest to him was the wider set of sliding doors that awaited him at the far end of the corridor. Beyond them lay the destination to which he had been summoned.

But as Shumar approached the doors, he found he could still hear a set of footfalls echoing behind him. He stopped and looked back. Could they be Dane's? he wondered. *Still?*

As if to confirm the commander's suspicion, the Cochrane pilot turned the corner and appeared in the hallway. Then he made his way toward Shumar, eyes straight ahead. If he was looking for one of the intervening offices, he gave no sign of it.

The commander glanced at the set of double doors, then at Dane again. No, he thought. It can't be. Who in their right mind...?

Despite Shumar's dismay, the Cochrane pilot didn't stop. He walked past the commander without a word and kept going, until the double doors parted for him and he was able to enter the briefing room.

The commander couldn't believe that Dane had been asked to attend the same meeting. There had to be some

mistake. Hell, he thought, the man was a disaster waiting to happen. He couldn't take care of himself, much
less worry about a crew.

Yet there he was. And it didn't seem to Shumar that
there was a lot he could do about it.

As the doors started to slide together again, the former commander of Earth Base Fourteen took a deep
breath and followed the Cochrane jockey into the room.
Sensing his approach, the doors retracted into their wall
slots, giving him an unobstructed view.

And for the first time, Shumar was able to get a
glimpse of what he had gotten himself into.

CHAPTER
8

AARON STILES WAS STANDING BETWEEN HAGEDORN AND Matsura, not far from the six chairs that had been set up in the center of the room, when the first of the butterfly catchers walked in.

He found himself sizing up the competition. But after a moment, he decided the guy looked familiar. And the more he looked at the newcomer, the more certain he was that he had met him before.

Suddenly, he placed the face. "Son of a…" he began, then remembered where he was and checked himself.

Hagedorn looked at him. "What is it?"

Stiles grunted. "An old friend. Pardon me." And without another word, he moved to intercept the newcomer.

The man's eyes narrowed as he saw Stiles approach him. "Something I can do for you?" he asked.

Stiles smiled, trying to be as friendly as possible. "You can give me back my gun," he said.

The man's forehead crinkled. "Excuse me?"

Out of the corner of Stiles's eye, he saw another butterfly catcher walk in. But he was too intent on the first one to take much notice.

"Your name is Dane?" asked Stiles.

The man nodded. "What about it?"

"Three years ago," Stiles explained, "you were in a poker game under Marsdome. According to security files, you won a twentieth century revolver from a man named Peter Stiles."

Dane shrugged. "So?"

"So Peter Stiles was my cousin and the revolver was a family heirloom," Stiles said reasonably. "He had no business gambling with it. I want it back—and just to be fair, I'm willing to pay for it."

The other man smiled a slow, thin smile. "I remember now. Your cousin's a lousy poker player."

"Was a lousy poker player," said Stiles. "But fortunately for you and me and the populations of a dozen planets, he was one hell of a space fighter. Now about that gun...I'll give you two and fifty hundred credits. It can't be worth more than that."

Dane shook his head. "Forget it."

Stiles felt as if he had been slapped across the face. "I beg your pardon?"

"I won the gun fair and square," Dane told him. "What's more, I've grown attached to the thing. You want it," he went on in a casual, almost arrogant tone, "you're going to have to take it from me."

And he started to move past Stiles.

But before the newcomer could get very far, the captain put his hand on the man's shoulder. "I just may do that," he said, barely controlling a hot surge of anger.

Dane looked at him for a moment. Then he brushed off Stiles's hand. "You're welcome to try, amigo."

Abruptly, a deep, resonant, and almost musical voice filled the room. "Welcome, gentlemen. Please be seated."

Stiles turned and tracked the voice to its source—a short, slender man in a gray suit. He had very dark skin, an aquiline nose, and a shock of gray hair. And he was looking directly at Stiles and Dane.

Stiles glared at Dane, warning him with a look that their business wasn't finished. Then, because he was every bit as disciplined as he was determined, he took a seat as the slender man had advised.

As the civilian took his place before the assembled chairs, Hagedorn and Matsura placed themselves on either side of Stiles in the front row. Dane and the other butterfly catcher secured seats behind them.

But that only made five of them, Stiles noted. Putting his ire over the revolver aside, he turned to Hagedorn and whispered, "I thought there were supposed to be six of us."

"So did I," said his wingmate, never taking his eyes off the man in the gray suit.

"Maybe they changed their minds," Matsura suggested.

Hagedorn seemed to ponder the possibility for a moment. Then he shook his head. "I doubt it, gentlemen. Three of us, three of them. More than likely, the beggar's just—"

Before he could get out another word, the doors slid

open again and someone else entered the room. Stiles wasn't surprised to see that the man wore a loose-fitting black jumpsuit, which was plainly civilian garb. What *did* catch him off guard was the rest of the newcomer's appearance, which indicated that he was a denizen of Rigel IV...

And not of Earth.

"—late," Hagedorn finished lamely, unable to conceal a note of raw surprise in his voice.

Stiles had known that humans would be serving alongside aliens, of course. Admiral Walker had made that clear to them. But no one had mentioned that humans would be serving *under* aliens.

"Captain Cobaryn," said the man with the hawklike nose. "I was wondering if your orders had somehow failed to reach you."

The Rigelian shook his bony, silver-skinned head. "They reached me without incident, sir. I simply had a little difficulty finding this facility. Of course, I regret any inconvenience I may have caused."

"None at all," the slender man told him. "We were just about to start. Please, sit down."

The exchange was a little too polite for Stiles's taste. In the service, officers were more blunt. But then, it was becoming increasingly evident that Starfleet was a different animal.

At least for the time being, he reminded himself.

The Rigelian deposited himself in a chair beside Dane. Unless Stiles was mistaken, there was a spark of recognition between the two. And not just between *them,* but between Cobaryn and the other butterfly catcher also.

"If I may have your attention," said the man in the gray suit, "my name is Chinua Abute. I am the Director of Starfleet. As the first half-dozen captains in our organization, you will all report directly to me."

Abute, thought Stiles. He had heard the name before. Judging by the grunts from the back row, the butterfly catchers had heard of it, too.

"Some of you," said Abute, "may know me for my work as Chief Protocol Officer at Earth Command. Of course, I served in that capacity some time ago. Immediately afterward, I resigned my commission to command the first civilian exploration vessel assigned to the Aratain Sector."

Stiles nodded, putting the facts together. Aratain was the sector where the Tellarite and Andorian homeworlds were located. Abute was probably responsible for making contact with those races—no doubt, a couple of big feathers in the man's cap.

"So as you can see," Abute concluded, "my experience straddles the various types of responsibilities our fleet will be undertaking. I understand the value of security as well as science."

Stiles frowned. A chief protocol officer was a military man in name only. Clearly, Abute was a butterfly catcher at heart.

What's more, he doubted the man had any real clout. More likely, he was a compromise between the military and scientific camps—and the real power rested in the hands of others.

"Now," said the director, "enough about me. Let's talk about our fleet...and what it expects of *you.*"

In the next few minutes, Abute introduced each of

them to the group and outlined their duties. They would each patrol a particular precinct of the newly formed Federation, alert to both alien threats and scientific opportunities. And as Walker had surmised, they would make use of Earth's Christopher fleet until Starfleet could build its own vessels.

Abute smiled with what seemed like genuine fervor. "Which brings me to the *Daedalus*," he said.

Fishing a small remote control device from his pocket, he pressed a button and dimmed the lights in the room. Then he pressed another button and produced a three-dimensional image in the air beside him.

It was an image of a spacegoing ship—but one that looked nothing like a Christopher. Whereas the latter resembled an old-fashioned hip flask with a couple of warp nacelles tucked underneath it, this vessel was comprised of an elegant central cylinder, two powerful-looking nacelles suspended above it, and a roomy, globelike appendage in front.

"The *Daedalus*," Abute repeated, a distinct note of pride in his voice, "is at this very moment under construction at the Utopia Planitia Shipyards in orbit around Mars. When completed, she will be capable of speeds up to *warp three*—thanks to increased plasma flow through the injectors and greater efficiencies in the warp field generator coils."

Stiles was impressed, to say the least. Even with the latest round of improvements, his Christopher had been lucky to maintain warp *two*.

"The *Daedalus*' will also boast state-of-the-art tactical systems," Abute told them. "These include six tight-beam laser generators which are fifty percent more powerful than anything we've used to date, improved launcher assemblies for our atomic detonation devices, and four additional layers of electromagnetic deflector shielding."

Six layers of deflectors, Stiles thought wonderingly. If they'd had that kind of protection against the Romulans, the war wouldn't have dragged on half so long.

"In addition," said Abute, "we have installed long-range scanners capable of probing thermal, gravimetric, and electromagnetic phenomena at distances of up to a light-year from the ship."

"What about passive neutrino imaging?" asked the Rigelian.

"Up to half a light-year," the director replied.

"Remarkable," said one of the butterfly catchers, a man with wavy black hair and dark, intense features.

"And on the short-range front," said Abute, "similarly remarkable improvements have been made in our optical, quark-resonance, and gamma-radiation scanning capabilities. Clearly, our ability to recognize and categorize planetary lifeforms will be greatly enhanced."

"Clearly," Cobaryn agreed.

"Communications?" asked Hagedorn.

Abute looked almost apologetic. "That is one of the few functions we have been unable to improve to any great degree—so far, at least."

"Too bad," said Cobaryn.

"On the other hand," Abute said, perking up noticeably, "we have cut short-range transport times by more than twenty-nine percent. And our quantum-resolution transporter range has been expanded to thirty-eight thousand kilometers, allowing for site-to-surface transports of living organisms—ship's personnel included."

Stiles couldn't help being skeptical. "You mean we can establish orbit around a world and just beam down?"

The director nodded. "I know. I had a hard time believing it myself at first. But we've been transporting volunteers at that range without negative effects for several weeks now. And in the next day or so, we'll be installing a site-to-surface transporter here at Earth Command—so if you like, you can try it yourself."

"Not *me*," Matsura breathed.

Abute smiled at him. "Not yet, Captain. But soon enough." He pointed to a spot on the *Daedalus*'s globe. "And just in case something goes wrong, you'll be glad to know you'll have a fully equipped sickbay on board—with six medical diagnostic tables that our engineers have dubbed biobeds."

"Six?" echoed Hagedorn. "Why so many?"

The director shrugged. "You may need them—considering this vessel is expected to carry a crew of no less than two hundred and thirty."

"My God," Stiles said out loud. His hometown back in Tennessee had fewer people than that.

Abute regarded him. "Quite a responsiblity, I agree. But then, the *Daedalus* isn't just another ship. It's going to be the prototype for all of Starfleet—the vehicle that's going to carry our fledgling Federation far beyond the bounds of known space."

"Who's going to command it?" asked Hagedorn.

The director's smile faded a little as he considered the man. "You've hit the nail on the head, haven't you, Captain?"

"I believe in being blunt," said Hagedorn.

"Very well, then," Abute responded. "Let us be blunt." He eyed each of the six individuals assembled before him, one at a time. "Only one of you will command the *Daedalus*—the one who best exemplifies the virtues of a Starfleet captain in the eyes of a special board of review."

"And the rest of us?" asked Matsura.

"The rest of you," said Abute, "will receive *Daedalus*-class vessels as they become available."

Stiles was no fool. It didn't take him long to understand what was at stake in such a competition—and it wasn't just pride or prestige.

If one of the captains with a military background was given command of the *Daedalus,* he would become the template for all Starfleet captains to come. But if one of the butterfly catchers got the nod, the prototypical Starfleet captain would be a scientist first and last.

That meant only one thing. Stiles or one of his wingmates would get the *Daedalus*. Any other outcome was unacceptable.

"Of course," Abute noted, "it would be foolish to finalize our designs for the *Daedalus* and her sister ships until we've heard from the men who will command them. If you check the computer terminals in your quarters, you will find all the information you'll need. Study it and come up with recommendations. I look forward to hearing what you have to say."

I'll bet you do, thought Stiles.

Shumar considered the holographic image of the *Daedalus,* with its sleek, strangely majestic lines and the amazing capabilities those lines suggested—and he began to understand what it represented.

To the victor goes the spoils, he mused. *All* of them.

"Any questions?" asked Abute.

There weren't any.

Abruptly, the director manipulated his remote control device, causing the three-dimensional image to vanish. A moment later, he turned the lights back on as well.

"Then that concludes our briefing," said Abute. "Thank you for your attention. I will see you in the large conference room at this same time tomorrow. Until then, you are dismissed."

With that, the hawk-nosed man made his way out of the room—leaving Starfleet's six captains alone with each other. That state of affairs didn't last long, however.

Hagedorn, Stiles, and Matsura got up and exchanged glances—but only with each other. Then they headed for the door together and followed Director Abute out of the room.

"Well," said Shumar, "that was rather friendly of them."

Cobaryn tilted his head. "You are joking, yes?"

Dane didn't answer. He just stood there and frowned. More than likely, Shumar reflected, the Cochrane jockey was only sticking around to give the military men a head start. Then, when he left, too, he wouldn't have to run into them in the hallway.

"Listen," said Shumar, "we've all spoken with Clarisse Dumont, right?"

Cobaryn nodded. "Indeed."

Dane's frown deepened. "What about it?"

"I just wanted to make sure," Shumar told him, trying not to let the man get to him. "Because if we *have* spoken with her, we should all understand the significance of this business about the *Daedalus*."

Cobaryn nodded. "Whoever receives it will have a great deal of influence on the objectives of the fleet. That much is clear."

"So?" asked Dane.

"So if we want Starfleet to be a force for knowledge, one of us has to wind up in command of the *Daedalus*. And the only way we're going to achieve that goal is to work together."

The Rigelian thought about it for a moment. Then he nodded again. "As you say, my friend, we must work together."

Shumar looked at Dane. "What about you, Captain? Are you in?"

The Cochrane jockey chuckled. "Let's get something straight, all right? I care about the advancement of science as much as I care about babysitting the galaxy— which is not very much."

Shumar didn't get it. "Then why did you agree to join Starfleet in the first place?" he wondered.

Dane didn't answer for a long time. Then he shrugged. "I keep asking myself that question."

With that, the man left the room. Sighing, Shumar turned to Cobaryn and said, "He's some piece of work."

"As I noted once before," Cobaryn remarked, "our Captain Dane is something of a loner."

Shumar had to agree. "I guess it's up to the two of us, then."

The Rigelian smiled his awkward smile. "Yes. And let us hope that will be enough."

CHAPTER
9

DOREEN BARSTOWE GAZED ACROSS THE WHITE-AND-RED checkered tablecloth at the large and imposing figure of Barnett Harrington Shaw.

"So," she said, "it seems you've made quite a name for yourself."

Shaw shrugged his broad shoulders, which had looked even broader before he developed a paunch of the same magnitude. "If you recall," he said, "I wanted to be a third baseman. I would've been good at it, too—better than a lot of those who came before me. Law is just something I dabble in while I mourn the passing of the major leagues."

Barstowe smiled. "Don't give me that, Barney. You eat and breathe and dream about the Law, and God help any attorney on the other side of the aisle who believes you're just a frustrated third sacker."

It was Shaw's turn to smile, his teeth white and perfect in the dark nest of his beard. "Sorry. I guess I forgot to whom I was speaking." He leaned across the table. "What brings you to Earth?"

"What else?" she said. "The Federation."

He sat back in his chair as if recoiling from something mildly distasteful. "Ah, yes. *That* little thing."

"You don't like my Federation?" Barstowe asked sweetly.

Shaw gazed out the open window beside them, which afforded a view of the quainter parts of San Francisco all the way down to the bay. The plunging streets were lined with narrow Victorian houses painted in soft, cheerful pastels. Gulls flew overhead. Somewhere down the hill, a streetcar bell was ringing as if it had something to complain about.

"It's not your Federation I don't like," Shaw said after a moment. "It's what it seems likely to bring with it."

"And what's that?" Barstowe asked. "Aliens?"

He shot her a look that said he meant nothing of the sort. "Curiosity-seekers," he replied. "Corporate bigwigs with trade contracts in their pockets. Entrepreneurs with grand ideas, God help us."

"And that's bad?"

"This is a sleepy little town, Doreen. I like it that way."

"You might be right," she conceded. "The place may change a bit. But not much, not in the ways you think. We're doing our best to set up facilities in other parts of the world so San Francisco doesn't end up bearing the burden of interstellar commerce all by herself."

The bearded man smiled a tight smile. "I hope it'll work as well as you believe it will."

"You've got my word on it," Barstowe said. "Remember, this was my town, too."

"Before you took off for the stars." He chuckled. "I remember how hopeful you were, how determined to bring the galaxy together. And now you've done it, haven't you?"

"With a little help," she reminded him.

"So now what? Do you plan to stay a while...I hope?"

The ambassador blushed. She had never been good at handling flirtations, even when they came from an old friend. Alien relations were more her style.

"Well," she said, forging ahead, "now that we've received commitments from all the other species we contacted, we attempt to set up an organization."

Shaw nodded. "A structure."

"And a set of bylaws everyone can live with. In fact, there's a conference scheduled for a week from now, where representatives of Earth and seven other member-worlds will bang out a constitution."

"Sounds nasty," Shaw observed.

"Nasty?" Barstowe echoed.

"Eight different species in one room? With eight different cultural perspectives, each as different from the others as Death Valley is from Kilimanjaro?" The attorney shivered. "I pity the poor soul who has to make sense of *that* mess."

She hadn't intended to raise the question so soon, but it was just as well it had come up. She knew from experience that one didn't beat around the bush with Barney Shaw.

"Ask not for whom the bell tolls," Barstowe said, and let her words fall through the air like bombs.

Her friend's jaw dropped as he realized what she was asking of him. "You're kidding, right? Please tell me you're kidding."

She shook her head from side to side. "It tolls for thee, Barney. And before you say no, hear me out."

Shaw's brow creased down the middle, but he didn't stop her. She drew encouragement from that.

"You're the best," she said. "We both know that, modesty and baseball stories aside. And beyond being the best, you've proven you can look at the law in ways other people can't. That's why you were able to defend that man accused of murder on Alpha Eridani Two."

"The first and last time you'll see me venture into space," the bearded man assured her.

"But you *did* it," the ambassador insisted, "because you were one of the few attorneys on Earth who could grasp that unusual set of circumstances and effectively wrap the Law around it. All I'm asking is that you take that nimble mind of yours and apply it to a challenge worthy of your abilities."

He raised an eyebrow. "Flattery?"

"If that's what it takes," she told him.

"But I've never dealt with aliens before," Shaw pointed out. "Hell, I've never even *met* an alien."

"Neither have the other representatives," Barstowe told him. "Sedrik of Vulcan would be the only exception, and the only alien *he* ever met was *me*."

Her friend frowned in his beard. "I'm only mildly acquainted with space law, Doreen."

"And those who *are* acquainted with it are too accustomed to turning it to their advantage, because they've been working all along for those corporate bigwigs you mentioned. You'll come to the task with a fresh point of view, untainted by previous experiences."

He looked impressed. "You have all the answers, don't you?"

"It's my job," she reminded him.

Shaw drummed his fingers on the table, weighing the offer. "Who's your backup in case I say no?"

"There's no backup, Barney. There's only you."

His eyes narrowed. "What kind of strategic planning is that?"

"Will you do it?" Barstowe asked, cutting to the chase.

Her friend took a while before answering. "On one condition," he said at last. "That you stay here on Earth and help me out."

She hadn't expected that. "I'm an ambassador," she pointed out. "I can't be of any use to anyone if I stay here on Earth."

Unexpectedly, Shaw leaned forward and took her hand in his. "You can be of use to *me*," he said softly.

It was only then that the ambassador realized what he was talking about. Suddenly, she found it hard to breathe. It was only with great effort that she found the words to fashion an answer.

"Where did *this* come from?"

He smiled. "It was always there. You just never noticed it."

"Barney," Barstowe began to protest, "I can't—"

"I'm serious," he insisted. "If you want me to represent Earth, you'd better stick around. I'm adamant about it."

She reached for her water glass and slid some of its contents down her throat. It helped.

All her life, she had made her way by convincing other people to do what she wanted. It was strange that when someone else came at her with the same approach, she found herself so unprepared.

So defenseless.

Nor was this an easy answer, the kind she might toss off and never have to worry about. It was an answer the ambassador would have to live with for some time to come.

But when she considered it, considered what it might lead to, she found—much to her surprise—that she wasn't so adverse to it after all. In fact, in a funny, nervous kind of way, she found herself looking forward to it.

And while it was true that her talents would be best applied on other worlds, there would also be a need for people of her talents here on Earth. At least, that was the way things seemed to be shaping up.

Barstowe looked at Barney Shaw. She had always liked him, hadn't she? How much, she couldn't say. But maybe this was the time in her life when she needed to find out.

"Well?" he asked. "Do we have a deal?"

She managed a smile. "You're going to love Sedrik of Vulcan."

T'pau was the highest-ranking official in the Vulcan planetary government. She was also one of the loveliest females Sammak had ever seen. He was reminded of both those facts as he entered her soaring, sandstone audience chamber in the city of ShariKahr and beheld her on her seat of ancient seekasa wood.

"Sammak," T'pau said, acknowledging his presence. Though she spoke softly, her voice echoed in the chamber.

"T'pau," he replied, his voice echoing as well.

If one had regarded T'pau from a distance, one might have said that she was girlish in appearance. Indeed, she was shorter in stature and smaller-boned than most females her age.

But even from a distance, she was a striking figure in her dark, sleeveless gown and traditional Vulcan headdress. In ancient days, warriors would have fought to the death for the right to possess her.

"Approach," she instructed him.

He crossed the white flagstone expanse that separated them and inclined his head out of respect. "I am grateful that you were able to see me on such short notice," he told her.

"I understand that this is a matter of some importance." In the light from torches set into the walls, her dark eyes seemed to glitter beneath delicate, upswept brows.

Youth, beauty, and an ability to command respect, Sammak reflected. A rare combination indeed.

"It is a Federation matter," he explained.

T'pau didn't comment on the relative importance of the Federation in the scheme of things Vulcan. She merely said, "I am listening."

"As you know," Sammak proceeded, "the Federation has called on all of its member worlds to present candidates for service in its Starfleet."

"A request we have respectfully declined," she remarked.

"That is true," Sammak said. "However, the Federation is again calling on us to present candidates—this time for its Starfleet Academy, where it will train the future officers of its vessels."

T'pau considered the request. "Is the Federation unaware of the existence of the Vulcan Science Academy? Or the honor that attends those students who are granted admission to it?"

"I have made mention of the Science Academy personally," he informed her. "Though even before that, the administrators of the Federation were aware of our Academy and its virtues. Nonetheless, it has been pointed out to me that the *Federation* Academy will provide a different range of opportunities, some of them beyond the scope of any planetbound institution."

T'pau cocked an eyebrow at his response. "The opportunity to leave Vulcan, I suppose?"

"And to experience other worlds," he added. "To do so firsthand, rather than to be restricted to the information available in computer files."

"And you believe our young people will find this alternative appealing?" she asked, her voice tinged with incredulity. "Would you?"

Sammak shrugged. "Of course not."

"Then perhaps we should advise the Federation that Vulcan declines in this instance as well."

"Perhaps we should," he allowed. "But then, would we not be closing a door it is just as easy to leave open?"

T'pau's eyes narrowed. "Explain."

"It may be," Sammak said, "that a very unusual Vulcan will surprise us and express a wish to join Starfleet after all."

"And in that instance," she concluded, "we will wish we had made it possible for him to do so."

"Precisely," he replied.

T'pau gave the matter some thought. Finally, she spoke. "I find it unlikely that any Vulcan would wish to make use of Starfleet's Academy. But as you say, it is not difficult to leave this door open."

Sammak inclined his head again. "You are most wise, excellency."

"And you are wise to say so," she returned. "But you need not flatter me, Sammak. You will always be welcome in my audience chamber."

"I am grateful," he told her.

Of course, Sammak hadn't told T'pau of another opportunity the Federation was likely to extend to them. He had been informed that she would be offered a seat on the Federation Council in the near future.

No doubt, T'pau would turn the seat down, and it would again be Sammak's job to convince her to reconsider her position. But he would deal with that matter when it became necessary.

For now, he had achieved something of a victory. He believed his friend Doreen Barstowe would be pleased.

"If there is nothing else...?" T'pau prodded. After all, there were other matters that required her attention.

"There is but one other subject to be discussed," Sammak said. "That of Skon and T'lara, whom you know. I have been asked to inform you that T'lara has given birth to a male child."

T'pau absorbed the news. "That is pleasant news indeed. What have Skon and T'lara decided to call the child?"

"His name is Sarek," Sammak told her.

"Sarek," she repeated. She nodded approvingly. "Perhaps he will be the youth who makes use of the Federation's invitation."

It was an ironic remark. But then, even the highest official in Vulcan's planetary government could lean toward sarcasm now and then.

"Perhaps," Sammak replied.

It didn't matter if a score of generations passed and no one availed himself of the opportunity to enter Starfleet Academy. Logic dictated that one prepare oneself for all eventualities.

No matter how unlikely they might seem.

Chinua Abute was cautiously pleased with the way his briefing had gone.

The Starfleet Commission could have handed him six fat, juicy lemons. Instead, they had given him six very capable individuals, a foundation for success if he was any judge of such things.

Of course, it was difficult to assess a man's character on the basis of a single meeting, much less six men all at once. They might yet turn out to be lemons of one kind or another. However, as Abute closed the door to his office at Earth Command and desposited himself in a chair by his workstation, it seemed to him that the Federation's fleet had made a good start.

Now he was curious to see how the morning's *other* meeting was going. Tapping out the requisite commands on his keyboard, the director opened a closed-circuit link to the Earth Command Executive Chamber, a stately, golden-walled room with a high ceiling and a black oval table at its center.

There were eight people seated around the table. Seven of them were denizens of other worlds. The lone Earthman was a prominent San Francisco attorney named Barnett Shaw.

At the moment, Shaw was addressing the group, his hands pressed together in front of him. Large and full-bearded as he was, he made an impressive figure, and his voice was no less commanding than his appearance.

"If there's no further comment pertaining to Guarantee Six," he said, "I would like to make a suggestion with regard to Guarantee Seven."

The others exchanged glances, then turned to him. "Please do," replied Ducheddet of Andor, inclining his white-haired head so that his antennae drooped in front of his blue-skinned face.

"Thank you," said Shaw.

He consulted his note padd for a moment. The other delegates waited patiently for him to speak—even the Tellarite, whose people were notoriously short on the virtue of patience.

"In our society," he said, "we grant each of our citizens the right to refrain from any action or statement that might identify him as the perpetrator of a criminal act. I propose that we embrace this right by making it our constitution's seventh guarantee."

The others looked at him with unconcealed skepticism. "The right to...refrain from self-incrimination?" said Erendi, the black-and-white striped representative from Dedderai.

"That's correct," Shaw told her.

"But why would we grant such a right?" asked Ducheddet, his head cocked to one side.

The Earthman looked uncomfortable, Abute thought. Perhaps he hadn't expected his proposal to meet with resistance.

"Why?" Shaw echoed. "For any number of reasons. For one thing, confessions can be coerced. For another, thcy can bc madc falsely, perhaps in the interest of protecting someone else. But mainly because self-incrimination sidesteps the other rights we've granted."

"What you earlier referred to as due process," observed Sedrik of Vulcan, a lean and thoughtful specimen.

Shaw nodded. "A person deserves a fair trial, my friends. No one should be able to take that away from him."

"But are we not depriving the accused of another right?" asked Odronk the Tellarite. "The right to admit the commission of a crime and have one's guilt expunged through punishment?"

"A good question," Erendi noted. "If this suggestion were to be codified as a guarantee, such an individual would have to resort to other forms of proof to identify himself as the guilty party."

"Also," said Aspartha of Rigel IV, whose people had been the last to join the Federation, "why should we provide a shield for those who seek to avoid punishment? If someone has committed a crime, he should be revealed as a criminal by any means possible."

"Even when his testimony may be needed as proof against someone who has committed a greater crime?" Shaw asked.

Ducheddet made a sound of disbelief deep in his throat. "Are you saying that we must tolerate *injustice* in one instance in order to ensure *justice* in the other?"

Clearly, that's what Shaw had suggested. "That's the way it works sometimes," he was forced to concede.

Before Ducheddet could press his point, Tirontis of Vobilin added his two cents. "I find it difficult to believe," he said, his protruding jaw-tusks moving as he spoke, "that an individual would refrain from identifying a murderer simply to protect himself."

Odronk snorted with amusement. "A Tellarite would," he said with a sneer. "In a heartbeat."

Tirontis looked at him with horror in his eyes. No doubt, he was reconsidering the wisdom of entering an agreement with a culture that accepted such perfidy.

"A Vobilite would *not*," Tirontis said.

"Nor would a Dedderac," Erendi added.

"We have incorporated your other suggestions into the constitution," said Cabbol of Osadj, his dark, recessed eyes fixed on Shaw. "We have stipulated that the accused must be judged by a jury of his peers, that he must be granted an opportunity to confront his accuser, and that he must be allowed to see the evidence brought against him. However, I am inclined to dismiss this notion."

"As am I," Ducheddet added.

"It simply makes no sense," Aspartha concluded, his hands held apart in an appeal for reason.

But Shaw didn't seem inclined to take no for an answer. "If you don't see this as a critical element in our constitution," he said calmly, even contritely, "it's only because I've failed to explain its value. Please allow me to try again."

None of the other representatives objected. However, the expressions on the aliens' faces told Abute that Shaw would have an uphill fight on his hands—not only over this matter, but perhaps over others as well. Now that an atmosphere of moral outrage had tainted the negotiations, it would be difficult to obtain a consensus on *anything*.

The director broke the comm link, that much more determined to hold up *his* end of the bargain.

CHAPTER
10

ALONIS COBARYN GRUNTED SOFTLY TO HIMSELF AS HE
studied the scale hologram of the *Daedalus*-class prototype. Somehow, the two-meter-long hologram had
looked more impressive in the darkened briefing room
where he had seen it the day before.

Here at the center of Earth Command's primary conference room, a grand, solemn amphitheater with gray
seats cascading toward a central stage from every side,
the hologram seemed small and insignificant. And with
two dozen grim, lab-coated engineers occupying a scat-
tering of those seats, already making notes in their handheld computer pads, the Rigelian had to admit he was
feeling a little insignificant himself.

He saw no hint of that insecurity in the other captains
standing alongside him. But then, Hagedorn, Stiles, and

Matsura were used to the soberness of Earth Command environments and engineers. And while neither Shumar nor Dane could make that claim, they were at least Earthmen.

Of all those present, Cobaryn was the only alien. And while no one in the facility had done anything to underline that fact, he still couldn't help but be aware of it.

For some time, the Rigelian had been fascinated by other species. He had done his best to act and even think like some of them. However, after having spent an entire day on Earth, he was beginning to wonder if he could ever live as one of them.

Cobaryn's thoughts were interrupted by a loud hiss. Turning, he saw the doors to the amphitheater slide open and produce the slender form of Starfleet Director Abute.

As the dark-skinned man crossed the room, the engineers looked up from their pads and gave him their attention. No surprise there, the Rigelian reflected, considering Abute was their superior.

"Thank you for coming, ladies and gentlemen," the director told the lab-coated assemblage, his voice echoing almost raucously from wall to wall. "As you know, I have asked the six men who are to serve as captains in our new fleet to critique your work on the *Daedalus*. I trust you'll listen closely to what they have to say."

There was a murmur of assent. However, Cobaryn thought he heard an undertone of resentment in it. Very possibly, he mused, these engineers believed they had already designed the ultimate starship—and that this session was a waste of time.

Abute disagreed, or he wouldn't have called this

meeting. The Rigelian found himself grateful for that point of view, considering he was one of the individuals who would have to test the engineers' design.

The director turned to Matsura. "Captain?" he said. "Would you care to get the ball rolling?"

"I'd be happy to," said Matsura. He took a step closer to the hologram and pressed the flats of his hands together. "Let's talk about scanners."

It seemed like a reasonable subject to Cobaryn. After all, he had some opinions of his own on the matter.

Matsura pointed to a spot on the front of the ship. "Without a doubt, the long-range scanners that have been incorporated into the *Daedalus* are a big improvement over what we've got. But we can go a step further."

Abute seemed interested. "How?"

"We can devote more of our scanner resources to long-range use," Matsura answered. "That would allow us to identify threats to Earth and her allies with greater accuracy."

The engineers nodded and made notes in their pads. However, before they got very far, someone else spoke up.

"The problem," said Shumar, "is that additional long-range scanners means fewer short-range scanners—and we need that short-range equipment to obtain better analyses of planetary surfaces."

Cobaryn couldn't help but agree. Like his colleague, he was reluctant to give up any of the advantages Abute had described the day before.

Matsura, on the other hand, seemed to feel otherwise. "With due respect," he told Shumar, "you're equating expedience with necessity. It would be nice to be able to get more information on a planet from orbit. But if we could detect a hostile force a fraction of a light-year further away . . . who knows how many Federation lives might be saved someday?"

Shumar smiled. "That's fine in theory, Captain. But as we all know, science saves lives as well—and I think you would have to admit, there's also a tactical advantage to knowing the worlds in our part of space."

Matsura smiled, too, if a bit more tightly. "Some," he conceded. "But I assure you, it pales beside the prospect of advance warning."

Cobaryn saw the engineers trade glances. Clearly, they hadn't expected this kind of exchange between two captains.

Abute frowned. "Perhaps we can table this topic for the moment." He turned to the engineers. "Or better yet, let's see if there is a way to increase both long- and short-range scanning capabilities."

Grumbling a little, the men and women in the lab coats made their notes. Then they looked up again.

The director turned to the Rigelian. "Captain Cobaryn? Can you provide us with something a bit less controversial?"

That got a few chuckles out of the engineers, but not many. They seemed to the Rigelian to be a rather humorless lot.

As Matsura stepped away from the hologram, looking less than pleased, Cobaryn approached it. Glancing at the crowd of engineers to make sure they were listening, he indicated the hologram's warp nacelles.

"While I am impressed," he said, "with the enhancements made in the *Daedalus's* propulsion system, I believe we may have placed undue emphasis on flight speed."

Abute looked at the Rigelian, his brow creased. "You mean you have no interest in proceeding at warp three?"

His comment was met with a ripple of laughter from the gallery. Cobaryn did his best to ignore it.

"In fact," he replied diplomatically, "I have *every* interest in it. However, it might be more useful to design our engines with range in mind, rather than velocity. By prolonging our vessel's ability to remain in subspace, we will actually arrive at many destinations more quickly—even though we have progressed at a somewhat slower rate of speed.

"What's more," he continued, "by shifting our emphasis as I suggest, we will be able to extend the scope of our operations...survey solar systems it would not otherwise have been practical to visit."

Stiles chuckled. "Spoken like a true explorer," he said loudly enough for everyone to hear him.

Cobaryn looked back at the man. "But I *am* an explorer," he replied.

"Not anymore," Stiles insisted. "You're a starship captain. You've got more to worry about than charts and mineral analyses."

Abute turned to him. "I take it you have an objection to Captain Cobaryn's position?" he asked a little tiredly.

"Damned right I do," said Stiles. He eyed the Rigelian. "Captain Cobaryn is ignoring the fact that most missions don't involve long trips. They depend on short, quick jumps—at ranges already within our grasp."

"Perhaps that is true now," Cobaryn conceded. "However, the scope of our operations is bound to grow. We need to range further afield for tactical purposes as well as scientific ones."

Stiles looked unimpressed with the argument. So did Hagedorn and Matsura. However, Stiles was the one who answered him.

"We can worry about the future when it comes. Right now, more speed is just what the doctor ordered."

There was silence for a moment. Without meaning to do so, the Rigelian had done exactly what Abute had asked him not to do. Like Matsura, he had become embroiled in a controversy.

"Thank you, gentlemen," the director said pointedly. "I appreciate the opportunity to hear both your points of view."

Cobaryn saw Stiles glance at his Earth Command colleagues. They seemed to approve of the concepts he had put forth. But then, that came as no surprise. It was clear that they were united on this point.

"Since Captain Stiles seems eager to speak," Abute added, "I would like to hear his suggestion next."

"All right," Stiles told him. He came forward and indicated the hologram with a generous sweep of his hand. "Two hundred and thirty people. Entire decks full of personnel quarters. An elaborate sickbay to take care of them when they get ill." He shook his head. "Is all this really necessary? Our Christophers run on crews of thirty-five—and most of the time, we don't need half that many."

"Your Christophers don't have science sections," Shumar pointed out abruptly, his arms folded across his chest. "They don't have laboratories or dedicated computers or botanical gardens or sterile containment chambers."

It was a challenge and everyone in the room knew it. Stiles, Shumar, the other captains, Abute... and the gathering of engineers, of course. Their expressions told Cobaryn that this was much more entertaining than any of them might have expected.

Stiles lifted his chin, accepting the gauntlet Shumar had thrown down. "I read the data just as you did," he responded crisply. "I heard the argument for all those research facilities. My question is... how much of it do we need? Couldn't we cut out some of that space and come up with a better, more maneuverable ship?"

Shumar shook his head. "Maybe more maneuverable, Captain, but not better—not if you consider all the capabilities that would be lost if the *Daedalus* was sized down."

"And if it's *not* sized down," Stiles insisted, "the whole ship could be lost... the first time it engages the enemy."

Again, Director Abute intervened before the exchange could grow too heated. He held up his hand for peace and said, "I would say it's your turn, Captain Shumar. To make a suggestion, I mean."

Shumar cast a last baleful glance at Stiles. "Fine with me," he replied. Taking a deep breath, he pointed to the hologram. "As we learned yesterday, we've improved our tactical systems considerably. Thanks to all the extra graviton emitters on the *Daedalus*, we've now got six layers of deflector protection—and as someone who's been shot at with atomic missiles, I say that's terrific."

Cobaryn hoped there was a "but" coming in his colleague's declaration. He wasn't disappointed.

"But what if we were to convert one or two of the extra emitters to another use?" Shumar suggested. "Say ... as tractor beam projectors?"

Matsura made a face. "*Tractor* beams?"

"Tightbeam graviton projections," Hagedorn explained, his voice echoing easily throughout the amphitheater. "When their interference patterns are focused on a remote target, they create a certain amount of spatial stress—which either pulls the target closer to the source of the beam or pushes it farther away."

Shumar nodded approvingly. "That's exactly right."

"However," said Hagedorn in the same even tone, "tractor beams are very much in the development stage right now. Some people say it'll be a long time before they can be made practical...if ever."

The Rigelian saw some nods among the engineers. It wasn't a good sign, he told himself.

Shumar frowned. "Others say tractor beams will be made practical in the next few months. Those are the people I prefer to put my faith in."

Hagedorn shrugged with obvious confidence. "I was simply putting the matter in perspective, Captain."

"As we all should," Abute said hopefully.

"Is it my turn now?" Hagedorn asked.

The director shrugged. "If you like."

Hagedorn began by circling the hologram in an almost theatrical fashion. For a few seconds, he refrained from speaking...so when he began, his words had a certain weight to them.

"You've made some interesting improvements in the ship's transporter function," he told the assembled engineers. "Some *very* interesting improvements. For instance, it'll be a lot easier to shoot survey teams and diplomatic envoys to their destinations than to send them in shuttles.

"But frankly," he continued, running his hand over the *Daedalus*'s immaterial hull, "I don't think these enhancements will be of any use to us in combat. As we proved during the war, it's impossible to force-beam our personnel through an enemy's deflector shields."

"Not everything is intended to have a military application," Director Abute reminded him, anticipating an objection from Shumar or Cobaryn.

"I recognize that," Hagedorn told him, as expressionless as ever. "However, transporters *can* have military applications. Are you familiar with the work of Winston and Kampouris?"

Abute's eyes narrowed. "It seems to me I've heard their names..."

So had Cobaryn. "They are military strategists," he stated. "They have postulated that we can use transporter systems to penetrate deflector shields by sending streams of antimatter along their annular confinement beams."

Shumar made a sound of derision. "Talk about being in the development stage. Transmitting antimatter through a pattern buffer is and always will be suicide."

Hagedorn shrugged. "Not if the buffer has been built the way we might build a warp core."

"In which case it would have to *be* a warp core," Shumar insisted. "The same elements that would protect the pattern buffer would make it impermeable to matter transmission."

"Not according to Winston and Kampouris," Hagedorn remarked.

But this time, Cobaryn observed, the engineers seemed to rule in Shumar's favor. They shook their heads at Hagedorn's comment.

Taking notice of the same thing, Abute scowled. "Which leaves us at another impasse, I take it."

Shumar eyed Hagedorn, then Stiles and Matsura. "I guess it does."

The director turned to Dane. "We have one more captain to hear from. Perhaps he can put forth a design recommendation on which we can all agree before we call it a day."

He didn't sound very optimistic, the Rigelian noted. But in his place, Cobaryn wouldn't have been very optimistic either.

Like everyone else in the amphitheater, he looked to Dane. The man considered Abute for a moment, then glanced at the engineers. "Communications," he said simply. "You say you can't do anything to improve what we've got. I say you're not trying hard enough."

The director seemed taken aback—but not nearly as much as the crowd of engineers. "I've been assured by our design team," he replied, "that nothing can be done at this time."

Dane regarded the men and women sitting all around him in their white lab coats. "I've got an assurance for your engineers," he said. "If they don't come up with a quicker way for me to contact headquarters, they can find themselves another starship captain."

Cobaryn had to smile. The Cochrane jockey had not shown himself to be a particularly charming individual. However, he did seem to have more than his share of vertebrae.

Abute looked at Dane for a second or two. Then he turned to his engineers. "You heard the man," he told them. "Let's see what we can do."

There was a rush of objections, but they died out quickly. After all, any engineer worth his degree relished a challenge. Even Cobaryn knew that.

"Thank you again," the director told the people in the gallery. "You may return to your work."

Clearly, that was the engineers' signal to depart. The Rigelian watched them toss comments back and forth as they descended to the level of the stage and filed out of the room. Then he turned to Abute, expecting to be dismissed as well.

But Abute wasn't ready to do that yet, it seemed. He regarded all six of his captains for a moment, his nostrils flaring. Finally, he shook his head.

"Gentlemen," he said, "we obviously have some differences. Honest ones, I assume. However, we must make an effort to seek common ground."

Cobaryn nodded. So did Shumar, Hagedorn, Stiles, and Matsura—everyone except Dane, in fact. But the Rigelian knew that Dane was the only one who was being honest with the director.

After all, there was a war raging. The first battle had been fought to a standoff there in the amphitheater, but Cobaryn didn't expect that it would be the last.

CHAPTER
11

DANIEL HAGEDORN YAWNED AND STRETCHED. THEN HE pushed his wheeled chair back from his monitor and the blue-and-gold ship schematics displayed on it.

True, the captain and his colleagues had submitted their recommendations regarding the *Daedalus* earlier in the day. But that didn't mean their responsibility to Director Abute was fully discharged—at least not from Hagedorn's point of view.

He meant to come up with further recommendations. A whole slew of them, in fact. By the time he set foot on the bridge of the *Daedalus* or one of her sister ships, he would know he had done everything he could to make that vessel a dead-sure success.

Abruptly, a red message box appeared against the blue-and-gold background. It was from Abute, advising each of his six captains that they would begin interviewing prospective officers the following day.

Hagedorn nodded. He had been wondering when the process would get underway.

There were to be a few rules, however. For instance, Abute wanted each vessel to reflect the variety of species represented in the Federation, so no captain could bring aboard more than a hundred human crewmen.

Also, Hagedorn couldn't draw on established military officers for more than half his command team. Clearly, the director wanted both the defense and research camps represented on each vessel's bridge.

The captain grunted. They could keep their Christopher crews intact after all, but only if some of their officers were willing to accept a demotion. Clearly, practicality would be taking a backseat to politics in this new Starfleet—not that he was surprised, given the other developments he had seen up to that point.

On the other hand, no one would be foisted on him— neither alien nor Earthman. That was one point on which Hagedorn wouldn't have given in, even if Abute had handed the *Daedalus* to him on a silver platter.

After all, the lives of the captain and his crew might one day depend on a particular ensign or junior-grade lieutenant. He wanted that individual to be someone who had earned his way aboard, not a down payment in some interplanetary quid pro quo.

With a tap of his keyboard, Hagedorn acknowledged receipt of the director's message. Then he stored the *Daedalus*'s schematics and accessed the list of officer candidates Abute had compiled.

Frowning, the captain began to set up an efficient interview schedule. He promised himself that by noon the following day he would know every bridge officer under his command.

Cobaryn was relaxing in his quarters, reading Rigelian triple-metered verse from an electronic book, when he heard the sound of chimes.

It took him a moment to remember what it meant—that there was someone in the corridor outside who wished to see him. Getting up from his chair, the captain crossed the room and pressed a pad on the bulkhead. A moment later, the doors slid apart.

Cobaryn was surprised to see Connor Dane standing there. "Can I help you?" the Rigelian asked.

The Cochrane jockey frowned. "You drink?" he asked.

Cobaryn looked at him. "You mean... do I partake of alcoholic beverages? In a public house?"

Dane's frown deepened. "Do you?"

"In fact," the Rigelian replied, "I do. That is to say, I have. But why are you inquiring about—?"

The human held up a hand for silence. "Don't ask, all right? Not where we're going, or why—or anything. Just put the damned book down and let's get a move on."

Cobaryn's curiosity had been piqued. How could he decline? "All right," he said. Then he put the book down on the nearest table, straightened his clothing, and accompanied Dane to their mysterious destination.

Dane tossed back a shot of tequila, felt the ensuing rush of warmth, and plunked his glass down on the bar.

The Afterburner's bartender, a man with a bulbous nose and a thick brush of gray hair, noticed the gesture. "Another?" he growled.

"Another," Dane confirmed.

He turned to Cobaryn, who was sitting on a stool alongside him. The Rigelian was nursing a nut-flavored liqueur and studying the human with his bright red eyes. They were asking a question.

"I know," said Dane, scowling. "You still don't understand why I asked you to come along."

Cobaryn smiled sympathetically. "I confess I don't."

"Especially since I never said a word to you the whole way from Rigel to Earth Base Fourteen."

"That does compound my curiosity, yes," the Rigelian admitted. "And even after our battle with the Romulans—"

"I sat in the bar by myself," Dane said, finishing Cobaryn's thought.

He watched the bartender replace his empty shot glass with a full one. Picking it up, he gazed into its pale-green depths.

"Why do I need company all of a sudden?" the human asked himself. "Because I'm out of my element here, that's why." He looked around the Afterburner. "Because I have no business trying to be a Starfleet captain."

The Rigelian shrugged. "From where I stand, it seems you would make an excellent captain. You have demonstrated intelligence, determination, the courage to speak your mind...."

"You mean at that meeting this morning?" Dane dismissed the notion with a wave of his hand. "That wasn't courage, pal. That was me losing my patience. I got hacked off at the idea of a bunch of lab coats telling me what I could and couldn't have."

"Nonetheless," Cobaryn insisted, "you said what no one else would have thought to say. You saw a danger to your crew and you did not hold back. Is that not one of the qualities one should look for in a captain?"

The human chuckled humorlessly. "Anyone can open a big mouth. You don't have to be captain material to do that."

"Perhaps not," the Rigelian conceded. His mouth pulled up the corners. "But it does not hurt."

Dane hadn't expected Cobaryn to make a joke. He found himself smiling back at his companion. "No," he had to allow, "I guess it doesn't."

Cobaryn's grin faded a little. "And what about me?"

The human looked at him askance. "What *about* you?"

"I am hardly the obvious choice for a captaincy in Starfleet. The only vaguely heroic action I ever undertook was to ram my ship into that Romulan back at Earth Base Fourteen—and that was only after I had determined with a high degree of certainty that I could beam away in time to save myself."

Dane was starting to feel the effects of the tequila. "Listen," he said, leaning closer to the Rigelian, "they didn't pick you for your courage, Cobaryn. They may have picked you for a whole lot of reasons, but believe me...courage wasn't one of them."

The Rigelian looked at him thoughtfully. "You are referring to my ability to command a vessel in deep space?"

"Maybe that's part of it," the human conceded, "but not all of it. Just think for a second, all right? This

United Federation of Planets they're building...it's not just about Earth. Technically, we humans are only supposed to be a small part of the picture."

"A small part...yes," said Cobaryn. His bony, silver brow furrowed a bit. "That is why Director Abute imposed a quota on the number of humans who can serve under us."

Dane pointed at him. "Exactly. And if they're encouraging us to include nonhumans in our crews and command staffs..."

For the first time, the Rigelian actually frowned in his presence. "You are saying I was picked to be a captain because I am an alien?"

"No," said Dane, "you're better than that. You're an alien who's demonstrated that he can work alongside humans—who's demonstrated that he actually *likes* to work alongside humans. Do you have any idea how many people fit that particular description?"

"Only a few, I imagine."

"A few?" The Earthman sat back on his stool. "You may be the only one in the whole galaxy! To the mooks who are engineering the Federation and its Starfleet, you're as good as having another human in the center seat—which is what they'd *really* like."

Cobaryn weighed the comment. "So I am a concession to the nonhuman species in the Federation? A token appointment, so they will not feel they have been ignored in the selection process?"

"Hey," said Dane, "it seems pretty clear to *me*. But maybe that's just the cynic in me talking."

The Rigelian didn't say anything for a while, though the muscles writhed in his ridged temples. Finally, he turned to his companion again. "I take it a human would resent the situation as you have described it?"

"Most would," Dane confirmed.

A knot of silver flesh gathered at the bridge of Cobaryn's nose. "And yet," he said, "I find I do *not* resent it. Earth's pilots clearly have more tactical experience than the pilots of any other world. And if a nonhuman is to work with them, why not choose one who has already shown himself capable of doing so?"

Dane drummed his fingertips on the mahogany surface of the bar. "You can find the bright side of anything, can't you?"

"So I have been told," the Rigelian conceded.

The human shook his head. "Pretty amazing."

Cobaryn smiled at him again—or rather, did his best impression of a smile. "Amazing for a human, yes. But as you will recall, I am a Rigelian. Among my people, everyone looks on the bright side."

Dane rolled his eyes. "Remind me not to stop at any drinking establishments on your planet."

The Rigelian looked as if he were about to tender a response to the human's comment. But before he could do that, someone bellowed a curse at the other end of the bar.

In Dane's experience, people bellowed curses all the time, almost always for reasons that didn't concern him. Unimpressed, he threw back his tequila and felt it soak into him. But before long he heard another bellow.

This time, it seemed to come from a lot closer.

Turning his head, the Cochrane jockey saw a big, balding fellow in black-and-gold Earth Command togs headed his way. And judging by the ugly, pop-eyed expression on the man's face, he was looking for trouble.

"You!" he said, pointing a big, blunt finger directly at Dane. "And you!" he growled, turning the same finger on Cobaryn. "Who do you think you are to imitate space captains?"

"I beg your pardon?" said the Rigelian, his tone flawlessly polite.

"You heard me!" roared the big man, pushing his way through the crowd to get even closer. "It's because of you two butterfly catchers that I wasn't picked to command a Starfleet vessel!"

Cobaryn looked at Dane, his face a question. "Butterfly catchers?"

Keeping an eye on their antagonist, who was obviously more than a little drunk, the Cochrane jockey made a sound of derision. "It's what Stiles and the other military types call us."

Call *you,* he corrected himself inwardly. He had never had an urge to do a stitch of research in his life.

"Well?" the balding man blared at them. "Nothing to say to Big Andre? Or are you just too scared to pipe up?"

By then, he was almost within arm's reach of his targets. Seeing that there would be no easy way out of this, Dane got up from his seat and met "Big Andre" halfway.

"Ah," grated the balding man, his eyes popping out even further. "So the butterfly catcher has some guts after all!"

"Actually," said Dane, "I was going to ask if I could buy you a drink. A big guy like you must get awful thirsty."

Big Andre looked at him for a moment, his brow furrowing down the middle. Then he reached out with lightning speed and grabbed the Cochrane jockey by the front of his shirt.

"I don't need any of your charity," the big man snarled, his breath stinking of liquor as he drew Dane's face closer to his. "You think you can take away what is mine and buy a lousy drink to make up for it?" He lifted his fist and the smaller man's shirt tightened uncomfortably. "Is that what you think, butterfly catcher?"

Dane had had enough. Grabbing his antagonist's wrist, he dug his fingers into the spaces between the bones and the tendons and twisted.

With a cry of pain and rage, Big Andre released him and pulled his wrist back. Then the expression on his meaty face turned positively murderous. "You want to fight me? All right—we'll fight!"

"No," said Cobaryn, positioning himself between Dane and the balding man. "That will not be necessary." He glanced meaningfully at his companion. "Captain Dane and I were about to leave...were we not?"

"I don't think so," said a sandy-haired civilian, who was half a head shorter than Big Andre but just as broad. "You'll leave when Captain Beschta gives you permission to leave."

"That's right," said a man with a thick, dark mustache, also dressed in civilian garb. "And I didn't hear him give you permission."

Dane saw that there were three other men standing behind them, all of them glowering at the Starfleet captains. Obviously, more of Big Andre's friends. Six against three, the Cochrane jockey mused. Not exactly the best odds in the world—and as far as he knew, the Rigelian might be useless in a fight.

"You want to leave?" the big man asked of Cobaryn, his expression more twisted with hatred than ever. "You can leave, all right—when they carry you out of here!"

And with remarkable quickness, he launched his massive, knob-knuckled fist at the Rigelian's face.

CHAPTER
12

WHEN DANE SAW BIG ANDRE TAKE A SWING AT COBARYN, he couldn't help wincing. The human looked big and strong enough to crack every bone in the Rigelian's open, trusting countenance.

But to Dane's surprise, Big Andre's blow never landed. Moving his head to one side, Cobaryn eluded it—and sent his antagonist stumbling into the press of patrons that had gathered around them.

Big Andre roared in anger and came at the Rigelian a second time. Dane tried to intervene, tried to keep his new-found friend from getting hurt, but he found himself pulled back by a swarm of strong arms.

Fortunately for Cobaryn, he was able to duck Big Andre's second attack almost as neatly as he had the first. Again, the human went hurtling into an unbroken wall of customers.

But Big Andre's friends were showing up in droves and pushing their way toward the altercation. Some of them, like Big Andre himself, wore the black and gold of Earth Command. Others were clearly civilians. But they all had one trait in common—a rabid desire to see Dane and the Rigelian pounded into something resembling pulp.

"Surround them!" one man called out.

"Don't let 'em get away!" barked another.

Dane tried to wriggle free of his captors. But before he could make any headway, he felt someone's boot explode in his belly. It knocked the wind out of him, forcing him to draw in great, moaning gulps of air.

Then he felt it a second time. And a third.

When his vision cleared, he could see Big Andre advancing on Cobaryn all over again. The man's hands were balled into hammerlike fists, his nostrils flaring like an angry bull's.

"I'll make you sorry you ever heard of Starfleet!" Big Andre thundered.

"That's enough!" called a voice, cutting through the buzz of the crowd the way a laser might cut an unshielded hull.

Everyone turned—Dane, Cobaryn, the big man, and everybody else in the place. And what they saw was the commanding figure of Dan Hagedorn, flanked by Hiro Matsura and Aaron Stiles.

Hagedorn eyed his former wingmate. "Leave it alone," he told Beschta.

The big man turned to him, his eyes sunken and red-rimmed with too much alcohol. "Hagedorn?" he snapped.

"It's me," the captain confirmed. "And I'm asking you to stop this before someone gets hurt."

Beschta laughed a cruel laugh. "Did they not hurt *me?*" he groaned, pointing at Dane and Cobaryn with a big accusing finger. "Did they not take what should rightfully have been mine?"

"Damned right!" roared a civilian whom Hagedorn had never seen before in his life.

A handful of other men cheered the sentiment. The captain had never seen them before either. Apparently, Beschta had picked up a few new friends in the last couple of weeks.

If the big man had been the only problem facing him, Hagedorn would have felt confident enough handling it on his own. But if he was going to have to confront an unknown number of adversaries, he wanted to make sure he had some help—and to that end, he glanced at his companions.

First he looked at Stiles, who knew exactly what was being asked of him. But Stiles shook his head from side to side. "This isn't any of our business," he said in a low voice.

"Like hell it isn't," Hagedorn returned. Then he turned the other way and regarded Matsura.

The younger man seemed to waver for a moment. Then his eyes met Stiles's and he shook his head as well. "I can't fight Beschta," he whispered, though he didn't seem entirely proud of his choice.

Hagedorn nodded, less than pleased with his comrades' responses but forced to accept them. "All right, then. I'll do this myself."

Turning sideways to make his way through the crowd, the captain tried to get between Beschta and his intended victim. But some of Beschta's new friends didn't like the idea.

"Where do you think you're going?" asked one of them, a swarthy man with a thick neck and broad shoulders.

Hagedorn didn't answer the question. Instead, he drove the heel of his hand into the man's nose, breaking it. Then, as the man recoiled from the attack, blood reddening his face, the captain collapsed him with a closed-handed blow to the gut.

If anyone else had had intentions of standing in Hagedorn's way, the incident changed their mind. Little by little, Hagedorn approached Beschta, who didn't look like he was in any mood to be reasoned with.

"Don't come near me!" the big man rumbled.

The captain kept coming. "That's not what you said when I saved your hide at Aldebaran."

"I'm warning you!" Beschta snarled, his eyes wide with fury.

"You won't hit me," Hagedorn told him with something less than complete confidence. "You can't. It would be like hitting yourself."

"Stay away!" the big man bellowed at him, his voice trembling with anger and pain.

"No," said the captain. "I won't."

For an uncomfortable fraction of a second, he thought Beschta was going to take a swing at him after all. He tensed inside, ready for anything. Then his former comrade made a sound of disgust.

"I thought you were my friend," Beschta spat.

"I am," Hagedorn assured him.

"They turned me away," the big man complained. "The bastards rejected me. *Me*, Andre Beschta."

"They were wrong," said the captain. "They were stupid. But don't take it out on these..." With an effort, he kept himself from using the term *butterfly catchers,* "...gentlemen."

Beschta scowled at Cobaryn and Dane, who was still in the grip of some of his allies. "You're lucky," he said. "Had Captain Hagedorn not come along, you would have been stains on the floor."

The Cochrane jockey had the good sense not to answer. Hagedorn was happy about that, at least.

The big man indicated Dane with a lift of his chin. "Let him go. He's not worth our sweat."

The men holding Dane hestitated for a moment. Then they thrust him toward Hagedorn. The Cochrane jockey stumbled for a step or two, but caught himself before anyone else had to catch him.

Off to the side, Beschta's friends were picking up the man Hagedorn had leveled. He looked like he needed medical attention—though that wasn't the captain's concern.

"Come on," he told Dane and Cobaryn. "Let's get out of here."

As they headed for the exit, the Rigelian turned to Hagedorn. "Thank you," he said with obvious sincerity.

"You're welcome," Hagedorn replied.

As he left the place, he shot a look back over his

shoulder at Stiles and Matsura. They were guiding the hulking Beschta to a table, taking care of their old wing-mate.

A part of Hagedorn wished he could have done the same.

Hiro Matsura felt more torn over what he had seen than he cared to admit. In the heat of the moment, he had taken the side of one trusted colleague over another. And on reflection, he wasn't at all sure that he had settled on the right decision.

Soberly, he watched Hagedorn and the two butterfly catchers leave the Afterburner. Then he negotiated a course to the bar.

"What'll it be?" asked the bartender.

"Brazilian coffee," said Matsura. "Black."

The bartender smiled. "For Beschta?"

Matsura nodded. Obviously, his friend had made a name for himself. "Sorry about the brawl."

The bartender dismissed the apology with a gesture and went to pour out some coffee. "It's okay," he said. "We haven't had a good knock-down-drag-out in weeks." Then he laid a hot, steaming mug on the wooden bar.

Picking up the coffee, Matsura paid the bartender and made his way back to Beschta's table. Stiles had pulled out a chair opposite the big man and was trying to calm him down.

"Listen," the captain was saying, "how long do you think those butterfly catchers are going to last? A month, Andre? Two, maybe? And when they're gone, who do you think they're going to call for a replacement?"

Beschta shook his head stubbornly. "Don't patronize me, Aaron. I may be drunk, but I'm not an imbecile. I have no chance. Zero."

"Here," said Matsura, placing the mug of coffee in front of the big man. "This will make you feel better."

Beschta glared at him, bristling with the same kind of indignation he had shown earlier. Then, unexpectedly, a tired smile spread across his face. "Some example I'm setting for you, eh, Hiro?"

Matsura didn't know what to say to that. A couple of days ago, he had still thought of himself as Beschta's protégé. Now, he was beginning to feel that he might be more than that. "Drink your coffee," was all he could come up with.

The big man nodded judiciously. "That's a good idea. I'll drink my coffee. Then I'll go home and sleep for a week or two."

"Now you're talking," said Stiles.

Seeing that Beschta was all right for the moment, he clapped him on his broad back and went over to Matsura. "Hagedorn was out of line," he said in a low voice.

"You think so?" asked the younger man.

Stiles looked at him with narrow-eyed suspicion. "Don't *you?*"

Matsura folded his arms across his chest. "The more I think about it, the more I wonder. I mean, Dane and Cobaryn could have gotten hurt. What would that have proved?"

Stiles looked like a man who was trying his best to exercise patience. "Listen," he said, "I didn't want to see people injured any more than you. But this is war, Hiro, and those two butterfly catchers are the enemy."

Matsura considered his colleague's position. "If it's a war, I'll do my best to help win it. You know that. But standing there while Dane and Cobaryn needed our help...it was just wrong."

His colleague considered him for a while longer. "You know," he said at last, "I disagree with you a hundred percent. If I had to do it over again, I'd do exactly the same thing."

Matsura started to protest, but Stiles held up a hand to show that he wasn't finished yet.

"Nonetheless," the older man continued, "this is no time for us to be arguing. We've got to be on the same page if we're going to get the kind of fleet we're aiming for."

Stiles was right about that, Matsura told himself—even if he was wrong about everything else. "Acknowledged."

His colleague smiled a little. "Come on. Let's get Beschta home."

Matsura agreed that that would be a good idea.

Aaron Stiles tapped the touch-sensitive plate on the bulkhead next to the set of sliding doors.

He desperately needed a workout—and it wasn't because he was feeling even the least bit out of shape. Even now, in his middle thirties, he could outbox, outwrestle, and outrun just about everyone he had ever known.

So it wasn't a physical need that had brought the captain here to Earth Command's little-used South End gymnasium. It was a need to let off steam, to drain off all the anger he'd felt the night before, when he saw

Hagedorn take the butterfly catchers' part in the After-burner.

Only then could he see the matter clearly. And only then could he decide what to do about it.

As it turned out, Stiles wound up with a lot less thinking time than he had bargained for—because as the doors to the gym slid apart, he saw a sweaty, red-faced Dan Hagedorn toweling off in front of the parallel bars.

The other man saw him, but didn't acknowledge him at first. Clearly, he was as surprised to see Stiles as Stiles was to see him. And like his colleague, he probably hadn't thought things out enough to know what to say.

Still, Hagedorn was the one who spoke first. "Aaron." Just that, evenly and without inflection.

Stiles nodded. "Dan."

He knew his friend well enough to glean that Hagedorn had been angry, too. And Stiles could understand why. When a guy went into a fight, he expected his wingmen to go in with him.

But you don't go into a fight to protect the enemy, he insisted bitterly. And if someone was crazy enough to consider it, he shouldn't expect help—from anyone.

All the arguments he had been mulling began bobbing to the surface of his mind. *They're not like us, dammit. They're the enemy. Starfleet would be a lot better off without them and you know it.*

But he didn't give voice to them. He didn't have to. Hagedorn would know exactly what he was going to say.

Likewise, Stiles knew what his friend would tell him. *Should I have stood there and watched Dane and Cobaryn get hurt? Was that what my duty to Starfleet demanded of me?*

In the end, they didn't have to say anything at all. They had already run through it all in their minds. And if they hadn't resolved anything, just as Stiles and Matsura hadn't resolved anything immediately after the fight, they had at least put the matter to rest.

"You done here?" Stiles asked.

Hagedorn thought about it, then shrugged. "I should probably take another shot at the rings."

"They get the better of you?"

Hagedorn worked his shoulder in its socket. "A little."

"Then," Stiles concluded, "you've got work to do."

So Hagedorn stayed there in the gym with him. And as the two of them worked out on apparatus after apparatus, Stiles and his friend wordlessly repaired the bonds of trust between them.

CHAPTER
13

BRYCE SHUMAR WALKED INTO THE SMALL, GREEN-WALLED cubicle and saw that his first interview was already waiting for him.

Circumnavigating the room's sleek, black desk, the captain took his seat in a plastiform chair and eyed the tall blond man seated opposite him. "Welcome," he said, "Mr.—"

"Mullen. Lieutenant Commander Steven Mullen. It's a pleasure to make your acquaintance, sir."

The man spoke in a clipped, efficient voice. A distinctly military voice, if Shumar was any judge of such things.

"Likewise," the captain responded.

He brought up Mullen's personnel file on the small screen built into the desk. It showed him everything... and nothing.

"You've got a degree from West Point," said Shumar, reading from the file. "You graduated with honors. Then you signed up with Earth Command, where you flew seventeen missions against the Romulans."

Mullen nodded. "That's correct, sir."

Shumar read on. "At the Battle of Aldebaran, you took command of the *Panther* after your captain and first officer were killed. Despite your lack of experience, you destoyed two enemy warships, not to mention a major Romulan supply depot." He looked at Mullen. "It says here that you were given a Medal of Valor for that action."

"That's true as well," the blond man replied solemnly. "But it was the crew who deserved that medal, sir. I just gave the orders. They're the ones who carried them out."

Shumar studied Mullen. "Do you mean that, Commander?"

The man's forehead puckered. "I beg your pardon, sir?"

The captain shrugged and leaned back in his chair. "Every Earth Command officer I've ever met gives his crew credit for his success. It's an unwritten code, I think."

"Perhaps it is, sir," Mullen answered earnestly. "But in this case, I mean it. My crew was responsible for that victory."

Shumar liked the man's approach. And Mullen's record was impeccable. There was only one more thing he needed to know.

"Tell me something, Commander," said the captain, "and for heaven's sake, please be honest."

Mullen nodded. "Of course, sir."

Shumar leaned forward again. "How would you feel taking orders from a man who's never commanded a starship?"

The blond man seemed to mull it over. "I don't know, sir," he said at last. "I suppose it would depend on the man."

The captain considered Mullen's response. Then he stood up and extended his hand. "Thank you, Commander."

Mullen stood, too, and shook Shumar's hand. There was a trace of disappointment in his eyes. After all, they had only conversed for a couple of minutes—normally not a very good sign.

"Thank you for your time," said the commander. "And good luck, sir."

"My luck will depend," the captain told him.

Again, Mullen's brow puckered. "On what, sir?"

"On you," said Shumar. "I'd welcome you aboard, Commander, but I don't have a ship yet. All I have is a first officer."

Finally, Mullen allowed himself a smile. "Yes, sir. I'll do my best not to disappoint you, sir."

The captain smiled back at him. "I'm sure you will, Commander."

Cobaryn scanned the personnel file displayed on the screen in front of him. "You have quite an impressive résumé, Mr. Emick."

The sturdy-looking, sandy-haired man on the other side of the table smiled at him. "Thank you, sir."

The Rigelian regarded Emick for a moment. The fellow was pleasant enough and his transport piloting credentials were clearly first-rate. What else could he possibly need to know?

"I am not the sort of person who requires a great deal of time to make a decision," Cobaryn declared. "I would like to sign you on as my primary helmsman."

Emick's smile widened. "I'd be delighted, sir."

Cobaryn smiled back at him. "Excellent. As soon as I know when and where you must report, I will send word to your superiors."

"Thank you, sir," the helmsman said. He got up to go, then stopped and looked back at the Rigelian. "May I ask a favor, sir?"

Cobaryn shrugged. "Of course."

"I'd like permission to exceed the weight and size parameters allotted to personal effects by about thirteen percent. That is," said Emick, "if it's not too much trouble, sir."

The captain looked at him. "Like you, Mr. Emick, I have never set foot on a Christopher, though I cannot imagine that a deviation of thirteen percent will be a problem. But if I may ask...what is it that you have in your possession that is both so large and so precious to you?"

"It's a book collection," the man told him. "You see, sir, I like to read a lot—and I like it even better when I can read from an actual volume and not a computer screen."

Cobaryn nodded. He had heard that there was a movement of bound-paper book aficionados on Earth. Apparently, Emick was one of them.

"Do you have any special interests?" he asked.

"Quite a few, actually," the man told him. "Antarctic

zoology. Aboriginal music. Religious art. Organized crime."

The last subject piqued the Rigelian's interest more than the others. "Organized crime?" he echoed. "What is that?"

"A phenomenon of Earth's early twentieth century," said Emick. "Some of Earth's larger urban centers were plagued by a number of illegal and often violent organizations."

Cobaryn absorbed the information. "I see. And you are in some way attracted to these organizations?"

The man recoiled. "No, sir. I'm appalled by them... of course. But they're still fascinating when viewed as a subculture."

The captain didn't see the appeal. "I suppose I will have to take your word for it."

"Or," Emick suggested as an alternative, "you could borrow one of my favorite books on the subject—*Chicago Mobs of the Twenties,* by Billings and Torgelson. Then you could judge for yourself."

Cobaryn effected another smile. "It would be my pleasure to do so. And by the way, your request for additional storage space is granted."

The helmsman's eyes crinkled at the corners. "I'm grateful for your understanding, sir."

"You and I and the other members of our crew have a lot of hard work ahead of us," the Rigelian noted. "I want us all to be as comfortable on our vessel as possible."

"I will certainly be more comfortable knowing I've got my books around me," Emick assured him. "Thank you again, sir."

"Think nothing of it," Cobaryn told the fellow graciously. "Consider yourself dismissed."

He watched Emick leave the cubicle. Then he sat back in his plastiform chair and tried to imagine an Earth overrun by men dedicated to violence. It just didn't seem possible.

But then, in that same century, humans had supposedly inhaled the smoke of burning vegetation, built habitations on geological faults, and destroyed herbivores for sport...so he had to concede that anything was possible.

Matsura felt funny as he stepped out of the shuttle pod and waited for the woman who had accompanied him to do the same.

Her name was Martha Megapenthes and she was the leading candidate for the job of chief engineer on his ship—a position formerly held by a man named Warneke, who had opted for retirement once the war was over.

Normally, Matsura would have conducted the woman's interview entirely in a room back on Earth, where he had conducted all his other interviews. Nor was he the type to break with convention very often. But in this instance, he felt circumstances demanded it.

As Megapenthes extracted herself from the pod, she looked a little out of place. But then, she had spent the war teaching warp theory at a university back on Earth.

"Looks interesting," she said of the shuttle bay.

Matsura smiled and gestured in the direction of the exit. "This way."

He led the way out of the bay and into the corridor beyond, which took them to the nearest turbolift. As soon as both of them were inside the compartment, Matsura pressed the button that would direct the lift system to take them to their destination.

Megapenthes looked at him as the compartment began to move. "Begging the captain's pardon, but you haven't told me where we're going."

"It's no mystery," he said. "We're headed for the supply room on Deck Six. That's where we keep—"

"The ship's complement of containment suits," she finished for him. "I know that. But—"

"But why are we going there?" Matsura asked. "Actually, I want to test your abilities as an engineer."

Megapenthes looked confused. "In a supply room?"

He nodded. "In a supply room."

"But my qualifications—"

"Are impressive," he told her. "You know warp field physics as well as anyone I've ever met. But it's been my experience that good engineers are good with their hands, with fixing things that are broken—because on a ship like this one, things are breaking all the time."

"I see," she said.

Matsura felt a bit of a jolt as they reached Deck Six. He waited for the doors to open, then emerged from the lift compartment and turned in the direction of the supply room.

Megapenthes didn't ask any other questions as they followed the curve of the corridor. Obviously, he thought, she was trying to figure out what the captain had up his sleeve.

When they reached the supply room, Matsura

tapped the pad on the bulkhead and the titanium doors parted for them, revealing two rows of gold-colored metal lockers. The door to one of the lockers was ajar.

The captain pointed to the open door and turned to Megapenthes. "Can you fix that?" he asked her.

The woman looked at him, a smile tugging at the corners of her mouth. "You mean the locker...?"

"I know," Matsura said. "It sounds like it should be easy compared to something like warp core physics. But that locker hasn't closed properly since we got knocked around in the Battle of Cheron. Nobody—I mean *nobody*—seems able to get it hung correctly, including the guy who was chief engineer on this ship for years before I got here."

Megapenthes advanced to the locker and took the door in her hand. She swung it back and forth a few times. Then she eyed the captain.

"Let me get this straight," she said. "If I can fix this locker, you'll make me chief of your engineering section?"

"That's the offer," Matsura confirmed.

She studied his face for a while, then shook her head from side to side. "No. There's got to be a catch."

"No catch," he assured her. "Can you do it?"

The woman laughed. "Well, yes...of course I can."

"Good. I'll see to it that you're supplied with tools. Then I'll check back in...say, an hour?"

That was fine with Megapenthes. "Piece of cake," she told him.

Unfortunately, even after an hour had gone by, the door to the locker still didn't close right. Megapenthes was at a loss to explain it, but there it was, as uncooperative as ever.

And Captain Matsura was forced to return to Earth to try to find another chief engineer.

Stiles went over Elena Ezquerra's file as he had gone over more than a dozen others that day.

He took note of the time she had put in on the *Timber Wolf* and the *Wildcat*. He saw the commendations she had received for bravery and initiative over the last couple of years. And he read the glowing praise that Captain Renault had heaped on her.

When Stiles was finished with the file, he looked up at the petite, dark-haired woman. She looked eager to see what he thought of her.

"I like what I see here," he told her. "I like it a lot."

Ezquerra's eyes lit up. "Very kind of you to say so, sir."

The captain shook his head. "It's not kind of me at all, Lieutenant. In fact, it's downright cruel."

The woman sat back in her seat. "I beg your pardon, sir?"

"It's cruel," he explained, "that despite all your considerable qualifications, I can't bring you aboard."

Ezquerra looked perplexed. "I'm afraid I don't understand, sir."

"It's very simple," Stiles told her. "Starfleet has put a cap on the number of Earth Command people we can take on as officers—and I've already filled my quota. So the only way I can add you to my crew is if you accept a demotion, which I would never ask you to do."

The lieutenant's shoulders slumped. "I see," she said.

But it was clear to him that she didn't like it. And for that matter, neither did he.

"There's one other thing I can do," Stiles said. "I can recommend you to one of the other captains in the hope they've still got room for you."

Ezquerra smiled a halfhearted smile. "You don't have to do that, sir."

"Actually," the captain replied, "I *do*, Lieutenant—because the alternative is to go track down my superior and vent my considerable frustration on him and maybe get myself court-martialed in the process. And as you can imagine, I don't see that as a viable option."

The woman took a moment to figure out what he had just said. When she was done, she nodded. "In that case, thank you, sir."

"It's the least I can do," Stiles told her.

Then he tapped the communications stud on the side of the desk and put in a call to Matsura.

Dane walked straight into his bedroom and hit the sack without even taking his boots off.

For a while, he just lay there, his mind reeling after an entire day spent staring at strange faces and personnel files that had begun to blur together all too quickly.

If Dane had needed further proof that he had no business in Starfleet, he had now received it in ample supply. How was he supposed to know who would be a good officer and who wouldn't? By making small talk for a few minutes? By counting the commendations in a damned computer file?

In some cases, he had picked the candidates with the most experience. In others, he had gone with a gut feeling. And as the day wore on, he had simply picked anyone who could do the job.

Dane was pretty sure that wasn't the way it was supposed to work. He was certain that none of his fellow captains had handled it that way. But then, he wasn't anything like his fellow captains.

Which is why, years from now, they would be flying the *Daedalus* and her sister ships...and he would be back in his Cochrane escorting cargo tubs through the worst neighborhoods the galaxy had to offer.

"Captain Dane?" came a voice, jolting him out of his reverie.

Dane swore under his breath. "That's me."

"This is Captain Fitzgerald in Earth orbit. I've got orders to turn the *Maverick* over to you at your earliest convenience."

Dane grunted. The *Maverick*, eh? Was that his uncle's idea of a joke?

"When should I expect you?" Fitzgerald asked.

Dane swung his legs out of bed. "Now," he said.

There was a pause. "Now?"

"Now," Dane confirmed. "Or, to be more accurate, as soon as I can get to a working transporter platform."

"Transporter? I'm afraid I don't—"

"I know, it sounds crazy. But the eggheads here have developed a transporter that can reach ships in orbit."

It had actually been designed for the *Daedalus*. However, Dane didn't think Fitzgerald needed to know that.

There was another pause—one that seemed to reek of resentment. "Acknowledged, Captain. Fitzgerald out."

In the silence that followed, Dane actually felt nervous. His heart was beating harder than it should have and there was an unfamiliar weakness in his knees. But it didn't stop him.

He made his way out of his quarters, followed the corridor to another corridor and then another, and finally found the facility's main transporter room. It was manned by a single operator, a muscular man with dark, neatly combed hair.

"Can I help you, sir?" the man asked Dane.

"You can indeed," the captain told him. "You can send me up to the *Maverick*. She's in Earth orbit."

He stepped up onto the transporter disc and waited for the operator to comply. But it didn't happen.

"I wasn't notified of any transports this evening," the man said.

Dane looked at him. "So?"

The transporter operator frowned. "My orders require me to follow a schedule, sir. You're not on my schedule."

Dane came down off the disc and crossed the room. "Let's see that schedule you're talking about."

The man pointed it out on his monitor. "You see, sir? There's no mention of any transports this evening."

"That's funny," said Dane, punching in a little-known access code and then tapping his name out. Letter by letter, it appeared on the screen. "It looks to me like you've got a transport scheduled after all."

The operator read Dane's name. Then he looked at the captain, amazed. "How did you do that?"

Dane smiled a thin smile. "I've been doing it since I was ten. It's one of the perks of growing up a Command brat. Now are you going to transport me or do I have to do it myself?"

The dark-haired man hesitated for a moment. Then he said, "I'm ready when you are, sir."

"Thanks a bunch," Dane told him.

Crossing the room again, he stepped up onto the transporter disc. A moment later, he saw the operator go to work.

In less than a minute, the captain's surroundings vanished—and he found himself in a much smaller chamber. He recognized it as the transporter room of a Christopher-class starship.

How about that, he thought, *I'm still in one piece. Guess those eggheads knew what they were doing.*

There was a tall, balding man in a black-and-gold Earth Command uniform standing beside the control console. "Welcome to the *Maverick,*" he said. "I'm Captain Fitzgerald."

His tone told Dane that he wouldn't have minded waiting until morning to bring his replacement aboard. In fact, he probably wouldn't have minded waiting until the millennium.

"I imagine you'll want to see the ship," Fitzgerald said.

Descending from the disc, Dane made his way across the room. "Look," he told his predecessor, "I know my way around a Christopher. You don't have to hold my hand if you've got something better to do."

He had meant it as a magnanimous gesture. If it were his vessel, he would have hated the idea of giving his successor a tour.

But Fitzgerald obviously didn't see it that way. "It's my duty to show you around, Captain. I'm going to see that duty done."

Dane shrugged. "Suit yourself."

Together, they left the transporter room and headed down the corridor to the nearest turbolift. En route, they passed a couple of lieutenants who acknowledged Fitzgerald but didn't so much as glance at Dane.

"Friendly crew you've got here," he noted. "I guess they're no more thrilled about giving up their ship than you are."

Fitzgerald shot him a stern look. "Frankly, it's not just a matter of giving up the *Maverick*. It's that we're giving it up to someone who's never worn the uniform."

Dane stiffened at the unexpected arrogance behind the rebuke. Who did these Earth Command types think they were? A superior species?

"It's funny," he said, refusing to rise to the bait. "I seem to hear that sort of thing a lot lately."

"And how do you respond?" Fitzgerald asked.

"Is that meant to be a gibe?" Dane countered bluntly.

"No. I'd really like to know," said Fitzgerald, allowing only the merest note of irony to creep into his voice.

Dane opened the doors with a tap of the pad on the bulkhead beside them. "Usually," he said in a matter-of-fact tone, "I tell them to go to hell. But that's only when they're not performing a life or death service like playing tour guide."

Fitzgerald's eyes became daggers as the doors finished sliding open. "Understand something, Captain. This vessel saw us through the worst of the war. If I hear you're mistreating her, I'll personally shove you out a missile tube."

Dane tried to keep a lid on his emotions as he entered the lift compartment. "Let's make a deal," he said as calmly as he could. "You don't make any more stupid threats and I'll treat this ship better than you ever did. I'll bring her flowers twice a week, wine her and dine her, bring her chocolates, the works. What do you say?"

Fitzgerald reddened. "That's not what I meant."

"Oh?" said Dane, feigning surprise. "Then what *did* you mean? That I was purposely going to bounce her through an asteroid belt?"

The other man scowled, accentuating the lines in his face. "I meant this ship is a whole lot more than you deserve."

"Maybe so," Dane replied evenly. "But then, the galaxy seldom plays fair, Captain. As someone who's fought a war all by himself, you should appreciate that." He indicated the inside of the turbolift with a flourish. "Care to join the tour?"

Biting his lip, Fitzgerald stepped inside and pressed the stud that closed the doors. Then he punched in a destination.

But before he could send the lift on its way, Dane canceled the command and instituted one of his own. "Let's go straight to the bridge," he said. "That's the part I'm *really* looking forward to."

Fitzgerald didn't say anything—either at that moment or any other—as the lift made its way to the *Maverick*'s command nexus. When they arrived, Dane took it on himself to open the doors.

As they slid apart, he absorbed the sight of his new bridge—a gold enclosure full of sleek, black consoles. Of course, it looked a lot like the bridges he had seen on a half dozen other Christophers in his lifetime. But there was something about *this* one that made Dane's heart skip a beat.

"Captain on the bridge," someone announced.

Dane didn't know if the man was talking about him or Fitzgerald. What's more, he didn't much care.

"At ease," he said, speaking up before his counterpart could.

There were eight officers on the bridge. They all looked at him—none of them with the least bit of kindness.

"This is Captain Dane," Fitzgerald pointed out dutifully. "The new commanding officer of—"

"They don't care who I am," Dane interjected. "They're like you in that regard, Captain. They just want to know me well enough to hate me for taking their ship away."

The bridge officers stared at him disbelievingly. Obviously, they had never heard anyone speak that way to their superior.

"So let's do everyone a favor," Dane went on. "Now that Captain Fitzgerald has given me my tour—and let me tell you, what a splendid tour it was—why don't you all take a last look around the ship? Go ahead. I can handle the bridge by myself."

Fitzgerald glared at him. "You're out of your mind. This is a Christopher, man. If something goes wrong—"

"I'll take my chances," Dane told him. "And unless I'm mistaken, it's my option to do that...since this vessel officially stopped being Earth Command property *the moment you slipped into orbit.*"

The muscles worked furiously in Fitzgerald's jaw. "That's exactly right," he conceded. "I commend you on your grasp of protocol, Captain."

"Please," said Dane. "You'll give me a swelled head. Now go. Get out of here, all of you."

The officers glanced at Fitzgerald, who nodded reluctantly. Then, little by little, they filed into the turbolift. It took two trips for the compartment to take them all away, but eventually it did its job.

When the doors slid closed on the second group, Dane walked over to the captain's chair and sat down. He looked around at the empty duty stations, both fore and aft, and imagined them full of the officers he had signed a few hours earlier, their faces turned to him for orders.

Dane wouldn't have admitted it out loud, but he had never been so scared in all his life.

CHAPTER
14

WEAPONS OFFICER MORGAN KELLY TOOK A DEEP BREATH and considered herself in the full-length mirror.

Like everyone else on the Christopher-class vessel *Peregrine,* she wore an open-collared blue uniform with a black mock-turtle pullover underneath it. A gold Starfleet chevron graced the uniform's left breast, and Kelly's rank of lieutenant was denoted by two gold bands encircling her right sleeve.

She tilted her redhaired head to one side and frowned. She had worn the gold and black of Earth Command for so long she had come to think of it as part of her natural coloring. A blue uniform looked as inappropriate as a hot-pink atomic missile.

But there it was, Kelly mused, her frown deepening. And she would get used to it. She would *have* to.

The sound of chimes brought her out of her reverie. Kelly turned to the double set of sliding doors that separated her quarters from the corridor beyond and wondered who might be calling on her.

Maybe it was the engineer she had met earlier, who had gotten lost looking for the mess hall. Or yet another lieutenant j.g., wondering if she had received her full complement of toiletries...

It couldn't be a friend. After all, the lieutenant only had one of those on the ship...and he was waiting for her on the bridge.

"I'm coming," she sighed.

Crossing the room, Kelly pressed the pad in the bulkhead beside the sliding doors and watched them hiss open. They revealed a silver-skinned, ruby-eyed figure in a uniform as blue as her own.

"Captain Cobaryn—?" she said, unable to conceal her surprise.

He inclined his head slightly. "May I come in?"

Kelly hesitated for a moment. Then she realized she really had no choice in the matter. "Of course. But I should tell you, I'm—"

"Due on the bridge in ten minutes," the Rigelian said, finishing her declaration for her. He fashioned a smile, stretching the series of ridges that ran from his temple to his jaw. "I know. I spoke with Captain Shumar before I transported over."

"Did you?" the lieutenant responded, getting the feeling that she had been the victim of some kind of conspiracy. *I'll be the first officer in Starfleet to kill my captain,* she told herself.

"Yes," Cobaryn rejoined. "I wish to speak with you."

Of course you do, she replied inwardly.

After all, Cobaryn had taken every opportunity to speak with her back on Earth Base Fourteen in the aftermath of the Romulan assault. It hardly came as a shock that he wanted to speak with her *now.*

And he had gone to some pretty great lengths to do so. All six of the fleet's Christophers were supposed to leave Earth orbit in less than an hour, and the Rigelian had a command of his own to attend to. There might even have been a regulation prohibiting a captain from leaving his vessel at such a momentous juncture.

If there was, Cobaryn seemed unaware of it... or else, for the sake of his infatuation with Kelly, he had decided to ignore it.

"Look," she said, "I—"

He held up a three-fingered hand. "Please," he insisted gently, "I will not be long, I promise."

The lieutenant regarded her visitor. He seemed to mean it. "All right," she told him, folding her arms across her chest.

Cobaryn offered her another smile—his best one yet. "First," he said, "I would like to apologize for my behavior back at Earth Base Fourteen. In retrospect, I see that my attentions must have been a burden to you. In my defense, I can only state my ignorance of human courtship rituals."

An apology was the last thing she had expected. "Don't worry about it," she found herself saying. "In a way, it was kind of flattering."

The captain inclined his hairless head. "Thank you for understanding. There is only one other thing...."

But he didn't say what it was. At least, not right away. Whatever it was, he seemed nervous about it.

As much as he had annoyed her at the base, Kelly couldn't help sympathizing with the man. "One other thing?" she echoed, trying to be helpful.

"Yes," said Cobaryn. He seemed to steel himself. "If it is not too much trouble, I would like a favor from you."

She looked at him askance, uncertain of what he was asking but already not liking the sound of it. "What kind of favor?"

His eyes seemed to soften. "The kind a knight of old received from his lady fair, so he could carry it with him on his journeys and accomplish great things in her name."

Kelly felt her heart melt in her chest. It was far and away the most romantic thing anyone had ever suggested to her, and it caught her completely off guard. For a second or two, she couldn't speak.

Cobaryn winced. "You do not think it is a good idea?"

The lieutenant shook her head, trying to regain her composure. "I...I'm not sure what I think."

He shrugged. "Again, I must apologize. It seemed like a good solution to both our problems. After all, if I had a favor, I could perhaps feel content worshiping you from afar."

Kelly sighed. She hadn't intended to. It just came out. *This is crazy,* she told herself. Cobaryn was an alien—a being from another world. What did he know of knightly virtues? Or of chivalry? And yet she had to admit, he embodied them better than any human she had ever met.

"I...see you've been doing some reading," she observed.

"A little," Cobaryn admitted. He looked sad in a peculiarly Rigelian way. "Well, then, good luck, Lieutenant Kelly. I trust you and I will meet again someday."

He extended his hand to shake hers. For a moment, she considered it. Then, certain that she had gone insane, she held up her forefinger.

"Give me a second," she said.

There was a set of drawers built into the bulkhead beside her bed. The lieutenant pulled open the third one from the top and rifled through it, searching for something. It took a while, but she found it.

Then she turned around and tossed it to Cobaryn. He snatched it out of the air, opened his hand, and studied it. Then he looked up at Kelly, a grin spreading awkwardly across his face.

"Thank you," he told her, with feeling.

She smiled back, unable to help herself. "Don't mention it."

Still grinning, the captain tucked her favor into an inside pocket of his uniform, where it created only a slightly noticeable bulge. Then, with obvious reluctance, he turned, opened the doors to her quarters, and left her standing there.

As the doors whispered closed again, Kelly had to remind herself to breathe. *Come on,* she thought. *Get a grip on yourself.*

Cobaryn's gesture was a romantic notion, no question. But it hadn't come from Prince Charming. It had come from a guy she didn't have the slightest feelings for.

A guy from another planet, for heaven's sakes.

Now, the lieutenant told herself, if it had been the Cochrane jockey who had asked for her favor...*that* would have been a different story. That would have been unbelievable.

Chuckling to herself, she pulled down on the front of her uniform and put on her game face. Then she tapped the door controls, left her quarters, and reported to the bridge.

Where she would, in her own unobtrusive way, give Captain Shumar the dirtiest look she could muster.

Hiro Matsura got up from his center seat on the *Yellowjacket* and faced his viewscreen, where the image of Director Abute had just appeared.

The captain wasn't required to get up. Certainly, none of his bridge officers had risen from their consoles. But Matsura wanted to show his appreciation of the moment, his respect for its place in history.

For weeks they had talked about a Starfleet. They had selected captains and crews for a Starfleet. And now, for the first time, there would actually *be* a Starfleet.

"I bid you a good morning," said Abute, his dark eyes twinkling over his aquiline nose. "Of course, for the United Federation of Planets it is *already* a good morning. More than two hundred of our bravest men and women, individuals representing fourteen species in all, are embarking from Earth orbit to pursue their destinies among the stars.

"Before long," the director told them, "there will be many more of you, plying the void in the kind of ships we've only been able to dream about. But for now, there is only you—a handful of determined trailblazers who will set the standard for all who follow. The Federation is watching each and every one of you, wishing you the best of good fortune. Make us proud. Show us what serving in Starfleet is all about."

And what *was* it about? the captain wondered. Unfortunately, it was still too soon to say.

Of course, Matsura knew what he *wanted* it to be. The same thing Admiral Walker wanted it to be—a defense force like no other. But as long as Clarisse Dumont's camp had a say in things, that future was uncertain.

Abute smiled with undisguised pride. "You have my permission to leave orbit," he told them. "Bon voyage." A moment later his image vanished, and their orbital view of Earth was restored.

Matsura didn't take his eyes off the viewscreen. He wanted to remember how the sunlight hit the cloud-swaddled Earth when he left on his first Starfleet mission. He wanted to tell his grandchildren about it.

"Mr. Barker," he said finally, "bring us about."

There was no response.

The captain turned to his left to look at his helmsman. The man ensconced behind the console there was staring back at him, looking a little discomfited. And for good reason.

His name wasn't Barker. It was McCallum. Barker had piloted Matsura's ship when it flew under the aegis of Earth Command.

The captain had wanted to take the helmsman with him when his ship became Starfleet property. However, he had been forced to adhere to Abute's quotas, and that meant making some hard decisions.

"Mr. *McCallum*," he amended, "bring us about."

"Aye, sir," said the helmsman.

The view on the screen gradually slid sideways, taking the clouds and the sunlight and a blue sweep of ocean with it. In a matter of moments, Earth had slipped away completely and Matsura found himself gazing at a galaxy full of distant suns.

They had never seemed so inviting. "Full impulse," he told McCallum.

"Full impulse," the man confirmed.

The stars seemed to leap forward, though it was really their Christopher 2000 that had forged ahead. As it plunged through the void, reaching for the limits of Earth's solar system and beyond, Matsura lowered himself into his captain's chair.

McCallum, he told himself, resolving not to forget a second time. *Not Barker. McCallum.*

CHAPTER
15

AARON STILES EYED THE COLLECTION OF HAPHAZARDLY shaped rocks pictured on his viewscreen, some of them as small as a kilometer in diameter and some many times that size. A muscle twitched in his jaw.

"Mr. Weeks," he said, glancing at his weapons officer, "target the nearest of the asteroids and stand by lasers."

"Aye, sir," came the reply.

Out of the corner of his eye, the captain could see Darigghi crossing the bridge to join him. "Sir?" said the Osadjani.

Stiles turned to look up at him. "Yes, Commander?"

Darigghi tilted his long, hairless head, his deepset black eyes fixed intently on the captain's. "Sir, did I hear you give an order to target one of the asteroids?"

166

Stiles nodded. "You did indeed, Commander." Then he turned back to Weeks. "Fire lasers, Lieutenant."

The weapons officer tapped a control stud. On the viewscreen, a red-tinged chunk of rock was speared mercilessly by a pair of blue energy beams. Before long it had been transformed into space dust.

Stiles heard the Osadjani suck in a breath. "Sir," he said, "are you certain you wish to do this?"

The captain shrugged. "Why wouldn't I?"

Darigghi licked his fleshy lips. "This asteroid belt is a most intriguing phenomenon," he replied. "I believe that is why we were asked to analyze it in the first place."

"And analyze it we did," Stiles pointed out. Then he glanced at Weeks again. "Target another one, Lieutenant."

The weapons officer bent to his task. "Aye, sir."

The first officer licked his lips a second time. "But, sir, it is irresponsible of us to destroy what natural forces created."

The captain eyed Darigghi. "Irresponsible, you say?"

The Osadjani nodded. "Yes, sir."

"I suppose that would be one way to look at it. But let me offer you another one, Commander. You see, during the war, the Romulans used this asteroid belt to hide their warships. When we finally found them and dug them out, it cost us the lives of three good captains and their crews."

Darigghi's eyes narrowed. "But what—?"

"What does that have to do with the activity at hand?" Stiles said, finishing his exec's question for him. "Simple, Commander. No hostile force is ever going to hide in this belt again."

The alien didn't know what to say to that. Of course, that was exactly the result the captain had desired.

Turning to the viewscreen, Stiles settled back in his seat. Then he said, "Fire, Mr. Weeks."

The weapons officer fired. As before, their lasers ate away at a sizable hunk of rock, reducing it to debris in no time.

Darigghi looked on helplessly, licking his lips like crazy. Ignoring him, Stiles ordered Weeks to target another asteroid.

Alonis Cobaryn sat at a long rough-hewn table in the gargantuan Hall of the Axe, which was located on a world called Middira.

By the light of the modest braziers that lined the soaring black walls, Cobaryn could make out the immense crossed set of axes wielded in battle by the founder of Middiron civilization—or so the legend went. He could also make out the pale, hulking forms of his hosts and the mess of monstrous insect parts they considered a delicacy.

First Axe Zhrakkas, the largest and most prominent member of the Middiron Circle of Axes, offered the captain a brittle, amber-colored haunch. "Eat," he said insistently.

Truthfully, Cobaryn had no desire to consume the haunch. However, his orders called for him to embrace local customs, so he took it from the First Axe and sank his teeth into it.

He found that it was completely tasteless—at least to his Rigelian senses. Considering this a blessing, he ripped off a piece of the haunch with his teeth and began chewing it as best he could.

"Have you reviewed our proposal?" the captain asked Zhrakkas, speaking with his mouth full in the manner of his dining companions.

The First Axe's slitted blue eyes slid in his guest's direction. "I have," he growled, spitting insect splinters as he spoke.

"And what is your reaction?" Cobaryn demanded. After all, he had been told to be firm with the Middirona—firm and blunt.

"I did not see anything that made my blood run hot," said the First Axe. "There is that, at least."

The Rigelian took another bite of the insect haunch. "Then you understand we mean you no harm? That the creation of our Federation does not portend badly for you?"

Zhrakkas grunted. "I understand that you say it."

"I do more than say it," Cobaryn assured him, forcing a note of titanium into his voice. "I mean it."

The First Axe made a face. "We will see."

It was the best response the Rigelian could have hoped for. Pressing the matter might only have made his host wary, so he let it drop. Besides, there was another subject he wished to pursue.

"I want to ask you something," said Cobaryn.

Zhrakkas shrugged his massive, blue-veined shoulders. "Ask."

The captain leaned forward. "As I understand it," he said, "you trade regularly with the Anjyyla."

The First Axe lifted his protruding chin. "Among others."

"However," Cobaryn noted, "the area between here and Anjyyl is reputed to be rife with interstellar strings, which, as you know, would be most dangerous to a vessel passing near them. I was wondering—"

Zhrakkas's eyes grew dangerous under his brow ridge. "The space between here and Anjyyl is *ours*—no one else's. If your Federation has any intention of trespassing in Middiron territory—"

The captain hadn't expected such a violent reaction—though perhaps he should have. "You misunderstand, First Axe. We have no intention of trespassing. We merely seek to increase our store of knowledge."

The Middirona's mouth twisted with mistrust. "Why would you need to increase your knowledge of what takes place in *our* space?"

By then, Zhrakkas's fellow councilors had taken an interest in the conversation as well. They glared at their guest with fierce blue eyes, awaiting his response.

The Rigelian sighed. Obviously, he had placed his mission here in some jeopardy. He would have to salvage it somehow—and quickly—or be the cause of a potentially bloody conflict.

Unfortunately he could think of only one way to do that. Gritting his teeth, he pulled his fist back and drove it into Zhrakkas's shoulder with all the power he could muster.

Though he was clearly unprepared for the blow, the Middirona barely budged. Then he looked to Cobaryn for an explanation.

"The First Axe needs to hone his sense of humor," said the captain, effecting his best human grin.

Befuddled, Zhrakkas looked at him. "My sense of humor?"

"Absolutely," Cobaryn pressed. "I thought when I

poked my haft where it did not belong, you would find my impertinence amusing. But, no—you took my question seriously. Admit it."

The First Axe looked around the table at his peers. "I did no such thing. I knew it was a joke all along." He smiled, exposing his long, hollow fangs. "But I decided to turn the tables and play a joke on *you.*"

And then Zhrakkas expressed his feeling of good fellowship the way any Middirona would have—by hauling his meaty fist back and returning the captain's blow with twice the force.

Cobaryn saw it coming, but dared not try to get out of the way. Not if he wanted to hang onto the respect of the Middirona.

The First Axe turned out to be even stronger than he looked. His punch knocked the Rigelian backward head over heels. The next thing Cobaryn knew, he was sprawled on the floor—and his shoulder hurt too much for him to even contemplate moving it.

Seeing him lying there, Zhrakkas got up and walked over to him. Then he pulled the captain to his feet.

"I like you," the Middirona said. "Your people and mine will be two blades of the same axe."

Trying not to wince at the pain in his shoulder, Cobaryn nodded. "I certainly hope so."

Connor Dane leaned back in his chair and studied the stars on the screen in front of him. They didn't look much different from any other stars he had seen, even if they constituted the part of space now known as the Romulan Neutral Zone.

Dane's eyes narrowed. "Let me get this straight."

"All right," said his science officer, a white-haired man named Hudlin. He was standing next to the captain with his arms folded across his chest, an expression of impatience on his wrinkled face.

"Our long-range scanners," Dane began, "have detected a wormhole out there in the Neutral Zone. And like any other wormhole, it's probably not going to be there for long."

"That's correct," Hudlin confirmed.

"But while it *is* there," said the captain, "you'd like the chance to study it at close range—even if it means entering the Neutral Zone, violating the treaty we just signed, and risking another war."

The science officer frowned. "With all due respect, sir, we don't have to go very far into the Neutral Zone, and it's highly unlikely that the Romulans would notice us. As you're no doubt aware, the war served to thin out their fleet considerably."

True, Dane conceded. Of course, the same could be said of the Federation. "So you really don't think we'd get caught?"

"I really don't," said Hudlin.

The captain thought about it a moment longer. "I'll tell you what, pal—I think you're in luck. You see, between you and me and the bulkhead, I don't give a rat's fat patootie about this Romulan Neutral Zone everybody's so impressed with. On the other hand, I don't give a rat's fat patootie about your wormhole."

The science officer stared at him, clearly more than a little confused. "But you said I was in luck."

"You are. You want to get a little closer to that wormhole? Be my guest. Just don't get me involved, all right? I hate the idea of having to explain something like this to a court-martial."

And with that, Dane got up from his chair and headed for the turbolift. Naturally, he didn't get far before he heard from Hudlin again.

"Sir?" said the science officer, hurrying to catch up with his captain. He looked around at the other bridge personnel, who were looking on with undisguised curiosity. "Where are you going?" he asked.

Dane shrugged. "To my quarters. I figure I'll get a little shuteye. But don't worry—you've got all the leeway you need. Just try to bring the ship back in one piece, okay?"

Again he headed for the turbolift.

"No!" Hudlin exclaimed.

The captain looked back at him. "No?"

The science officer swallowed. "What I mean is...I can't command the ship. I'm only a science officer."

Dane feigned surprise. "Hang on a second, Mr. Hudlin. There's a wormhole out there just begging to be examined with short-range scanners—and you're going to let that kind of opportunity slip through your fingers? What kind of scientist are you?"

The man couldn't have looked more frustrated. "But I've had no tactical training. What if—"

The captain regarded him. "What if you run into some Romulans?" He allowed a note of irony to creep into his voice. "It's highly unlikely that they'd notice us, don't you think? Especially after the war thinned out their fleet so much."

The other man frowned. "There's no need to be abu-

sive," he responded. And without another word, he retreated to his science station.

Dane returned to his center seat, where he was
greeted again by the stars that filled the Neutral Zone.
"There's no need to be abusive, *sir,*" he said under his
breath.

Bryce Shumar was three weeks out of Earth orbit
when he finally found what he was looking for.

The Tellarite vessel on his viewscreen was a collection of dark, forbidding spheres, some bigger
than others. The deep creases between them served
as housings for the spacecraft's shield projectors,
weapons ports, scanner arrays, and audio-visual trans-
mitters, while a quartet of small cylinders, which
spilled golden plasma from unlikely locations among
the spheres, provided the ship with its propulsion capabilities.

More to the point, the vessel was far from any of the
established trade routes. And from the time it had picked
up Shumar's ship on its long-range scanners, it had done
its best to elude pursuit.

Unfortunately for the Tellarite, there wasn't a starfar-
ing vessel in the galaxy that could outrun a Christopher
2000. It hadn't ever been a question of whether Shumar's craft would catch up with its prey; the only question had been *when.*

Mullen, Shumar's first officer, came to stand beside
the captain's chair. "Interesting ship," he noted.

"Ugly ship," Shumar told him. "Probably the ugliest
I've ever seen. And when you run an Earth base, you see
all kinds."

The younger man looked at him, no doubt uncertain as to how to react to the remark. "I have to admit, sir, I'm no expert on esthetics."

"You don't have to be," said Shumar. "Some things are ugly by definition. That Tellarite is one of them."

"Weapons range," announced Wallace, the helm officer.

The captain leaned forward. "Raise deflector shields and route power to laser batteries."

Forward of his center seat, Morgan Kelly manipulated her tactical controls. "Aye, sir," came her reply.

Just like old times, thought Shumar. He turned to Klebanov, his navigator. "Hail the Tellarite, Lieutenant."

The woman went to work. A moment later, she looked up. "They're responding," she told the captain.

"On screen," he said.

Abruptly, the image of a porcine being with a bristling beard and a pronounced snout assaulted his viewscreen. "What is the meaning of this?" the Tellarite growled.

Shumar could tell the alien was covering something up. Tellarites weren't very good at duplicity.

"I'm Captain Shumar," he said, "of the starship *Peregrine*. I have reason to believe you're carrying stolen property."

"I'm Captain Broj of the trading ship *Prosperous*," the Tellarite answered, "and what I carry is my own business."

"Not so," the human pointed out. "It's also the business of the United Federation of Planets."

Broj's already tiny eyes screwed up even tinier.

"The United *What?*" he grunted, his tone less than respectful.

"The United Federation of Planets," Shumar repeated patiently. "An organization of which your homeworld is a charter member."

"Never heard of it," said the Tellarite.

Another lie, the human reflected. "Nonetheless," he insisted, "I need to search your vessel. If you haven't got anything to hide, you'll be on your way in no time. If—"

"Sir," said Kelly, a distinct note of urgency in her voice, "they're building up laser power."

Shumar wasn't the least bit surprised. "Target their weapons ports and fire, Lieutenant."

Out in space, the *Peregrine* buried her electric-blue fangs in the other ship's laser banks. But Shumar didn't see that. What he saw was the wide-eyed apprehension on Broj's face as he anticipated the impact of Shumar's assault and realized that the human had beaten him to the punch.

Suddenly, the Tellarite flung his arms out and lurched out of sight, revealing two other Tellarites on a dark, cramped bridge. A console behind them erupted in a shower of sparks, eliciting curses from Broj's crewmen and a series of urgent off-screen commands.

When Broj returned, his eyes were red-rimmed and his nostrils were flaring with anger. "How dare you fire on a Tellarite ship!" he snorted.

"As I indicated," said Shumar, "I'm acting under Federation authority. Now, are you going to cooperate...or do I have to take out your shield generators as well?"

Broj's mouth twisted with indignation. For a fraction of a second, he looked capable of anything. Then he seemed to settle down and consider his options—and come to the conclusion that he had none.

"All right," the Tellarite agreed with a snarl. He glanced at someone off-screen. "Lower the shields."

Shumar nodded approvingly. "That's better." He got to his feet. "Lieutenant Kelly, you're with me. Mr. Mullen, you've got the center seat. Keep our weapons trained on the Tellarite—just in case."

As Kelly slaved her weapons functions to the navigation console, the captain headed for the turbolift. To his surprise, his first officer insinuated himself in Shumar's path.

"Yes?" the captain asked, wondering what the man wanted.

"Begging your pardon, sir," said Mullen in a low, deferential voice, "but Earth Command regs called for commanding officers to remain on their ships. Generally, it was their subordinates who led the boarding parties."

"Subordinates like *you*, I suppose?"

The exec nodded. "That's correct, sir."

Shumar smiled at him. "This isn't Earth Command, Mr. Mullen. Starfleet has no regulations against captains leading boarding parties—at least, none that I'm aware of. Besides, I like to get my hands dirty."

By then, Kelly was ready to depart. Shumar clapped his exec on the shoulder and moved past him, then opened the lift doors with a tap on the bulkhead pad and went inside. After Kelly joined him, he closed the doors again and the compartment began to move.

The weapons officer glanced at him sideways. "So tell me," she said, "when was the last time you had occasion to use a laser pistol, Captain I-Like-To-Get-My-Hands-Dirty?"

Shumar patted the weapon on his hip. "Never, Lieutenant. That's why I brought you along."

CHAPTER
16

WHEN CAPTAIN BRYCE SHUMAR MATERIALIZED IN THE transporter room of the Tellarite trading vessel, he did so with his laser pistol drawn and leveled in front of him.

As it turned out, his concern was unfounded. Outside of Shumar, Kelly, and the three armed crewmen they had brought with them, there was only one other humanoid in the room—a Tellarite transporter operator.

"Come with me," he said.

"It would be my pleasure," said the captain.

He gestured with his weapon for his team to follow. Then he stepped down from the transporter disc and fell in line behind their guide.

The corridors of the vessel were stark and poorly illuminated, but very wide. It wasn't surprising, Shumar reflected, considering the girth of the average Tellarite.

Before long, they came to a cargo bay. As luck would have it, it was on the same level as the transporter room. The Tellarite opened the door for them and plodded off.

Broj, the vessel's captain, was waiting for them inside. He wasn't alone, either. There was a tall, green-skinned Orion with a sour expression standing next to him.

Not that there was anything unusual about that. Tellarite traders often took on financial backers from other species, and there never seemed to be a shortage of willing Orions.

However, this particular Orion didn't look like a financier. He looked more like a mercenary—which inclined Shumar to be that much more careful in his dealings here.

In addition to Broj and his green-skinned associate, the cargo bay contained perhaps two dozen metal containers. None of them were labeled. They could have contained apricots or antibiotics, though Shumar wasn't looking for either of those things.

Shumar nodded. "Captain Broj."

"This is an outrage," the Tellarite rumbled.

Shumar didn't answer him. He simply turned to Kelly and said, "Keep an eye on these gentlemen."

"Aye, sir," she assured him, the barrel of her laser pistol moving from the Tellarite to the Orion and back again.

Tucking his weapon inside his belt, Shumar crossed the room and worked the lid off a container at random. Then, still eyeing Broj, he reached inside. His fingers closed on something dry and granular.

Extracting a handful of the stuff, he held it out in front of him. It looked like rice—except for the blood-red color.

"D'saako seeds," said the Tellarite.

"I know what they are," Shumar told him. "When you run a starbase, you encounter every kind of cargo imaginable."

Taking out his laser, he pointed it at the bottom half of the container. Then he activated its bright blue beam.

Not even titanium could stand that kind of point-blank assault. The metal puckered and gave way, leaving a hole the size of a man's fist.

"What are you doing?" bellowed Broj, taking a step forward. He looked ready to charge Shumar, but couldn't because of the lasers trained on him. "I paid good money for that grain!"

"No doubt," the human responded, deactivating the beam and putting his pistol away again. "But I'm willing to bet there's more than d'saako seeds in this container."

After waiting a moment longer for the metal to cool, Shumar reached inside. What he found was most definitely not seeds. They were too big and hard. Smiling, he removed some.

"Gold?" asked Kelly.

"Gold," the captain confirmed.

There were perhaps a dozen shiny, irregularly shaped orange nuggets in his open hand, ranging in size from that of a pea to that of an acorn. Shumar showed them to Broj.

"Our informants say this gold is from Ornathia Prime."

The smuggler grunted disdainfully. "I don't know where it came from. I only know I was paid to take a cargo from one place to another."

"According to our informants," said Shumar, "that's a lie. You mined this gold yourself, ignoring the fact that you had no right to do so. Then you set out for the Magabenthus system in the hope of peddling it."

The Tellarite puffed out his chest. "Your informants are the ones who are lying," he huffed.

"In that case," said the captain, "you won't mind our checking your other cargo bay. You know, the one a couple of decks below us? I'll bet you we find some gold-mining equipment."

The smuggler scowled disdainfully. "Go ahead and check. Then you can apologize to my government for waylaying an honest businessman."

Shumar knew he would need the mining equipment as evidence, so he tilted his head in the direction of the exit. "Come on," he told Kelly and his other crewmen. "Let's take a look at that other bay."

"Aye, sir," said Kelly. She gestured with her laser for the Tellarite to lead the way.

But before Shumar had made it halfway to the exit, something occurred to him. He stopped dead—and his weapons officer noticed.

"What is it?" Kelly asked him.

The captain turned to Broj. "Where did those d'saako seeds come from?"

The Tellarite regarded him. "Ekkenda Four. Why?"

Why indeed, Shumar thought. *Because an immunologist at the University of Pennsylvania, back on Earth, is trying to cure Vegan choriomeningitis using the DNA of certain Ekkendan lizards—creatures whose entire diets seem to consist of adult sun-ripened d'saako plants.*

If Shumar could find lizard cells among the d'saako seeds, he might be able to conduct some experiments of his own. Maybe he could even expedite the discovery of a cure. It was the kind of work that would make people sit up and take notice....

And see the possibilities inherent in a science-driven Starfleet.

"Captain?" said Kelly, sounding annoyed at the delay.

"Hang on a moment," Shumar told her.

Returning to the open, laser-punctured container, he zipped down the front of his uniform almost to his waist. Then he scooped up a healthy handful of d'saako seeds, poured them carefully into an inside pocket, and zipped up his uniform again.

If there were lizard cells present, his science officers would be able to detect them and pull them out. And if there weren't, the captain mused, he hadn't lost anything.

That's when he felt the business end of a laser pistol poke him in the small of his back.

"No one move," rasped the Orion.

Apparently, he had had a concealed weapon on him. Shumar's detour had given him an opening to use it—but he would eventually have used it anyway. At least, that was what the captain chose to believe.

"I'll kill him if I have to," the Orion vowed.

Shumar didn't doubt it. "Easy," he said. "Stay calm."

"Don't tell me how to feel," the Orion snapped. "Don't tell me anything. Just tell *them* to move out of our way."

"*Our* way?" the captain echoed.

"That's right," said his captor. "You and I are going to take a little trip in an escape pod."

"What about me?" asked Broj.

"You're on your own," the Orion told him.

So much for honor among thieves, Shumar thought. Feeling the prod of the laser pistol, he began to move toward the exit.

Then he saw Kelly raise her weapon and fire.

The flash of blue light blinded him, so he couldn't tell what effect the beam had had. But a moment later, it occurred to him that the pistol in his back was gone.

"Are you all right?" asked a feminine voice, amid the scrape of boots and the barking of a warning.

The captain blinked a few times and made out Kelly through the haze of after-images. Then he looked down and saw the Orion lying unconscious on the deck. Broj had his hands up, kept in line by Shumar's crewmen.

"Fine," he told Kelly, "thanks to you. I was surprised you were able to get a clear shot at him."

The weapons officer grunted. "I didn't."

Shumar's vision had improved enough for him to see her face. It confirmed that she wasn't kidding.

"What would I do without you?" he asked sotto voce.

"I don't know," Kelly said in the same soft voice. "Exercise a little more care, maybe?"

"Come on," said the captain, understanding exactly what she was talking about. "There was no way I could have known the Orion was armed."

"All the more reason not to leave yourself open."

Shumar wanted to argue the point further. And he would have, except he knew that the woman was right.

Taking out his communicator, he flipped it open and contacted his ship. "Commander Mullen?"

"Aye, sir. Did you find what you were looking for?"

The captain glanced at the Orion, who was still sprawled on the floor. His actions were all the justification Shumar needed to seize the *Prosperous*.

"That and more," he told Mullen. "Send a couple of teams over. We've got a smuggling vessel to secure."

Daniel Hagedorn watched the cottony, violet-colored walls slide by on every side of his vessel, missing his titanium hull by less than thirty meters in any direction.

He and his crew were traveling the main corridor of a nebular maze—a gargantuan cloud of dust and destructive high-energy plasma that dominated this part of space. Unlike other nebulae of its kind discovered over the last thirty years, this one was rife with a network of corridors and subcorridors, the largest of which allowed a ship like Hagedorn's to make its way through unscathed.

Hence the term "maze."

The captain's orders called for him to remain in the phenomenon's main passageway, where he would gather as much data as possible. Normally, he was the kind of officer who followed instructions to the letter. Today, however, he planned to diverge from that policy.

For the last several minutes he had been scanning the cottony wall on his right for an offshoot that could give him some clearance. Unfortunately, that offshoot hadn't materialized.

Until now.

"Lieutenant Kendall," Hagedorn told his helm officer,

"we're going to change course. Take the next corridor to starboard." He consulted the readout in his armrest. "Heading two-four-two mark six."

Kendall glanced at the captain, his confusion evident. "Sir," he said, "that's not the way out."

"It is now," Hagedorn told him.

For a moment, the helmsman looked as if he were about to object to the course change. Then he turned to his console and dutifully put the captain's order into effect.

Instantly, the Christopher veered to starboard and entered the passageway, which was substantially narrower than the main corridor but still navigable. Satisfied, Hagedorn leaned back in his seat—and saw that his executive officer was standing beside him.

Her name was Corspa Zenar. She was an Andorian, tall and willowy, with blue skin and white hair. Her antennae were bent forward at the moment—which could have signified a lot of things, disapproval among them.

"You'd like an explanation," the captain guessed.

Zenar shrugged her bony shoulders. "That won't be necessary."

"And why is that?" Hagedorn asked, intrigued.

"Because I know what you have in mind," she said. "You're going to try to find the exit that will let us out near the Kryannen system."

He eyed her. "For what purpose?"

"During the war, the Pelidossians aided the Romulans. They sold them supplies, even helped them with repairs. Earth Command returned the favor by destroying a couple of Pelidossian ships."

The captain was impressed. "And now?"

"Now you want to reconnoiter—and you don't know

when you'll again be in a position to do so." Zenar glanced at the viewscreen. "Of course, our orders call for us to chart the main corridor only. But if you're waiting for me to object, you'll be waiting a long time."

It didn't take him long to figure out why. "Because you're a scientist first and foremost, and the more prodding around we do in these tunnels the better you'll like it."

The first officer nodded. "Something like that."

Hagedorn grunted. "I believe you and I are going to work well together, Commander Zenar."

The Andorian allowed herself a hint of a smile. "Nothing would please me more, sir."

Hiro Matsura had never fought the Shayal'brun, but he knew some captains who had. They were said to be a vicious species, capable of unpredictable and devastatingly effective violence whenever they perceived that their borders had been violated.

The problem, as Matsura understood it, was that their borders seemed to change constantly—at least from the Shayal'brun's point of view. As a result, Earth Command had felt compelled to monitor the aliens' movements every few months, sending patrols out to the Shayal'brun's part of space even at the height of the Romulan Wars.

But now, with Earth Command turning so many of its activities over to Starfleet, responsibility for keeping track of the Shayal'brun had fallen to Matsura. That was why he was slicing through the void at warp one, scanning the aliens' farthest-flung holdings for signs of hostile intent.

"Anything?" asked Matsura, hovering over his navigator's console.

Williams shook her head from side to side. "Not yet, sir," she reported, continuing to consult her monitor. "No new colonies, no new scanner platforms, no new supply depots..."

"And no sign of the Shayal'brun fleet," said Jezzelis, Matsura's long-tusked Vobilite first officer.

"Looks pretty quiet to me," Williams concluded.

Matsura straightened. "Then let's get out of here. The last thing we want to do is start an incident."

It was a real concern. The Shayal'brun were no doubt scanning them even as they scanned the Shayal'brun. The aliens would likely overlook a fly-by, as long as the ship remained outside their perceived borders.

But if the *Yellowjacket* lingered long enough, the Shayal'brun would attack. That much was certain.

"Mr. McCallum," said the captain, "bring us about and—"

Before Matsura could finish, his ship bucked and veered to starboard. The captain grabbed wildly for the back of Williams's chair and found a handhold there, or he would surely have lost his feet.

"What was *that?*" asked Jezzelis.

Williams examined her monitor again, hoping to give him an answer. But McCallum beat her to it.

"It's a subspace chute," said the helmsman.

Matsura looked at him. "A *what?*"

"A chute, sir," McCallum repeated, his fingers dancing across his control panel. The man looked excited, to say the least. "We ran into one on the *Pasteur* about a year ago."

"And what did you find out?" asked the captain.

"Not much, sir," said the helmsman. "Our instruments weren't nearly as powerful as the *Yellowjacket*'s." He looked up suddenly. "If I may say so, sir, this is a rare opportunity."

"You mean to turn back and study the chute?"

"Yes, sir." McCallum looked almost feverish in his desire to retrace their steps. "We may never come across one again."

Matsura frowned and turned to the viewscreen, where the stars burned brightly against the black velvet of space. He couldn't ignore the fact that some of those stars belonged to the Shayal'brun.

On the other hand, every captain in the fleet wanted to get a better handle on subspace anomalies, regardless of his background. Lives had been lost during the war because they hadn't known enough about such things.

And here was an opportunity to rectify that problem.

Jezzelis, who had enjoyed both military and scientific careers, didn't say anything. But his expression spoke volumes.

"All right," Matsura told his helmsman. "You've got ten minutes—not a second more."

McCallum started to argue, to say that ten minutes might not be enough for the kind of analysis he had in mind. Then he saw the captain's eyes and seemed to think better of it.

"Yes, sir," said the helmsman. "Ten minutes. Thank you, sir." And he brought the ship about.

Matsura glanced at the viewscreen again and bit his lip. With luck, he thought, their little detour wouldn't be a bloody one.

* * *

Sitting at the compact computer station in his quarters, Aaron Stiles called up the message he had received a few minutes earlier.

Normally, he waited until the end of his shift before he left the bridge to read his personal messages. But this one was different. This one had come from Big Ed Walker.

The first thing Stiles noticed was that the admiral was smiling. It was a good sign, he told himself.

"Hello, Aaron," said Walker. "I hope you're well. I've been doing my best to keep track of your exploits. It sounds like you're doing good work, considering the adverse circumstances."

Naturally, the admiral was referring to the butterfly catchers. He just didn't want to mention them by name, in case his message accidentally fell into the wrong hands.

"I just wanted you to know that everything is looking good back here on Earth," Walker continued. "Our side is gaining the upper hand. It's looking more and more like one of us will get that brass ring they've been dangling in front of you."

The brass ring, of course, was the *Daedalus*. The upper hand was control of the fleet. And if the Earth Command camp was winning the battle, Stiles wouldn't have to worry about Darigghi and his ilk much longer.

In the captain's opinion, it couldn't happen soon enough.

"Stay well, son," said the admiral. "Walker out."

Stiles saw the Earth Command insignia replace the man's image. Tapping out a command on his padd, he dumped the message. Then he returned to his bridge, his step just a little lighter than before.

CHAPTER
17

BRYCE SHUMAR REGARDED THE IMAGE OF DANIEL HAGE-
dorn on the computer monitor outside his bedroom.

"So," said Shumar, "Councillor Sammak arrived
safely?"

The esteemed Sammak of Vulcan was returning to his
homeworld for his daughter's wedding ceremony. He
had left San Francisco on an Earth Command vessel,
which had transferred him to the *Peregrine* two days
earlier. Now the *Peregrine* was transferring the councillor to the *Horatio*.

"He's being shown to his quarters now," Hagedorn
told him.

"How are your missions going?" asked Shumar, because he had to say *something*.

"Well enough," said his counterpart. "And yours?"

"We're getting by."

Neither of them spoke for a moment. After all, if it was a war they were fighting over the future of the fleet, neither of them wanted to give away any strategic information.

It was a shame that it had to be that way, Shumar told himself. Hagedorn wasn't a bad sort of guy. And he had taken Cobaryn's side in that brawl back in San Francisco.

Maybe the time he had spent with a crew half full of scientists had softened his position a little. Maybe with a little urging he could be made to see the other side of the issue.

There was only one way to find out.

"Actually," Shumar remarked, "I'm glad we've got a chance to compare notes. I think you and I are a lot alike."

"In what way?" Hagedorn asked, his expression giving away nothing.

"We're reasonable men, I'd say."

The other man's eyes narrowed ever so slightly. "Reasonable...?"

"We can see the other fellow's side of the story," Shumar elaborated. "Certainly *I* can."

"And what side is the *other* side?" Hagedorn inquired. He was beginning to look wary.

Shumar smiled in an attempt to put the man at ease. "I think you know what I'm going to say. That a strictly military-minded Starfleet would miss out on all kinds of scientific opportunities. That it would fail to embrace all the benefits the universe has to offer."

Hagedorn hadn't lodged an objection yet. Shumar interpreted that as his cue to go on.

"Mind you," he noted, "there's a lot to be said for combat smarts. I've learned that firsthand. But two hundred years ago, when man went out into space it was to expand his store of knowledge. It would be a shame if we were compelled to abandon that philosophy now."

Hagedorn regarded him. "In other words, you would like me to rethink my position on the nature of Starfleet."

"I would," Shumar admitted, "yes. And believe me, not because I want to win this little internecine war of ours. That doesn't matter to me one bit. All that matters is that the Federation doesn't get cheated out of the advancements it deserves."

The other man leaned back in his chair. "You know," he said, in a surprisingly tired voice, "I like you. What's more, I respect you. And I sure as hell won't try to tell you that you don't have a point."

Shumar's hopes fell as he heard a "but" coming. Clearly, the other shoe was about to fall.

"But," Hagedorn went on, "I believe that this fleet has to be a military organization first and foremost, and I can't tell you I'd ever advocate anything else. Not even for a nanosecond."

The scientist accepted the defeat. "Well," he responded in the same spirit of candidness, "it was worth a try."

The other man just looked at him. He seemed at a loss as to how to respond.

Shumar could see there was nothing to be gained by further conversation. "I ought to be getting on to my next assignment, I suppose. I'll see you around, no doubt."

Hagedorn nodded. "No doubt."

"Shumar out."

He was about to break the connection when the other captain said something. It was low, under his breath—as if it had escaped without his wanting it to.

"I didn't catch that," Shumar told him.

Hagedorn looked sympathetic. "I said it wasn't. Worth a try, I mean. The competition is already over."

Shumar felt his cheeks grow hot. "What are you talking about?"

"I mean it's over," Hagedorn said soberly. "I'd tell you more, but I've probably said too much already."

Shumar saw the undiluted honesty in the man's eyes. Hagedorn wasn't maneuvering, he realized. He really meant it.

"Thank you," Shumar replied. "I think."

For a moment it looked as if his colleague was going to say something else. Then he must have thought better of it.

"Hagedorn out," he said. And with that, his image vanished from the monitor and was replaced with the Starfleet insignia.

Suddenly, Shumar had a lot to think about.

Connor Dane made his decision and turned to his helmsman. "Take us out of orbit, Mr. Dolgin."

Dolgin shot a glance at him, his surprise evident on his florid, red-bearded face. "Sir?"

"Out of orbit," the captain repeated, with just a hint of derision. "That means *away*. More specifically, away from *here*."

The helmsman blushed. "Yes, sir," he said with an undercurrent of indignation, and got to work.

"Captain Dane?" said Nasir, his tall, dark-skinned blade of a first officer. He moved to Dane's side and leaned over to speak with him. "Would you say it's wise to move off so quickly?"

The captain looked up at his exec. *"Quickly?* We've been here for two entire days. If the Nurstim are going to take note of us, I'd say they've probably done it already."

Nasir frowned. "Begging your pardon," he said, "but the Nurstim may simply be waiting for us to move off."

"At which point they'll attack the Arbazans?"

"Precisely, sir."

"In that case," said Dane, "maybe we should stay here forever. Then we can be *sure* the Nurstim won't start anything."

Nasir smiled thinly. "Another day—" he began.

"Is a day too many," the captain told him. "Our orders called for us to stay two days—no longer."

His first officer nodded. "That's certainly true. But I assure you, anyone with a military background—"

"Can go straight to hell," said Dane.

That brought Nasir up short. "All I meant—"

"I *know* what you meant," the captain declared. "That I didn't wear black and gold during the war, so I can't possibly have the slightest idea of what I'm doing. Right?"

The first officer shook his head. "Not at all, sir. I just—"

Dane held his hand up. "Spare me the denials, Commander. I'm not in the mood." He turned to the science console, which was situated behind him and to his right. "Mr. Hudlin?"

Hudlin, who was hanging around the bridge as usual, looked up from his monitors. "Sir?"

"Didn't we pass something on the way here that you wanted to investigate? Some kind of cloud or something?"

The white-haired man smiled. "An ionized gas torus," he said. "It was trailing one of the moons around the seventh planet."

"Sounds intriguing," said Dane, though it didn't really sound intriguing to him at all. "Let's look into it."

Hudlin looked at him askance. "What about the Arbazans?"

"The Arbazans are as safe as they're going to be," the captain told him. He addressed his helmsman again. "Mr. Dolgin, head for the seventh planet. Three-quarters impulse."

"Aye, sir," came the faintly grudging response.

Next, Dane turned to his navigator. "Chart a course for the eighth and ninth planets as well, Lieutenant Ideko. They might have some interesting moons, too."

Ideko, a slender, graceful Dedderac, nodded her black-and-white-striped head. "Aye, sir."

Hudlin seemed unable to believe his ears. "If I may ask, sir...why the sudden interest in moons?"

The captain shrugged. "I've always been interested in moons, Mr. Hudlin. It's the scientist in me."

For Nasir, that appeared to be the last straw. He straightened and looked down at Dane with undisguised hostility. "It's only fair to inform you that I'll be lodging a formal protest."

The captain nodded. "Thanks for being fair, Commander. It's one of the things I like best about you."

The first officer didn't say anything more. He just moved away from the center seat and took up a position near the engineering console.

Inwardly, Dane cursed himself. Nasir was a strutting know-it-all he should never have hired in the first place—but still, he didn't deserve that kind of tongue-lashing. It wasn't his fault that his captain was a walking tinderbox lately.

It was Big Ed Walker's.

Dane's uncle was the one who had notified him that the Earth Command faction had carried the day. *As if I were one of them,* he reflected bitterly. *As if I had come around, just the way Big Ed always knew I would.*

Truth be told, Dane hadn't considered himself an ally of Shumar and Cobaryn either. But his uncle's message had sparked something inside him—and not just resentment.

It had made him realize that he had to take a stand in this war sooner or later. He had to choose between the cowboys and the butterfly catchers, or someone else would make the choice for him.

All his life, he had denied his family's glorious military history—but he hadn't embraced anything else in its place. Maybe it was time to make a commitment to something.

Maybe it was time to start chasing butterflies.

Bryce Shumar watched the small, slender woman take a seat in the anteroom of his quarters.

"Well," said Clarisse Dumont, "here I am. I hope this is as important as you made it out to be."

The *Peregrine* had been nearly a trillion kilometers from Earth when Shumar asked to speak with Dumont. Of course, it would have been a lot more convenient for them to send messages back and forth through subspace, but the captain had wanted to see his patron in person.

So Dumont had pulled some strings. She had made it to the nearest Earth base via commercial vessels. And now she was waiting to hear why she had made such a long and arduous trip.

Shumar found himself in the mood to be blunt. He yielded to it. "What's going on?" he asked unceremoniously.

Dumont's brow puckered. "What exactly do you mean?"

Shumar felt a surge of anger constrict his throat. "Don't play games with me," he said with forced calm. "I spoke with Hagedorn. He told me that the war for the fleet is over—that his side has already won."

He wanted Dumont to tell him he was crazy. He wanted her to say that Hagedorn didn't know what he was talking about. But she didn't do either of those things.

The only response she could muster was, "Is that so?"

"Was he right?" the captain pressed, feeling he knew the answer already. "Is the war already over?"

Dumont sighed. "Honestly, not yet. But it's getting there. Unless something changes—and quickly—Starfleet's going to be nothing more than Earth Command with a different name."

Shumar frowned. "You could have told me."

"I could have," she agreed. "But then, you might have stopped fighting—and whatever slim chance we had would have been gone."

It made sense in a heavy-handed, presumptuous kind of way. He asked himself what he would have done if he had been Clarisse Dumont. It didn't take him long to come up with an answer.

"You should have left that up to me," the captain told her. "I deserved to know the truth."

Dumont smiled a bitter smile. "How often do we get what we deserve?" She paused. "So now what, Captain? Are you going to pack it in, as I feared? Or are you going to keep fighting?"

Shumar grunted. "Do I have a choice?"

She nodded. "Always."

The woman was glib—he had to give her that. But then, she hadn't risen to such prominence by being shy.

"In that case," he told her, "I'll have to give it some thought."

"I hope you'll do that," said Dumont. "And I hope you'll come to the same conclusion you did before, odds or no odds."

He didn't pick up the gauntlet she had thrown down. Instead, he changed the subject. "Can I get you something to eat?"

She shook her head. "Thank you, but no. I should be getting back to the base. As always, I've got work to do." She smiled again. "Miles to go before I sleep and all that."

The captain nodded. "I understand."

He and Dumont talked about something on their way back to the transporter room—though afterward, he wasn't sure what. And he must have given the order for his transporter operator to return her to Earth Base 12, but he didn't remember issuing it.

All Shumar remembered was what Dumont had said. *Unless something changes—and quickly—Starfleet's going to be nothing more than Earth Command with a different name.*

It was a depressing thought, to say the least.

* * *

In the privacy of his tiny suite on the *Cheyenne,* Alonis Cobaryn viewed a recorded message from his friend and colleague Captain Shumar. It didn't appear to be good news.

"Dumont confirmed it," said Shumar, his brow creased with concern. "Our side is losing the war for the *Daedalus.*"

Cobaryn eased himself back into his chair. He was sorry to hear such a thing. He was sorry indeed.

"She asked me whether I intended to stop fighting," Shumar continued, "since our cause was all but lost." He chuckled bitterly. "I told her I'd give it some thought."

And what decision did you make? the Rigelian wondered.

Shumar shrugged. "What could I do except stick it out? I made a commitment, Alonis. I can't give up now."

Cobaryn nodded. *Bravo,* he thought.

"I'll expect the worst, of course," the Earthman told him. "But that doesn't mean I'll stop hoping for the best."

Cobaryn smiled. "And they call *me* a cockeyed optimist," he said out loud.

Shumar sighed. "Pathetic, isn't it?"

If it is, the Rigelian reflected, *then we are both pathetic. Like you, I will see this venture through to its conclusion.*

He had barely completed the thought when a light began to blink in the upper quadrant of his screen, signaling an incoming message. Responding to it, he saw that it was from Earth.

From Director Abute...

Aaron Stiles was peering at the tiny screen of a handheld computer, going over the results of his science section's analysis of the asteroid belt, when his navigator spoke up.

"Sir," said Rosten, a tall woman with long, dark hair, "I have a message for you from Director Abute."

Stiles turned in his seat to acknowledge her, glad for the opportunity to put the asteroid data aside. "Put it on-screen, Lieutenant."

"Aye, sir," said Rosten.

A moment later, the starfield on the forward viewer was replaced by Abute's dark, hawk-nosed visage. The man looked positively grim.

"Good morning, Captain Stiles," said the Starfleet administrator. "I have a mission for you."

Judging from the seriousness of the man's tone, Stiles guessed that it was a *real* mission this time. He certainly hoped so. He'd had enough asteroid-watching to last him several Vulcan lifetimes.

"I trust you're familiar with the Oreias system," Abute continued. "It's not far from your present position."

In fact, the captain *was* familiar with Oreias. A girl he had dated for a while had gone there to help establish an Earth colony.

"We have four scientific installations there, one on each of Oreias's class-M planets," the director noted. "Late yesterday, the Oreias Five colony was attacked by an unknown aggressor."

Unknown? thought Stiles. He felt his jaw clench.

"I know what you're thinking," said Abute. "That it may be the Romulans again. Frankly, I can't imagine what they would have to gain by such an action, but I concede that we cannot rule out the possibility."

Seeing a shadow fall across his lap, the captain traced it to its source. He found Darigghi standing next to him, his tiny Osadjani eyes focused on the Earthman's message.

"Fortunately," the director remarked, "no one died in the attack. However, the place is a bloody shambles and the colonists are scared to death—those on the other worlds as well as on Oreias Five. After all, whoever did this could be targeting the other colonies as well."

True, Stiles reflected. And if it *was* the Romulans, if he found even a hint that they were back on the warpath...

"Which is why we need a Starfleet presence there as quickly as possible," Abute declared, "to stabilize the situation, defend against further attacks, and try to determine who was responsible. Your vessel is the one closest to Oreias, Captain—"

Stiles smiled to himself. So I'll be the one who gets to check it out, he concluded. He was already beginning to savor the challenge when Abute completed his sentence.

"—so it looks as though you will be the first to arrive. However, I am deploying the remainder of the fleet to the Oreias system as well. A threat of this potential magnitude clearly dictates a team effort."

The captain slumped in his seat. Six ships...to investigate a single sneak attack? If they had worked that way during the war, they would never have had time to launch an attack of their own.

"Good luck," said the director. "I look forward to the report of your initial findings. Abute out."

Abruptly, the man's image was replaced with a starfield. Stiles frowned and turned to his navigator. "Lieutenant Rosten," he sighed, "set a course for the Oreias system. Top cruising speed."

"Aye, sir," said the navigator, applying herself to the task.

The captain leaned back in his seat. Then he looked up at Darigghi. "I don't suppose you've ever been in battle before?"

The Osadjani shook his head. "I have not."

"Well," said Stiles, "this may be your chance."

CHAPTER
18

AARON STILES CONSIDERED THE TINY BROWN-AND-BLUE sphere of Oreias Nine on his viewscreen.

"We are in communications range," Darigghi announced from his place at the captain's side.

Stiles nodded. "I know that."

"Shall I hail the colony administrator?"

"That won't be necessary," the captain told him.

The first officer looked down at him. "Do you not intend to communicate with the colonists?"

"That's correct," Stiles responded evenly. "I don't intend to communicate with them."

Darigghi licked his fleshy lips—a gesture that the captain had come to know all too well. "The people on this world have been living in fear," the Osadjani observed. "Knowledge of our presence in this system will give them a sense of security."

"I'm not here to hold anyone's hand," said Stiles. "I'm here to take care of whatever attacked Oreias Five. When that's done, the colonists will feel plenty secure."

Darigghi didn't seem satisfied with the captain's response. "Then what *will* you do? Proceed directly to Oreias Five?"

"I'll proceed in that *direction*," he told the Osadjani.

Darigghi tilted his head, confusion evident in his deep-set black eyes. "But you will not stop there?"

"I don't see any need."

"No need?" the first officer asked, a strain of incredulity in his voice. "When the colony may hold clues to its attacker's identity?"

Stiles chuckled dryly. "There are captains in this fleet who would give their eyeteeth to examine that colony—and I'm only too glad to give them the chance. Me, I'm going to sniff around this system and see if I can't pick up the enemy's propulsion trails."

Darigghi stared at him for a moment, as if weighing the utility of arguing the point. In the end, he must have decided that opposition was futile, because he made his way to the lift and disappeared inside.

The captain wasn't going to miss him. Turning to his navigator, he said, "Ms. Rosten, set a course for Oreias Eight. And scan for propulsion trails, maximum range."

Rosten got to work. "Aye, sir."

Sitting back in his chair, Stiles eyed his viewscreen again. Every vehicle known to man left some kind of residue in its wake. He was betting that his adversary's vessels were no exception.

With luck, he thought, he would get a notion of where the enemy had come from before the rest of the fleet arrived.

"Here he comes," said Cobaryn, as a gleam appeared in the sky over the pristine curve of a bone-white dome.

The husky, fair-haired individual standing beside him shaded his eyes against the brittle sunlight. His name was Sam Lindblad, and he was the administrator of the Oreias Five agricultural colony.

"I still don't get it," the fair-haired man told him.

"I beg your pardon?" said the captain.

"Why Earth Command didn't respond. This is an Earth colony, after all. And Earth Command knows how to fight."

"Starfleet can fight, too," Cobaryn pointed out.

Lindblad grunted disdainfully. "Not from what I've heard." He glanced at the Rigelian. "They say you're just a bunch of scientists."

"And that bothers you?" asked Cobaryn.

"Right now it does," said Lindblad.

"Even though you are a scientist yourself?"

"*Especially* because I'm a scientist myself. I know what I can do and what I can't do—and going toe to toe with some alien invader is one of the things I *can't* do."

By that time, the gleam in the sky had grown into a shuttlepod. As it descended toward the plaza in which they were standing, it raised a cloud of amber dust with its thrusters. Then it settled on the ground, joining the pod in which Cobaryn had come down from the *Cheyenne*.

"Perhaps we can change your mind," said the Rigelian.

The colonist frowned. "I sure as hell hope so."

A moment later, the pod door slid open and Cobaryn's colleague stepped out. Squinting as his eyes adjusted from the relative darkness of his vehicle, he said something to his crewmen, who were still inside. Then he made his way across the plaza.

"Administrator Lindblad," said the Rigelian, "this is Bryce Shumar, captain of the *Peregrine*."

Shumar shook hands with the colonist. "Sorry about all this," he said with what was obviously heartfelt sympathy. He turned to Cobaryn. "Have you had a chance to survey the damage yet?"

The Rigelian shook his head. "We just arrived ourselves."

Shumar looked to Lindblad. "Shall we?"

"This way," said the fair-haired man, gesturing for the Starfleet officers to follow him. Then he led them on the straightest possible course through the colony, a complex comprised mainly of large geodesic domes and the occasional pyramidal supply hut.

Cobaryn had sent his team ahead with its portable scanners to conduct their analyses while he waited for his friend to land. As a result, the Rigelian's only exposure to the stricken parts of the colony had been through the observation port of his pod.

Now, as he and Shumar followed Lindblad, Cobaryn began to see firsthand what had drawn the Federation's fledgling Starfleet to this planet. There were burn marks on the walls of some of the domes along with rents in the fabric from which they were constructed.

And the farther they went, the worse it got.

The punctures and scorch marks gave way to splintered supports and major structural damage. In fact, some of the domes seemed unsalvageable, though the teams of men and women attempting to make repairs might have taken issue with that verdict.

As Cobaryn and his companions went by, the colonists stopped and scrutinized them. The captain wondered if they were more fascinated with his alien appearance or the blue uniform he wore...and decided that neither answer would have surprised him.

"Here's the worst of it," said Lindblad, as they came around the shoulder of a half-shredded dome that still smelled of burning, and looked out toward the edge of the human settlement.

It was the worst, all right. There was no question about that in the Rigelian's mind. Perhaps a dozen of the colonists' residences, all of them situated between a pair of rounded hills, had been seared and pounded into the ground. What was left looked like a collection of blackened carcasses baking in the afternoon sun.

Cobaryn's landing party—his science officer and two crewmen—had all hunkered down among the wreckage with their scanners. After all, whatever residue had been left by the directed-energy weapons of the colony's assailants would be in greatest evidence here.

Shumar frowned as he gazed at the carnage. "And no one was hurt?"

"Miraculously, no one at all," said Lindblad. "But we were plenty scared, I can tell you that."

Shumar nodded soberly. "I've been fired on myself. I know what that can feel like."

The Rigelian negotiated a path through the ravaged domes and joined his science officer, a stern-looking woman named Kauff. Her scanner was cradled in her arms and she was playing it over a blackened strut.

"Anything yet?" Cobaryn asked.

Kauff put her scanner down and stretched out her back. The device was too heavy for a human to carry for very long, especially when one was working in such an obstacle course.

"One thing's for sure," said the science officer. "It wasn't the Romulans who did this."

"Why do you say that?" the captain inquired.

Kauff pointed to her scanner's digital readout. "The Romulans use electromagnetic beams, just like we do—and there's no electromagnetic beam in the universe that can cause this kind of molecular disruption."

The captain bent over and studied the readout. The woman was right. The colony's assailants boasted weapons much more advanced than those employed by the Romulans.

"So we know who it is *not*," he concluded. "Now all we need to determine is who it *is*."

"We'll get there," Kauff assured him. "Eventually." Then she bent, hefted her scanner again, and moved to another section of wreckage.

Next, Cobaryn went to check on Crewman Milosovich. The fellow was analyzing the soil to see if the aliens might have been after some kind of mineral wealth. They wouldn't have been the first group to try to scare a rival off a potentially valuable piece of land.

Stopping behind Milosovich, the Rigelian ventured a guess. "Precious metals?"

The crewman looked back over his shoulder at his commanding officer. "No, sir. At least, nothing to write home about. But there are heavy concentrations of organic materials."

"Oh?" said Cobaryn.

"Yes, sir. A certain polysaccharide in particular. It suggests that this area was once teeming with life."

The captain took a look around at the surrounding landscape, much of which had been turned into dark, carefully ordered farmland by Lindblad's people. Only in the distance was the terrain still dry and barren, a broad expanse of yellow plains dappled with dusky orange hillocks. Outside of a few small, spiky scrub plants, Cobaryn couldn't find any obvious signs of indigenous biological activity.

"Teeming with life," he repeated ironically. "That must have been a long time ago."

"That would be my guess as well, sir," said Milosovich. "Though I would have to conduct some lab tests to determine *how* long ago."

Catching a glimpse of blue out of the corner of his eye, Cobaryn turned and saw Shumar's team approaching. Their captain pointed to an as-yet-unexplored area with a gesture, then led the way.

After all, Shumar was a planetary surveyor by trade. When it came to performing scanner analyses, he was as qualified as anyone.

For that reason, Cobaryn disliked the idea of interrupting the man. Nonetheless, he walked over and knelt beside Shumar as the latter adjusted the data input on one of his scanners.

"So tell me," said Cobaryn, "how is Lieutenant Kelly?"

His friend looked at him, his expression one of surprise tinged with amusement. "You never give up, do you?"

Cobaryn smiled. "In my place, would *you?*"

Shumar thought about it for a moment, then shook his head. "Maybe not. But then, I haven't thrown in the towel yet insofar as the *Daedalus* is concerned, so I'm probably the *last* person you want to ask."

"Anything new on the Dumont front?" the Rigelian inquired.

"Nothing," his colleague told him. "And what happened here isn't going to help our cause one bit. If the Federation believes they've got a new enemy to contend with, they're not going to be devoting a lot of resources to science and exploration."

Cobaryn weighed the comment. "I suppose that's true," he was forced to concede.

"Look at the bright side," said Shumar, managing a humorless smile. "When the fleet becomes Ed Walker's toy, you and I can quit and do what we wanted to do all along."

"Explore the galaxy," the Rigelian responded.

"And forget about people like Walker and Clarisse Dumont." With a grunt, the human went back to work.

Quit Starfleet? Cobaryn thought. Somehow, "the bright side" didn't seem all that bright to him.

For the better part of an hour, he watched his men and Shumar's as they went through one pile of charred debris after another, gathering all kinds of data. During that time, Lindblad came and went a few times. So did some of the other colonists, including a few children, seeking to satisfy their curiosity or gain some sense of reassurance . . . or perhaps both.

Then, as the sun approached the horizon and they began to lose its light, both teams agreed that they had accumulated all the information they could. Lugging their scanners back through the heart of the wounded colony, they returned to their pods and prepared to analyze the data in greater depth.

But as Cobaryn took his leave of Lindblad, he knew that they hadn't uncovered anything that would lead them to the colony's attackers. For all intents and purposes, they had come up empty.

Hiro Matsura considered his viewscreen, where a bony-faced man with small eyes and thick brown hair looked back at him.

"So you've heard about what happened on Oreias Five," the captain recapped, "but you haven't seen any sign of alien vessels yourselves?"

"No sign at all," confirmed Tom Orlowski, the administrator of the Oreias Seven colony. "But that doesn't mean a thing. If they attacked Oreias Five, they may decide to attack us, too."

Matsura could hear the strain in the man's voice. Clearly, the last few days had been difficult ones for him.

"That's why we're here," the captain said. "To figure out who staged the Oreias Five attack and why...and to make certain that sort of thing doesn't happen again."

Orlowski frowned. "You sound so confident."

Matsura smiled. "And you don't."

That caught the administrator by surprise. "With all due respect," he said, "we asked for—"

"Experienced help," the captain noted. "And that's

what you're getting. Don't let the uniform and the age fool you, Mr. Orlowski. I was at the Battle of Cheron. So were two of the other captains assigned to this mission. Whatever it takes, we'll get the job done."

The statement seemed to calm the administrator a bit. "That's good to know," he told Matsura.

"Now," said the captain, "I'm going to send a team down to scan your colony and the area around it. When we're done, we'll compare notes with our teams at Oreias Five and the other colonies."

"And if you don't come up with anything?" Orlowski asked.

"Then we'll pursue other strategies," Matsura assured him. "In fact, at least one of our vessels is doing that already."

The captain looked forward to joining that pursuit— just as soon as his scanner team took a look around.

Hours after his visit to Oreias Nine, Dan Hagedorn could still see the faces of that planet's colonists, their eyes full of fear and uncertainty and the desperate hope that he could help them.

He had grown accustomed to that look during the war, seeing it at civilian settlements from one end of Earth space to the other, but there was something unsettling about seeing it now that the war was over. As hard as Earth had battled the invader, as high a price as she had paid, she should have earned a respite from armed conflicts.

Unfortunately, Hagedorn mused, it was a cruel universe—one that seemed to have a limitless supply of unpleasant surprises.

Just as he thought that, his navigator turned from her control console to look at him. "Sir," said Glendennen, a slender, dark-skinned woman, "we've picked up an unusual ion concentration. And unless our instruments are off, it seems to describe a pretty coherent line."

The captain felt a twinge of anticipation, but he was careful not to show it. "Sounds like a propulsion trail," he observed.

"It certainly could be," his navigator responded.

Hagedorn tapped his fingers on his armrest, considering the discovery from all angles. After he had rejected the idea of a trap, he said, "Get me Captain Stiles. He'll be interested to hear what we've found."

"Aye, sir," said Glendennen.

Hagedorn leaned back in his center seat. If this had been an Earth Command mission, its next stage would have been a simple one: seek out the enemy and destroy him.

But this was different, wasn't it? It wasn't just a matter of tearing their adversaries' ships apart. Somewhere along the line, they would have to find out why hostilities had begun in the first place.

It raised the level of difficulty considerably. But then, the captain reflected, that was the nature of the job.

Once, when he was a teenager, Aaron Stiles had seen a hawk pounce on a field mouse. Right now, he felt a lot like that hawk.

His viewscreen showed him four alien ships—the ones whose propulsion trails he and Hagedorn had been tracking. The vessels were small, dark, and triangular, with no visible nacelles. For all Stiles knew, they weren't even capable of faster-than-light travel.

He opened a communications link to his colleague's bridge. "I've got visual," he told Hagedorn.

"Same here," said his fellow captain. "And they don't seem to know we're on their tails."

"That's my impression, too," Stiles responded. "Remember that maneuver we pulled near Pluto?"

Hagedorn grunted audibly—as close as the man ever came to a laugh. "How could I forget? I'll work on their starboard flank."

"Acknowledged," said Stiles. He glanced at his helm officer, a woman named Urbina who wore her flaxen hair in a tightly woven braid. "Heading two-six-two-mark one, Lieutenant."

"Aye, sir," Urbina responded.

Over his comm link, the captain could hear Hagedorn giving the same sort of orders on the *Horatio*. Though Hagedorn was no longer Stiles's commanding officer, Stiles liked the idea that the man was working alongside him.

He regarded Weeks, who was sitting in front of him at the weapons console. "Deploy power to all batteries, Lieutenant."

"Power to lasers and launchers," Weeks confirmed.

"Range?" asked the captain.

Weeks consulted his instruments for a moment. "One minute and fifty-five seconds, sir."

"Thank you," said Stiles. Finally, he turned to his navigator. "Raise shields, Ms. Rosten."

"Raising shields," came Rosten's reply.

The captain studied the viewscreen. The enemy ships

were maintaining their course and speed. Apparently, they hadn't spotted the Christophers yet. Or if they had, they weren't giving any indication of it.

It felt good to be in battle again, he thought. It felt good to have an enemy in his sights. Stiles wasn't a scientist or a diplomat, and he didn't think he could ever become one.

He was a soldier, plain and simple.

And right now, he was in a situation that called for a soldier's skills.

"Range in one minute," said Weeks.

The words had barely left the weapons officer's mouth when the enemy squadron began to split up. The captain frowned.

"Stiles to Hagedorn. Looks like they're on to us."

"Looks that way. Let's go after the two nearest ships first, then worry about the other two."

"Agreed," said Stiles.

He pointed out one of the vessels on his screen. "That one's ours, Urbina. Get us in range."

"Aye, sir," the helm officer returned, her slender fingers dancing over her control console.

The *Gibraltar* veered hard to port and locked onto the alien's tail. It wasn't long before she began to gain on her prey, which seemed incapable of full impulse.

"Range?" asked Stiles.

"Twenty seconds," said Weeks.

"Target lasers," the captain ordered.

"Targeting," the weapons officer confirmed.

The Starfleet vessel continued to narrow the gap. Stiles remained as patient as he could, the muscles working in his jaw. Finally, he got the word he had been waiting for.

"Range!" called Weeks.

"Fire!" the captain barked.

Twin bolts of blue energy stabbed through the void. But somehow, the alien ship eluded them. And as it curled back around, it spewed a string of fiery crimson packets at the *Gibraltar.*

The charges loomed on Stiles's viewscreen until all of space seemed to be consumed in ruby-red fire. He took hold of his armrests, expecting the aliens' volley to send a brisk shudder through the *Gibraltar*'s forward shields.

Instead, the impact sent his ship heeling steeply to port and nearly tore him out of his chair. Amazed, he turned to his helm officer and called out, "Evasive maneuvers!"

Urbina sent them twisting away from the enemy, allowing them to escape a second blazing barrage. But before they knew it, another alien vessel had slid onto their viewscreen.

"Target and fire!" the captain snapped, instinctively grasping an opportunity to reduce the odds against them.

But the enemy was quicker, unleashing a stream of scarlet energy bundles that slammed into the *Gibraltar* with skull-rattling force. The Federation vessel reeled and a plasma conduit burst above the aft stations, releasing a jet of white-hot gas.

"Report!" Stiles demanded.

"Shields down eighty-four percent!" Rosten barked.

The captain swore beneath his breath. The enemy's weapons were more powerful than they had a right to be. One more hit like the last one and their hull would look like a sieve.

"What about the enemy?" he asked.

"No apparent damage," said the navigator, her expression one of disappointment and disgust.

Abruptly, the triangular shape of an alien ship swam into their sights again. But this time, Stiles wasn't so eager to confront it—especially when he sensed he was about to become the target of a crossfire.

"Move us off the bull's-eye!" he told Urbina. Then he leaned toward his comm controls. "Captain Hagedorn!"

As the *Gibraltar* swung sharply to starboard, avoiding another alien barrage, the other man's voice came crackling over a secure channel. "I'm here. What's your status?"

"Not good," said Stiles. "Shields are down to sixteen percent, and we haven't done any damage ourselves."

"We're taking a beating here, too," Hagedorn confessed. "We need to break off the engagement."

The idea of conceding defeat was poison to Stiles. During the war, his squadron had only done it twice—and on both occasions, they had been facing vastly superior numbers. This time, the odds were only two to one.

But the aliens hit harder and moved faster than any Romulan ship ever built. The Starfleeters didn't have any choice but to slink away with their tails between their legs....

At least for now.

"Get us out of here!" Stiles told his helm officer, each word like a self-inflicted wound.

Suddenly, the *Gibraltar* hurtled away from the battle, going back in the direction from which she had come. On her starboard flank, Hagedorn's ship followed a parallel course.

Stiles wasn't the least bit certain that the enemy wasn't going to come after them. But as it turned out, the aliens were perfectly content to let their adversaries escape.

For a moment, the triangular ships just cruised back and forth, as if defending an invisible border. Then, after the Federation vessels had put some distance between themselves and the aggressors, the aliens recreated their original formation and resumed their course.

They acted as if there hadn't been a battle at all…as if Stiles and Hagedorn weren't even there.

On Stiles's viewscreen, the enemy ships diminished rapidly with distance, shrinking to the point where they were barely visible. But the captain didn't have to see them to remember what they looked like.

Or to promise himself that they would meet again.

CHAPTER
19

HIRO MATSURA HAD RETRIEVED HIS POD AND WAS ABOUT to break orbit when his navigator notified him that the *Maverick* was in the vicinity.

Matsura hadn't expected any company at Oreias Seven. "On screen," he said, settling back into his center seat.

A moment later, Connor Dane's face filled the forward viewscreen. He didn't seem pleased.

"Tell me you had better luck than we did," said Dane.

Matsura shook his head. "My team didn't find anything of significance."

Dane scowled. "Maybe we'll figure something out when we compare notes with Shumar and Cobaryn."

Matsura couldn't keep from smiling a little. "You really think so?"

Dane looked at him. "Don't you?"

"With all due respect," Matsura told him, "I think we can sit and compare notes until the last days of the universe, and we'll still just be groping in the dark."

Dane's eyes narrowed. "And you've got a better way to dope out what happened?"

"I think Captain Stiles had the right idea," said Matsura. "The only way we're going to find the aliens is by going out and looking for them."

"It's not that big a system," Dane responded. "We don't *all* have to be looking for them."

"It would speed things up," Matsura noted.

"Or slow them down," said Dane, "by putting all our eggs in the wrong basket. Depends on how you look at it."

Matsura was surprised at the man's attitude. "I didn't know you had such deep respect for research scientists."

Dane's mouth twisted at the other man's tone. "You mean butterfly catchers, don't you?"

Matsura found himself turning red. "I don't use that terminology."

"But your buddies do," the other man observed. "And don't insult my intelligence by claiming otherwise."

"All right," said Matsura, "I won't."

That seemed to pacify Dane a bit. "At least you're honest," he conceded.

"Thanks. Now, I'm sorry you took the trouble to fly all the way over here, but I'm leaving to try to hook up with Stiles and Hagedorn. You're welcome to join me if you'd like."

Dane snorted. "I'll put my money on Shumar and Cobaryn."

"Suit yourself," said Matsura. "I'll—"

Suddenly, his navigator interrupted him. "Sir," said Williams, her face drawn with concern as she consulted her monitor, "we're picking up a number of unidentified vessels."

The captain saw Dane turn away from the viewscreen and spit a command at one of his officers. He didn't look happy.

For that matter, Matsura wasn't very happy either. "Give me visual," he told Williams.

A moment later, Dane's image vanished from the viewscreen, to be replaced by that of three small, triangular vessels. They were gleaming in the glare of Oreias as they approached.

The aggressors, Matsura thought. It had to be.

"Raise shields," he announced. "Power to all batteries."

"Raising shields," Williams confirmed.

"Power to lasers and launchers," said his weapons officer.

"You still there?" asked Matsura over their comm link.

"Yeah, I'm here," came Dane's response. "But I've got to tell you, I'm not much of a team player."

No big surprise there, Matsura told himself. "I'll try to work with you anyway. Leave your comm link open. If I see an alien on your tail, I can give you a holler."

"Acknowledged," said Dane.

Then the enemy was on top of them. Or rather, the triangular vessels were plunging past them—so intent on the colony, it seemed, that they were ignoring the Christophers above it.

Matsura took the slight personally. "Lock lasers on the nearest ship," he told his weapons officer.

"Targeting," said Wickersham, a bearded man with a narrow face and deep-set eyes.

"Fire!" the captain commanded.

Their electric-blue beams reached out and skewered the enemy vessel—failing to disable it, but getting its attention. It came about like an angry bee and returned fire, sending out a string of scarlet fireballs.

"Evade!" Matsura called out.

But they weren't fast enough. The energy clusters plowed into the *Yellowjacket*, sending a bone-rattling jolt through the deckplates.

The aliens packed a punch, the captain realized. He had made the mistake of judging their firepower by their size.

"Another one on our port beam!" said Williams.

"Split the difference!" Matsura ordered.

At the helm console, McCallum worked feverishly. What's more, his efforts paid off. The *Yellowjacket* sliced between the two triangular ships, preventing them from firing for the moment.

Suddenly, the third vessel loomed on Matsura's viewscreen, its underbelly exposed, filling the entire frame with its unexpected proximity. He had never had such an easy target and he might never have one again.

"Target lasers and fire!" he commanded.

At close range, their beams seemed to do a good deal more damage. The enemy staggered under the impact.

"Their shields are at twenty-eight percent," Williams reported.

A barrage of atomics might take the alien out of the fight, the captain speculated. But before he could launch one, the enemy was bludgeoned with blasts of white fury.

Dane, Matsura thought.

"Their tactical systems are offline," his navigator told him.

The captain could have finished off the alien then and there. However, the vessel wasn't in a position to hurt the colony anymore, and he still had two other marauders to worry about.

"Where are the others?" he asked Williams.

She worked at her console. "Right here, sir."

A moment later, he saw the two still-capable triangles on his viewscreen. They were going after the *Maverick* with their energy weapons blazing, trying to catch her in a deadly crossfire.

Unlike Matsura, Dane didn't make an attempt to dart between his adversaries. He headed straight for one of them, exposing his starboard flank to the other.

It was a maneuver that depended on the enemy's being caught by surprise and veering off. But if that didn't happen, it was suicide.

Had Matsura been fighting both the aliens on his own, he might have made an effort to do something similar. As it was, he found the move reckless to the point of insanity.

You idiot, he thought—and not just because Dane had endangered his own ship. By placing himself in jeopardy, he had made it necessary for the *Yellowjacket* to expose herself as well.

Matsura frowned. "Pursue the vessel to port, Mr. Wickersham! Target lasers and fire!"

Wickersham managed to nail the enemy from behind with both blue beams. He hit the triangle hard enough to keep it from striking the *Maverick* with an energy volley, but—unfortunately—not hard enough to cripple it.

As they dogged the alien ship, trying to lock on for another shot, the captain saw the other triangle peel off to avoid the *Maverick*—just as Dane had gambled it would.

But as surely as the *Maverick* had climbed out of the fire, the *Yellowjacket* was falling into it. As Wickersham released another laser barrage, the enemy to port looped around with amazing dexterity. Then it came for Matsura and his crew, its weapons belching bundle after bundle of crimson brilliance.

"Hard to starboard!" the captain called out, hoping to pull his ship out of harm's way.

But it was no use. The alien's energy clusters dazzled his screen and rammed the *Yellowjacket* with explosive force—once, twice, and again, finally wrenching Matsura out of his captain's chair and pitching him sideways across the deck.

Behind him, a control console erupted in a shower of sparks. Black smoke collected above it like a bad omen. There were cries of pain and dismay, punctuated by frantic status reports.

"Shields are down!"

"Hull breaches on decks five and six!"

"Lasers and atomics are inoperable!"

Dazed, Matsura watched someone grab a fire extinguisher from the rack on the wall. Ignoring a stinging wetness over his right eye, he dragged himself to his feet and made his way back to his center seat.

On the static-riddled viewscreen, the battle had advanced while Matsura was pulling himself together. Somehow, Dane had incapacitated another of the enemy's vessels because only the *Maverick* and one of the aliens were still exchanging fire.

Abruptly, the commander of the triangle decided to change tactics. The ship broke off the engagement and went hurtling out into the void. And just as abruptly, its sister ships departed in its wake.

Matsura's first instinct was to follow them. Then he remembered that the *Yellowjacket* was in no shape to pursue *anyone*.

Without shields and weapons, she was all but helpless. The captain looked around at his bridge officers. They looked relieved that the battle was over, especially the ones who had sustained injuries.

"Casualties?" Matsura asked, not looking forward to the response he might get.

Williams, who looked shaken but not hurt, consulted her monitor. "Sickbay has three reports, sir, but more are expected. No fatalities as far as the doctor can tell."

The captain frowned. It could have been worse. "Dispatch a couple of engineering teams to see to those hull breaches."

Williams nodded. "Aye, sir."

Matsura turned to Wickersham, who was holding a damaged left arm and grimacing. "Tacticals are a mess, sir," he got out. "I'll see to bringing them back online, but it's going to take a while."

"First," the captain said, "you'll get yourself to sickbay."

"But, sir," Wickersham protested, looking even more pained than before, "we're in need of—"

"Repairs? Yes, we are," Matsura told him. "But they can be carried out without you."

The weapons officer looked like he was going to put

up a fight. Then he said, "Aye, sir," and made his way to the lift.

Matsura was about to check on his propulsion system when Williams spoke up. "Sir, Captain Dane is asking to speak with you."

His jaw clenching, the captain nodded. "Link him in."

A moment later, Dane appeared on the viewscreen. "You look like you took a beating," he observed. "What's your situation?"

"The situation," said the captain, doing his best to keep his voice free of anger, "is I've lost my lasers, my atomics, and my shield generators. And that's just a superficial assessment."

Dane grunted. "Tough luck. We suffered a little damage ourselves." He began tapping a command into his armrest. "I'll contact the others and let them know what happened here."

Matsura's mouth fell open. That was it? No thanks? No recognition that he had put his ship and crew on the line to bail out a reckless fool of a comrade?

If this had been an Earth Command mission, Matsura's wingmates would have been quick to acknowledge what he had done. But this wasn't Earth Command, he reminded himself bitterly. It was something completely different.

And Connor Dane was still a Cochrane jockey at heart, taking low-percentage chances as if his life were the only one at stake.

Matsura was tempted to lash out at the man, to tell him how he felt; but he wouldn't do that with two complements of bridge officers privy to the conversation. He would arrange a better time.

"You do that," Matsura said. "And when you're done, I'd like to speak with you. In private."

For the first time, it seemed to dawn on the other man that his colleague might not be entirely happy with him. "No problem," Dane answered casually. "I'll tell my transporter operator to expect you."

"*Yellowjacket* out," said Matsura—and terminated the link.

A moment later, Dane's face vanished from the screen, replaced with a view of his Christopher. Matsura studied it for a moment, his resentment building inside him.

Then he got up from his center seat. "You've got the conn," he told Lieutenant Williams and headed for the *Yellowjacket*'s transporter room.

As far as he knew, *that* system was still working.

"I'd ask you to pardon the mess," Dane said, "but I might as well tell you, it's like this all the time."

Matsura didn't say anything in response. He just frowned disapprovingly, looked around Dane's cluttered anteroom, and found an empty seat.

Obviously, Matsura wasn't pleased with him. And just as obviously, Dane was about to hear why. Removing yesterday's uniform from his workstation chair, Dane tossed it into a pile in the corner of the room and sat down.

"All right," he told his fellow captain. "There's something you want to get off your chest, right? So go ahead."

Matsura glared at him. "Fine. If you want me to be blunt, I'll be blunt. What you did out there a minute ago was foolish and irresponsible. Leaving your flank exposed, forcing me to go in and protect it...you're lucky you didn't get us all killed."

Dane looked at him. "Is that so?"

"You're damned right," Matsura shot back. "No Earth Command captain would ever have taken a chance like that."

Dane shrugged. "Then maybe they should consider it."

"Are you out of your mind?" asked Matsura, turning dark with anger. "You're going to defend that gambit— after it crippled my ship and injured seventeen of my crewmen?"

Dane smiled a thin smile. "Given a million chances, I'd do it a million times...hands down, no contest."

Matsura was speechless.

"Of course," Dane went on, "I'm not one of the noble black and gold, so none of my skill or experience means a flipping thing. But I'll tell you what...I've met a few Romulans in my day, too. In fact, I was blasting them out of space long before you ever warmed your butt in a center seat."

Matsura's eyes narrowed. "There's a difference between experience and luck," he pointed out.

"Men make their own luck," Dane told him. "I make mine by pushing the envelope—by doing what they least expect. Come to think of it, you might want to think about pushing the envelope a little yourself."

"Me...?" Matsura asked.

"That's right. Dare to be different. Or do you want to spend the rest of your life living in your flyboy buddies' shadow?"

Matsura's jaw clenched. "I don't live in anyone's shadow—not Hagedorn's or Stiles's or anyone else's.

What I do is carry out my mission within the parameters of good sense."

Dane looked skeptical. "Right."

"You think otherwise?"

Dane shrugged. "I think good sense is what people hide behind when they can't do any better."

"Says the man who hasn't got any."

"Says the man who accomplished his mission," Dane countered.

Matsura flushed and got to his feet. "Obviously, I'm wasting my time talking to you. You know everything."

"Funny," said Dane, keeping his voice nice and even. "I was just about to tell you the same thing."

Matsura's mouth twisted.

"And just for the record," said Dane, "I didn't expect you to protect my flank. As I said, I'm not much of a team player."

The other man didn't respond to that one. He just turned his back on Dane, tapped the door control, and left.

The captain shook his head. Matsura had potential—anyone with an eye in his head could see that. But the way things were going, it didn't look like he was going to realize it.

Not that that's any of *my* headache, Dane told himself, leaning back in his chair and closing his eyes.

CHAPTER
20

MATSURA WAS STILL BOILING OVER DANE'S REMARKS AS he left the *Yellowjacket*'s transporter room...and on an impulse, headed for a part of his vessel he hadn't had occasion to visit lately.

Men make their own luck, Dane had told him.

But Matsura had done that, hadn't he? During the war, he had been as effective a weapon as Earth Command could have asked for. He had risen to every challenge thrown his way.

But Dane wasn't talking about efficiency or determination. He was talking about thinking outside the box. He was talking about a willingness to try something different.

You might want to think about pushing the envelope...

And, damn it, Matsura would do just that. He would show Dane that he could take the direction least expected of him—and do more with it than the butterfly catchers themselves.

Neither Shumar, Cobaryn, nor Dane had discovered anything of value with all their meticulous site scanning. But with the help of his research team, Matsura would turn up something. He would find a way to beat the aliens that his colleagues had overlooked.

Or do you want to spend the rest of your life living in your flyboy buddies' shadow?

Matsura swore beneath his breath. Dane was wrong about him—dead wrong—and he was going to make the arrogant sonuvagun see that.

The captain had barely completed the thought when he realized that his destination was looming just ahead of him. Arriving at the appropriate set of doors, he tapped the control pad on the bulkhead and watched the titanium panels slide aside.

Once, this relatively large compartment on Deck Eight had been a supply bay. It had been converted by Starfleet into a research laboratory, equipped with three state-of-the-art computer workstations and a stationary scanner that was three times as sensitive as the portable version.

It was all Clarisse Dumont's doing. If the fleet was going to conduct research in space, she had argued, it might as well enjoy the finest instruments available.

Matsura hadn't been especially inclined to make use of them before; he had left that to those members of his crew with a more scientific bent. But he would certainly make use of them now.

"Mr. Siefried," he said, addressing one of the three crewmen who had beamed down to the colony to collect data.

Siefried, a lanky mineralogist with sharp features and close-cropped hair, evinced surprise as he swiveled in his seat. After all, it wasn't every day that Matsura made an appearance there.

"Sir?" said Siefried.

"What have we got?" asked the captain, trying his best to keep his anger at Dane under wraps.

The mineralogist shrugged his bony shoulders. "Not much more than we had before, I'm afraid. At least, nothing that would explain why the aliens attacked the colony."

Matsura turned to Arquette, a compact man with startling blue eyes. "Anything to add to that?" he asked.

Arquette, an exobiologist, shook his head. "Nothing, sir. Just the same materials we saw before. But I'm still working on it."

"Perhaps if we had a context," said Smithson, a buxom physicist who specialized in energy emissions, "some kind of backdrop against which we could interpret the data."

"That would be helpful, all right," Matsura agreed. "Then again, if we knew something about these aliens, we probably wouldn't have needed to do site research in the first place."

The scan team looked disheartened by his remark. Realizing what he had done, the captain held his hand up in a plea for understanding. "Sorry. I didn't mean that the way it came out."

"It's all right, sir," said Smithson, in an almost motherly tone of voice. "It's been a frustrating time for all of us."

Matsura nodded. "To say the least."

But he wasn't going to accept defeat so easily. Not when Dane's smugness was still so vivid in his memory.

"Do you mind if I take a look?" he asked Smithson.

"Not at all," said the physicist, getting up from her seat to give the captain access to her monitor.

Depositing himself behind the workstation, Matsura took a look at the screen, on which the Oreias Seven colony was mapped out in bright blue lines on a black field. He hadn't actually seen the site in person, so he took a moment to study it.

Immediately, a question came to mind.

"Why does the perimeter of the colony follow these curves?" he asked, pointing to a couple of scalloped areas near the top of the plan.

"There are hills there," said Siefried, who had come over to stand behind him. "Not steep ones, mind you, but steep enough to keep the colonists from erecting their domes."

Makes sense, the captain thought. Why build on a slope when you can build on a flat?

Then again, why build near hills at all? Matsura presented the question to his mineralogist.

"Actually," Siefried noted, "it would have been difficult to do otherwise. All the regions suitable for farming have hilly features. The area the colonists picked is the flattest on the planet."

"I see," said the captain.

He studied the layout of the colony some more, looking for any other detail that might trigger an insight. Nothing seemed to do that, however. Without anything else to attract Matsura's eye, it was eventually drawn back to the two scalloped areas.

"What is it, sir?" asked Arquette, who had come to stand behind the captain as well.

Matsura shook his head, trying to figure out what it was about those two half-circles that intrigued him. "Nothing, really. Or maybe . . ." He heaved a sigh. "I don't know."

But it seemed that a visit to the colony was in order. And this time, he was going to go down there *personally*.

As Bryce Shumar materialized on the *Horatio*'s transporter pad, he saw Cobaryn standing alongside the ship's transporter technician. Obviously, the Rigelian had decided to wait there for him.

That came as no surprise to Shumar. What surprised him was that Connor Dane was waiting there too.

"Welcome to the *Horatio*, sir," said the transporter operator.

Shumar nodded to the man. "Thanks, Lieutenant."

"About time you got here," the Cochrane jockey added. "Hagedorn and Stiles have probably finished all the hors d'oeuvres."

The remark was unexpected—even more so than Dane's presence there in the first place. Shumar couldn't help smiling a little. "I didn't know you were a comedian," he said.

"Who's joking?" Dane returned.

"I hate to interrupt," Cobaryn told them, "but now that Captain Shumar is here, we should get up to Captain Hagedorn's quarters as quickly as possible. I wish to be present when the decisions are made."

Shumar agreed. Together, the three of them exited the transporter room and made their way to the nearest turbolift, which carried them to the appropriate deck. From there, it was a short walk to the captain's door.

They knew that because the ships they commanded were exact replicas of the *Horatio,* designed to be identical down to the last airflow vent and intercom panel. Anyway, that had been the intent.

As the doors to Hagedorn's quarters whispered open, Shumar saw that there were at least a few details there that diverged from the standard. More to the point, Hagedorn's anteroom wasn't anything like Shumar's.

It had been furnished economically but impeccably, the walls decorated with a series of small, ancient-looking iron artifacts, the clunky, standard-issue Earth Command table and chairs replaced with a simpler and earthier-looking version in a tawny, unfinished wood.

Interestingly, there weren't any of the *customary* personal effects to be seen. Not a medal—though Hagedorn must have won lots of them. Not an exotic liquor bottle, a musical instrument, an alien statuette, or an unusual mineral specimen. Not a hat, a globe, or a 3-D chessboard.

Not even a picture of a loved one.

Shumar found the place a little off-putting in its spartan outlook, in its minimalism. However, it looked considerably bigger than Shumar's own anteroom. So much so, in fact, that he didn't feel cramped sharing the space with his five colleagues.

Then it occurred to Shumar that only *four* of his colleagues were present. Matsura was conspicuous by his absence.

"Come on in," said Hagedorn, his manner cordial if a bit too crisp for Shumar's taste. "Can I get you anything?"

Shumar noticed that neither Hagedorn nor Stiles had

a drink in his hand. "Nothing, thanks. Where's Captain Matsura?"

Stiles frowned. "He'll be a few minutes late. He wanted to check out the Oreias Seven colony himself."

"Didn't he do that already?" asked Shumar.

"Apparently not," Hagedorn replied, obviously unperturbed by his colleague's oversight.

"You forget," said Stiles, "some of us aren't scientists."

Shumar hadn't forgotten. He just couldn't believe his fellow captains hadn't seen a value in examining the colonies firsthand.

"Why don't we get down to business?" asked Dane. "We can bring Matsura up to speed when he gets here."

Shumar had never heard Dane take such a purposeful tack before. Was this the same man who had lingered over his tequila while everyone around him was scrambling to fight the Romulans?

It seemed Connor Dane was *full* of surprises today.

Stiles glanced at Hagedorn. "I agree. It's not as if we don't know where Matsura will come down in this matter."

Hagedorn must have been reasonably sure of Matsura as well because he went ahead with the meeting. "All right, then," he said. "We're all aware of the facts. We've scanned all four colonies in this system, including the two the aliens have already attacked, and we haven't discovered anything to explain their aggressive behavior."

"Fortunately, we've shown we can track them down," said Stiles, picking up where his comrade left off. "But we can't match their firepower or their maneuverability unless we come at them with everything we've got."

"Even with the *Yellowjacket* damaged," Hagedorn noted, "we've still got five battleworthy ships left. I propose we deploy them as a group in order to find the aliens and defuse the threat."

"It's the only viable course of action open to us," Stiles maintained. "Anything less and we'll be lucky to fight them to a draw again."

Silence reigned in the room as they considered the man's advice. Then Hagedorn said, "What do the rest of you think?"

In other words, thought Shumar, you three butterfly catchers.

Cobaryn was the first to speak up. "I agree with Captain Stiles's assessment," he responded.

Shumar was surprised at how easily his friend had been swayed. It must have shown on his face because the Rigelian turned to him with a hint of an apology in his eyes.

"Believe me," said Cobaryn, "I wish we could have come up with another solution to the problem. However, I do not see one presenting itself, and the colonists are depending on us to protect them."

It was hard to argue with such logic. Even Shumar had to admit that.

Dane was frowning deeply, looking uncharacteristically thoughtful.

"You seem hesitant," Stiles observed, an undercurrent of mockery in his voice. "I hope you're not thinking of hanging back while the rest of us go into battle."

Obviously, thought Shumar, some bone of contention existed between Stiles and Dane. In fact, now that Shumar had occasion to think about it, he was reminded of an exchange of remarks between the two at the captains' first briefing back on Earth.

In response to Stiles's taunt, the Cochrane jockey smiled jauntily. "What?" he asked, his voice as sharp-edged as the other man's. "And let you have all the fun?"

Ever the cool head, Hagedorn interceded. "This is a serious situation, gentlemen. There's no place at this meeting for personalities."

"You're right," said Stiles. "I was out of line." But neither his expression nor his tone suggested repentance.

Hagedorn turned to Shumar. His demeanor was that of one reasonable man speaking to another.

"And you, Captain?" he asked.

As his colleagues looked on, Shumar mulled over the proposition before him. Part of him was tempted to do what Cobaryn was doing, if only for the sake of the colonists' continued well-being.

Then there was the other part of him.

Shumar shook his head. "Unfortunately, I'm going to have to break with the party line. I'll be beaming down to Oreias Seven in order to continue my investigation."

"Are you sure you want to do that?" asked Hagedorn.

Shumar nodded. "Quite sure."

"What about your ship?" Stiles inquired.

Shumar understood the question. Stiles wanted the *Peregrine* to go with the rest of the fleet to increase their chances of a victory. What's more, Shumar didn't blame him.

"My ship will go with you," he assured Stiles.

"Under whose command?" Stiles pressed.

"That of my first officer, Stephen Mullen. From what I've seen of him, he's more than qualified to command the *Peregrine*. In fact, considering all the military experience he's got under his belt, you'll probably feel more comfortable with *him* than you do with *me*."

But that didn't seem to be good enough for Stiles, who shot a glance at Hagedorn. "As it happens," he argued, "we've got an experienced commanding officer without a viable vessel. Why not put Captain Matsura in the center seat of the *Peregrine?*"

Shumar didn't like the idea. After all, Mullen had demonstrated an ability to work smoothly with the *Peregrine*'s crew. Besides, he wasn't going to let Stiles or anyone else decide whom to put in charge of his vessel.

But before he could say anything, the doors to Hagedorn's anteroom slid aside again and Matsura joined them, his forehead slick with perspiration. "Sorry I'm late," he said.

"It's all right," Stiles assured him. In a matter of moments, he brought his Earth Command comrade up to date. "So, since Captain Shumar has decided to stay here, we're talking about putting you in command of his ship."

"Which isn't going to happen," Shumar interjected matter-of-factly. "Captain Stiles may have missed it, but I've already decided who's going to command the *Peregrine*."

Stiles's look turned disparaging. "With all due respect, Captain—"

Matsura held up his hand, stopping Stiles in mid-objection. "There's no need to argue about it," he said. "As it happens, I'd prefer to stay here with Captain Shumar."

Stiles looked at Matsura as if he were crazy. "What the devil for?"

Shumar wanted to know the answer to that question himself.

CHAPTER
21

"I KNOW," SAID MATSURA, "THIS COMES AS A SURPRISE TO you." He glanced at his fellow captains, Dane included. "To *all* of you."

In their places, Matsura would probably have been surprised as well.

He was an Earth Command officer by training as well as inclination, not one of the research types Clarisse Dumont had foisted on the Federation's new Starfleet. And at that moment, with every Earth colony in the Oreias system threatened by a mysterious fleet of alien marauders, his military skills were needed more than ever.

But this one time, Matsura felt compelled to pursue a different course of action.

"Listen," he told the others, "I may be on to something. I was studying the Oreias Seven colony back on the *Yellowjacket* a little while ago, and I noticed there were two hills at the edge of the colony."

"Wait a minute . . ." said Shumar. "There were two hills outside the Oreias Five colony as well."

"I'm aware of that," Matsura replied. "I got the information from your first officer a few moments ago."

"Two hills," Stiles repeated quizzically. "And that *means* something?"

"It sure as hell might," said Shumar.

"So what did you see when you went to examine the terrain for yourself?" asked Cobaryn.

"I'm not sure," said Matsura.

Zipping open the front of his uniform, he delved into an interior pocket and pulled out a handful of what he had found. They were fragments of something, each piece rounded, amber-colored, and brittle.

"I did some digging with my laser," Matsura told the others, "and this is what I came up with. The hill was full of it."

Cobaryn held his hand out. "May I?"

Matsura deposited his discovery in the Rigelian's silver-skinned palm. Then he watched Cobaryn's ruby eyes glitter with curiosity as he held the material up to the light.

"Any idea what it is?" asked Shumar.

Cobaryn made a face. "I wish I did."

Shumar turned to their host. "Can we bring up a scanner?"

"Absolutely," said Hagedorn.

Before two minutes had elapsed, one of the *Horatio*'s security officers produced the device Shumar had requested. Shumar hefted it, pointed its business end at the stuff in Cobaryn's palm, and then activated it.

"What is it?" asked Matsura.

Shumar checked the scanner's readout. "It's organic." His brow creased. "A polysaccharide—one that we found in great abundance in the hardest hit area on Oreias Five."

The Rigelian's eyes lit up. "Of course. I recall Crewman Milosovich telling me about it."

"And now we've found it at both Oreias Five and Oreias Seven," Shumar observed. "The same two colonies the aliens went after."

"So we have a pattern," said Matsura.

"So it would seem," Cobaryn responded.

"Though it's one we don't understand yet," Hagedorn pointed out.

"True," Shumar conceded. "But if one of the other colonies is near a couple of hills, and the hills happen to have this stuff inside them, there's a good chance that colony will be a target soon."

Stiles scowled. "And if it is? You think we ought to sit in orbit and wait for an attack?"

Shumar shook his head. "No, because the aliens might go back to Oreias Five. Or Oreias Seven, for that matter."

"So what *should* we do?" asked Dane, who, in Matsura's memory, had never posed so earnest a question before.

"We use our five good ships to hunt the aliens down," said Shumar, "just as Captain Stiles proposed. That's the best approach to keeping *all* the colonies from harm."

"But at the same time," Matsura added, "Captain Shumar and I pursue our hill theory...and see if we can figure out why the aliens decided to attack Earth colonies in the first place."

Cobaryn smiled. "A reasonable strategy."

Hagedorn regarded Matsura. "You're certain about this? I could always use an experienced hand on my bridge."

"Same here," said Stiles.

Clearly, thought Matsura, they didn't think his services would prove critical to the research effort. Still, he shook his head. "Thanks," he told his former wingmates, "but you'll do fine without me."

Hagedorn seemed to accept Matsura's decision. "Suit yourself. We'll hook up with you when we get back."

"After we've plucked the aliens' tailfeathers," Stiles chipped in.

But Matsura had engaged the triangular ships, and he knew it wouldn't be as easy as Stiles was making it out to be. Not by half.

"Good luck," said Matsura.

It was only inwardly that he added, *You'll need it.*

Alexander Kapono had been overseeing the spring planting on Oreias Eight when he was called in from the fields.

As he opened the curved door to the administrative dome, he felt a breath of cool air dry the perspiration on his face. It was a welcome relief after the heat of the day.

"What is it?" he asked Chung, one of his tech specialists.

Chung was sitting on the opposite side of the dome

behind his compact communications console, a smaller version of the one used on the bridges of Earth Command vessels. "You've got a message from Starfleet."

"Captain Dane?" asked Kapono.

Dane had said he would be in touch when they figured out what had prompted the attack on Oreias Five. However, the administrator hadn't expected to hear from the captain so soon.

The technician shook his head. "It's from a Captain Matsura. He says he's on his way to take a look around."

"Doesn't he know Dane did that already?"

"He says he wants to visit anyway."

The administrator grunted. "I guess he thinks he's going to find something that Dane missed."

Chung chuckled. "I guess."

To Kapono's knowledge, Earth Command captains had never worked this way. It made him wonder if Dane, Matsura, or anyone else in Starfleet had the slightest idea of what he was doing.

Cobaryn peered over his navigator's shoulder at a pattern of tiny red dots on an otherwise black screen. "Are you certain?"

"As certain as I can be, sir," said Locklear, a man with dark hair and blunt features who had navigated an Earth Command vessel during the war. "This is almost identical to the ion concentration that led the *Horatio* and the *Gibraltar* to the aliens."

The captain considered the red dots. They seemed so innocent, so abstract. However, if Locklear was right, they would steer the *Cheyenne* and all her sister ships into a clash as real as flesh and blood.

"Contact the other ships," Cobaryn told his navigator. He returned to his center seat and sat down. "Let them know what we have discovered."

"Aye, sir," came the response.

The fleet had spread out as much as possible to increase its chances of picking up the enemy's trail. However, it would only take a few seconds for the *Cheyenne*'s comm equipment to span those distances.

"They're responding," said Locklear. "The *Horatio* is transmitting a set of convergence coordinates."

During the Romulan War, Hagedorn had led Earth Command's top Christopher squadron—the one that had secured the pivotal victory at the planet Cheron. It made sense for Cobaryn to defer to him in tactical matters. Anything else would have been the height of arrogance.

"Chart a course," the Rigelian told his navigator.

"Charting," said Locklear.

"Best speed, Mr. Emick."

"Best speed, sir," his helmsman returned.

Cobaryn sat back in his chair and regarded his viewscreen, where he could see the stars shift slightly to port. They were on their way to a meeting with their sister ships.

And after that, if all went well, they would attend a different kind of meeting...along with their mysterious adversaries.

Bryce Shumar wiped some sweat from his sunburned brow and considered the hole he was standing in—a ten-foot-deep burrow that descended into the heart of a tree-covered mound of red dirt.

Oreias Eight's sun was a crimson ball of flame, its sky a vast blue oven. The colonists who had come to watch Shumar work—a collection of children and their caregivers, for the most part—didn't seem to mind the relentless heat so much.

But then, they had had a few months to get used to it. The captain had been on the planet's surface less than half an hour.

Training his laser pistol at the unusually thick tree root at his feet, he pressed the trigger. The resultant shaft of blue energy pulverized the root and dug past it into the rocky red ground below.

"Why don't I take over for a while?" asked Matsura, who was sitting on a grimy shelf of rock at the level of Shumar's shoulders.

The former Earth base commander cast a glance at him. It was true that his wrist was getting tired from the backlash of all his laser use. However, he hated to admit that he was in any way less physically capable than Matsura, who was a good several years his junior.

"I'm fine so far," said Shumar.

"You sure?" asked Matsura.

"Quite sure," the older man told him. Setting his jaw against the discomfort in his arm, he continued his task.

Suddenly, the ground seemed to collapse beneath the onslaught of his laser beam and Shumar felt his feet slide out from under him. Before he knew it, he was sitting in a drift of loose red soil....

With something hard and amber-colored mixed into it.

"Hey!" cried Matsura, dropping down from his perch

to land on a ledge of dirt that was still intact. "Are you all right?"

Shumar took stock of his situation. "I'm fine," he concluded, though not without a hint of embarrassment.

The younger man reached down and picked up a molded piece of amber-colored material about a third of a meter long. "Look at this," he said.

Shumar's eyes narrowed as he considered the object. It was the substance they had been excavating for, but in aggregate form.

"Same stuff?" asked Matsura.

"Looks like it," Shumar told him.

He poked through the dirt with his fingers and dug out another fragment. This one had a molded look to it as well, and it was even bigger than the first piece. As he brushed it off, he came to a conclusion.

"It's part of a shell," he said.

"How do you know?" the other man asked him.

"It's too regular to be a random accretion," Shumar pointed out. "And it's not strong enough to be part of an internal skeleton."

Matsura nodded. "So how do you think it got in here?"

Shumar frowned. "Good question."

"If the shell belonged to an animal," the younger man speculated, "the thing could have burrowed in here and died."

"But, remember," said Shumar, "we found evidence of similar remains in and around all those other mounds. So burrowing would have to have been an instinctive behavior for this animal."

"And it would have to have been in existence on Oreias Five and Oreias Seven as well."

Shumar nodded. "Which means it was transported here by an intelligent, spacefaring civilization."

Matsura looked thoughtful. "For what purpose?"

For what purpose indeed? Shumar asked himself.

He turned the piece of shell over in his hands, watching it gleam with reflected sunlight...and an alternative occurred to him. "On the other hand," he muttered, "maybe it wasn't an animal at all."

"What do you mean?" asked Matsura.

But Shumar barely heard the man's question. He was still thinking, still following the logic of his assumption. Before he knew it, the mystery of the Oreias system had begun to unravel right before his eyes.

"Are you all right?" Matsura prodded, concern evident in his face.

"I've never been better," said Shumar. He turned to his colleague, his heart beating hard in his chest. "Have you ever heard of Underwood's Theory of Parallel Development?"

Matsura shook his head. "I don't think so."

"It encourages us to assume, in the absence of information to the contrary, that species develop along similar lines. In other words, if an alien has a mouth, it's likely he's also developed something along the lines of a table fork—even if his mouth doesn't look anything like your own."

"And if you find buried shells...?" asked Matsura.

"Then you have to ask yourself why *you* might have buried them—or more to the point, why you might have buried *anything*."

Suddenly, understanding dawned in the younger man's face. "Then that's it?" he asked. "That's the answer?"

Shumar smiled, basking in the glow of his discovery. "I'd bet my starship on it."

In fact, that was *exactly* what he would be doing.

Aaron Stiles shifted in his center seat. "Anything on scanners yet?" he inquired of his navigator.

Rosten shook her head. "Nothing yet, sir."

The captain frowned. It had been clear from the increasing integrity of the ion trail they had been following that the enemy wasn't far off. It could be only a matter of minutes before they picked up the triangular ships and got a handle on the odds against them.

Not that it mattered to Stiles how many aliens he had to fight. This time, there was no retreat. One way or the other, he and his comrades were going to put a stop to the attacks.

"Sir?" said Rosten.

The captain glanced at her. "You have them?"

"Aye, sir," his navigator assured him.

Stiles got up from his seat and went to stand by Rosten's console. Studying it, he could see a series of red blips on the otherwise black screen. He counted six of them.

Good odds, he thought. *Excellent* odds.

He returned to his seat and tapped the communications stud on his armrest. "Stiles to Hagedorn."

The captain of the *Horatio* responded a moment later. "I know," he said over their radio link. "We just noticed them. I'll contact the others."

"Bull's-eye formation?"

There was a pause on the other end. "You know me too well, Captain. Bull's-eye it is. Hagedorn out."

Stiles smiled grimly to himself, then turned to his weapons officer. "Power to all batteries, Mr. Weeks."

"Power to all batteries," Weeks confirmed.

"Maintain speed," the captain told his helm officer.

Urbina checked her instruments. "Full impulse."

Darigghi came over to stand by Stiles's side. "It would appear a confrontation is imminent," he observed.

The captain resisted the temptation to deliver a sarcastic comeback. "It would appear that way."

"I realize I was not very helpful in our last clash with the aliens," the Osadjani went on. "If there is something more I can do this time, please let me know."

Stiles looked up at Darigghi. It wasn't at all the kind of statement he had expected from his first officer.

"I'll do that," the captain assured him.

Darigghi nodded. "Thank you."

Stiles leaned back in his chair. Maybe a leopard could change its spots after all.

"Navigation," he said, "any sign that we've been spotted?"

"None, sir," Rosten replied. "It'll be—"

The captain waited a moment for his navigator to finish her sentence. When she didn't, he turned to her—and saw that she was focused on her monitor, her brow puckered in concentration.

"Lieutenant?" he prompted.

Rosten looked up at him. "Sir," she said, "I've received a message from Captain Shumar and Captain Matsura. They're asking all of us to return to Oreias Eight."

Stiles felt a spurt of anger. "Are they out of their minds? We're on the brink of a battle here!"

His navigator's cheeks flushed. "Yes, sir."

The captain hadn't meant to chew her out. It wasn't *her* fault that Shumar and Matsura had gone insane.

"Sorry," he told Rosten. "I should know better than to shoot the messenger."

The woman managed a smile. "No problem, sir."

"Why are we being recalled?" asked Darigghi.

Rosten shrugged. "They say they've discovered something that makes it unnecessary to confront the aliens."

His teeth grinding angrily, the captain opened a channel to the *Horatio* again. "This is Stiles," he snapped. "Did you receive a message from Shumar and Matsura?"

"I did," Hagedorn confirmed.

"And what do you think?"

"I think we've worked hard to track the aliens down. I also think we've got an opportunity here to end their activity in this system."

"Then we're on the same page."

He had barely gotten the words out when another voice broke into their radio link. "This is Captain Cobaryn."

Stiles rolled his eyes. "Go ahead," he said.

"I cannot imagine that the recommendation we received sits well with you. After all, we are close to engaging the enemy."

"Damned right," Stiles replied.

"Nonetheless," said the Rigelian, "I trust our colleagues' judgment. I do not believe they would have sent such a message unless the value of their discovery was overwhelming."

"Same here," a fourth voice chimed in.

Stiles recognized the voice as Dane's. It was just like the Cochrane jockey not to follow protocol and introduce himself.

"Ever heard the one about the bird in the hand?" Stiles asked. "Right now, we've got the aliens where we want them. We may never get another shot like this one."

"This isn't just Shumar talking," Dane reminded them. "It's Matsura, too. He knows how you feel about stamping the aliens out."

"And despite that," said Cobaryn, "he is asking us to turn around."

Try as he might, Stiles couldn't ignore the truth of that. If it had just been Shumar trying to rein them in, he wouldn't even have considered complying. But Matsura had an Earth Command officer's mentality.

For a moment, no one responded, the only sound on their comm link that of radio buzz. Then Hagedorn spoke up.

"I hate to say this," he said in a thoughtful, measured voice, "but it sounds like we don't have much of a choice in the matter. If there's a chance to avoid bloodshed, we've got to take it."

Stiles felt his stomach muscles clench. They were on the verge of completing their mission, for crying out loud. They were *this* close to showing the aliens that Starfleet wasn't an organization to be taken lightly.

But he couldn't argue with Hagedorn's logic. Even in war, one had to seize the bloodless option if it became available.

Stifling a curse, he said, "Agreed. *Gibraltar* out."

And with a stab of his finger, he severed the link.

He was about to give Urbina instructions to come about when Darigghi saved him the trouble. As the captain looked on, doing his best to contain his bitterness, he saw the stars swing around on their viewscreen.

One thought kept going through his mind, over and over again: *Shumar had damned well better know what he's talking about.*

Hiro Matsura could feel a bead of perspiration trace a stinging path down the side of his face.

"Let me get this straight," said Stiles, who was studying the amber-colored shell fragment that Matsura had just handed him. "You dug this out of a mound of dirt and decided to call us back from an imminent confrontation with the enemy?"

He didn't sound impressed. But then, Matsura reflected, Stiles hadn't heard Shumar's theory yet. Neither had Hagedorn, Dane, or Cobaryn, who looked a little befuddled themselves as they stood by a gutted mound in the blazing light of Oreias.

"It wasn't just what we found," Shumar responded patiently. "It's what it all represents."

"And what *does* it represent?" asked Hagedorn, who seemed inclined to exercise patience as well.

Matsura picked up another of the orange-yellow fragments that he and Shumar had laid on the ground beside the ruined hill. This piece was more rounded than some of the others, more obviously designed to fit the anatomy of a living creature.

"We asked ourselves the same question at first," he told Hagedorn. "What was it about these shells that compelled someone to bury them? And who did the burying? Then Captain Shumar came up with an explanation."

Shumar picked up on his cue. "There's a scientific theory that alien species exhibit remarkably similar behavior, even when they're separated by many light-years."

"I believe I've heard of it," said Hagedorn. "Underwood's Theory of Parallel Development, isn't it?"

"Exactly right," Shumar confirmed. "And with Underwood's thinking in mind. I asked myself why I would have buried these shells—why I would have buried anything, for that matter."

"To honor the dead," Cobaryn blurted. He looked around at his fellow captains. "I am quite familar with human customs," he explained.

"Captain Cobaryn is right," said Shumar, smiling at his colleague's enthusiasm. "We demonstrate our respect for our deceased friends and relatives by burying them."

Dane looked perplexed. "But I don't see any bodies lying here. Just a bunch of shells."

"True," Matsura conceded. "But maybe that's where the resemblance to human customs ends. Maybe this species *sheds* its shells, like certain insects on Earth—and feels it has to bury them, because their shells were once a living part of their anatomy."

"And if it's true," said Shumar, "that these shells have some spiritual value to this species, is it any wonder that it would object to offworlders intruding on its burial grounds?"

"In other words," Cobaryn added, following his friend's logic, "the aliens who attacked Oreias Five and Oreias Seven...did so because we encroached on their sacred property?"

"It looks that way," said Shumar.

The captains exchanged glances as they mulled what Shumar and Matsura had told them. No one was outwardly incredulous.

"Makes sense, I suppose," said Dane, speaking for everyone.

"But we're not certain this is the answer," Hagedorn reminded them. "We have no conclusive proof."

"Scientists seldom do," Shumar pointed out. "Often, they have to go with what their instincts tell them. And right now, my instincts are telling me we've hit the mark."

The sun beat down on the six of them as they absorbed Shumar's comment. Matsura, of course, had already accepted his colleague's explanation. He was thinking about the next step.

"So," he said, "what do we do now?"

Matsura had barely gotten the words out when his communicator started beeping. In fact, *all* their communicators started beeping.

He took his own device out, flipped it open, and spoke into it. "Matsura here," he replied.

"Captain," said Jezzelis, his voice taut with apprehension, "there is an alien armada approaching Oreias Eight."

Matsura's mouth went dry. "Exactly what constitutes an armada?"

"I count fourteen ships, sir. And according to our scanner readings, their weapons have already been brought to full power."

Matsura looked at the others, all of whom seemed to have received the same kind of news. Their expressions were grim, to say the least. And it wasn't difficult to figure out why.

With the *Yellowjacket* all but useless, they were outnumbered almost three to one. Not promising, Matsura thought.

Not promising at all.

CHAPTER
22

As soon as Hiro Matsura reached the *Yellow-jacket*'s bridge, he took stock of its viewscreen.

He could see what his first officer had described to him via communicator minutes earlier—a formation of fourteen alien ships, each one a deadly dark triangle. And without a doubt, they were bearing down on the colony world from which Matsura's pod had just returned.

The last time he had seen the aggressors, they had all but crippled his ship—a setback from which the crew of the *Yellowjacket* was still trying desperately to recover. The ship's shields, lasers, and atomic weapon launchers had yet to be brought back online, and her impulse engines were too sluggish to be effective.

In short, the *Yellowjacket* wasn't fit to engage the

enemy. If she entered the field of battle, she would be nothing more than a target—and therefore a liability to her sister ships.

The odds against Matsura's comrades were considerable. It galled the captain to have to hang back at a safe distance and watch the aliens tear chunks out of their Christophers.

But it didn't seem like he had much of a choice.

Aaron Stiles glared at his viewscreen, which showed him so many tightly packed enemy ships that they seemed to blot out the stars.

It would have been a daunting sight even if three of his fellow captains weren't butterfly catchers. As it was, only he and Hagedorn could point to any real combat experience—a deficit which prevented the five of them from executing maneuvers as a group.

Stiles would have much preferred to fly alongside his old wingmates—veteran space fighters like Andre Beschta and Amanda McTigue and his brother Jake. Then they would have *had* something.

Of course, Shumar, Dane, and Cobaryn had plenty of former Earth Command officers on their bridges. If they paid them some mind, they might have a chance to come through this.

Yeah, right, Stiles thought. *And I'm the King of Tennessee.* If he and Hagedorn couldn't beat *four* of the triangle ships, how was their little fleet supposed to beat *fourteen?*

He scowled and began barking out orders. "Raise shields. Power to all batteries. Mr. Weeks, target atomics."

"Atomics targeted," came Weeks's reply. And a moment later, he added, "Range, sir."

"Fire!" bellowed Stiles.

A black-and-gold missile erupted from the *Gibraltar* and shot through the void in the enemy's direction. For a fraction of a second, it was on its own. Then four other missiles came hurtling after it.

Apparently, the captain's colleagues were all thinking along the same lines he was. It was more than he had expected.

As his missile found a target, it vanished in a burst of blinding white light. The other missiles struck the enemy in quick succession, each one swallowed up in a light show of its own.

But when the alien armada became visible again, it wasn't clear if the atomics had done any damage. The enemy vessels looked every bit as dangerous as they had before.

A voice came through the comm grate in Stiles's armrest. "Stay outside them," Hagedorn advised the group. "The longer they remain bunched that way, the better our chances."

The man was right, of course. Stiles regarded his weapons officer. "Fire again!" he snapped.

The *Gibraltar* sent a second black-and-gold missile hurtling toward the alien formation. Over the next couple of heartbeats, the other captains followed Stiles's example.

Unfortunately, their second barrage wasn't any more productive than the first. It lit up the void for a moment, but the enemy shook off its impact and kept coming.

And by then it was too late to launch a third barrage anyway. They were too close to the aliens to risk atomics.

"Target lasers!" Stiles roared.

As if the enemy had read his mind, the triangle ships abandoned their formation and went twisting off in pairs. Suddenly, they weren't such easy targets anymore.

"Fire at will!" the captain told Weeks.

The weapons officer unleashed the fury of their laser batteries on the nearest pair of enemy vessels. At the last possible moment, the triangles peeled off and eluded the beams.

Then they came after the *Gibraltar*.

Stiles glowered at them. "Evade!" he urged his helm officer.

Urbina did her best to slip the aliens' knot, but it tightened altogether too quickly. The *Gibraltar* was wracked by one fiery assault after another, each barrage like a giant fist punishing the vessel to the limits of her endurance.

A console exploded directly behind the captain, singeing the hairs on the back of his neck. As sparks hissed and smoke billowed darkly, his deck lurched one way and then the other like a skiff on a stormy sea.

But Stiles held on. They all did.

By the time the enemy shot past them, the *Gibraltar* was in a bad way. The captain knew that even before he was told that their shields were down eighty-five percent, or that they had lost power to the starboard nacelle.

"They're coming about for another shot at us!" Rosten called out abruptly, her voice hoarse and thin with smoke.

Stiles swore beneath his breath. "Shake them!" he told Urbina.

The helm officer sent them twisting through space, even without any help from their damaged nacelle. And somehow, she did what the captain had demanded of her. She shook the triangles from their tail.

It looked as if they were safe, at least for a moment. Then Stiles saw the two alien vessels sliding into view from another quarter, setting their sights on the poorly shielded *Gibraltar.*

"Enemy to port!" Rosten called out.

The captain felt his throat constrict. This must have been how his brother Jake felt before the Romulans blew him to pieces.

"Target and fire!" he thundered.

If they were going to go down, it wouldn't be without a fight. Stiles promised himself that.

But before the aliens could get a barrage off, a metallic shadow swept between the *Gibraltar* and her antagonists. It took Stiles a second to realize that it was one of the other Christophers, trying to shield him and his crew from the enemy.

He couldn't see the triangles' weapons ports as they fired, but he saw the ruddy flare of light beyond the curve of the other Christopher's hull and the way the Starfleet vessel shuddered under the impact.

The captain didn't know for certain which of his colleagues was risking his life to save the *Gibraltar.* However, he guessed that it was Hagedorn. It was the kind of chance only a soldier would take.

The aliens pounded the interceding ship a second time and a third, but Stiles wouldn't let his comrade protect him any longer. Glancing at Urbina, he said, "Get us a clear shot, Lieutenant."

"Aye, sir," came the reply.

"Ready lasers," the captain told Weeks.

"Ready, sir."

"Fire as soon as you've got a target," Stiles told him.

As Urbina dropped them below the level of the other Christopher, Bagdasarian didn't hesitate for even a fraction of a second. He unleashed a couple of devastating blue laser volleys that struck the enemy vessels from below, forcing them to give ground—at least for the time being.

Stiles turned to Rosten, taking advantage of the respite. "Raise Captain Hagedorn," he said. "See how badly he's damaged."

But when the navigator bent to her task, she seemed to find something that surprised her. "It's not the *Horatio*," she reported crisply. "It's the *Maverick*, sir."

Stiles looked at her. *Dane?*

A moment later, the Cochrane jockey's voice came crackling over the *Gibraltar*'s comm system. He sounded as if he were talking about a barroom brawl instead of a dogfight.

"Looks like I bit off more than I could chew," said Dane. "Everything's down . . . shields, weapons, you name it. I'm not going to be much help from here on in."

"I'll do what I can to protect you," Stiles assured him.

There was a pause, as Dane seemed to realize whom he was talking to. "You just want to make sure nothing happens to that pistol I won."

"Damned right," said Stiles.

But, of course, the pistol was the farthest thing from his mind. He was trying to figure out how he was going to repay Dane's favor without getting his ship carved up in the process.

Hiro Matsura had never felt so helpless in his life.

The other captains were fighting valiantly, dodging energy volley after energy volley, but it wasn't getting them anywhere. With one of their ships disabled—perhaps as badly as the *Yellowjacket*—the tide of battle was slowly but inexorably turning against them. In time, the aliens would blow them out of space.

But Matsura couldn't do anything about it—not with his ship in its current state of disrepair. With his weapons down and his shield generators mangled, he would only be offering himself up as cannon fodder.

He wished he could speak to the aliens. Then he would let them know that he understood the reason for their hostility. He would make them see that it was all a misunderstanding.

But he *couldn't* speak to them—not without programming their language into his ship's computer. And if he knew their language, he wouldn't have required the computer's help in the first place.

As Matsura looked on, Hagedorn's ship absorbed another blinding, bludgeoning barrage. Then the same thing happened to Shumar's ship, and Cobaryn's. Their deflector grids had to be failing. Pretty soon, they would all be as helpless as the *Yellowjacket*.

The captain's fists clenched. *Dammit,* he thought bitterly, *there's got to be* something *I can do.*

His excavation of the mound on Oreias Eight had put the key to the problem in his hands. He just had to figure out what to unlock with it.

Unlock...? he repeated inwardly.

And then it came to him.

There might be a way to help the other ships after all. It was a long shot, but he had taken long shots before.

Swinging himself out of his center seat, Matsura said, "Jezzelis, you're with me." Then he grabbed the Vobilite's arm and pulled him in the direction of the lift.

"Sir?" said Jezzelis, doing his best to keep up.

The captain punched the bulkhead pad, summoning the lift. "I need help with something," he told his exec.

"With what?" asked Jezzelis.

Just then, the lift doors hissed open. Moving inside, Matsura tapped in their destination. By the time he was finished, his first officer had entered the compartment, too.

"Captain," said Jezzelis, "I would—"

Matsura held up a hand for silence. Then he pressed the stud that activated the ship's intercom. "Spencer, Naulty, Brosius, Jimenez...this is the captain. Meet me on Deck Six."

A string of affirmative responses followed his command. All four of the security officers would be there, Matsura assured himself.

His exec looked at him askance, no doubt trying to figure out what could be so pressing about Deck Six. After all, there was nothing there except cargo space and supply rooms.

"Mr. McDonald," the captain went on, "report to the transporter room and stand by."

"The transporter...?" Jezzelis wondered out loud.

Then they reached Deck Six and the doors opened. Spencer, Naulty, Brosius, and Jimenez were just arriving.

"Follow me," said Matsura, swinging out of the lift compartment and darting down the corridor.

He could hear the others pelting along after him, matching him stride for stride. No doubt, the four security officers were every bit as curious as Jezzelis. Unfortunately, there was no time for an explanation.

If his plan was going to stand a chance, he had to move quickly.

The captain negotiated a couple of turns in the passage. Then he came to a door and pounded on the bulkhead controls beside it. A moment later, the titanium panel slid aside, revealing two facing rows of gold lockers in a long, narrow cabin.

And one of the locker doors was defiantly hanging open, though he had been convinced his chief engineer had repaired it.

Matsura knew exactly what each locker contained—a fully charged palm-sized flashlight, a small black packet of barely edible rations, and an Earth Command emergency containment suit.

There were two dozen of the gold-and-black suits in all, each one boasting a hood with an airtight visor. As bulky as they were, a normal man wouldn't be able to carry more than four of them at once—which was why Matsura had brought help along.

As Jezzelis and the others caught up with him, the captain tapped a three-digit security code into a pad on the nearest locker. When the door swung open, he grabbed the suit inside the locker and gestured for his assistants to do the same.

"Take them to the transporter room," he barked.

Invading one locker after the other, including the uncooperative one, Matsura dragged out three more suits. They weighed his arms down as if they were full of lead. Satisfied that he couldn't carry any more, he made his way back to the lift.

Jezzelis was right behind him. With his powerful Vobilite musculature, the first officer didn't seem half as encumbered as his captain did. As Matsura struck the bulkhead panel and got the doors to open for them, Jezzelis helped the human with his ungainly burden.

"Thanks," Matsura breathed, making his way to a wall of the compartment and leaning against it for support.

The Vobilite took advantage of the respite to pin the captain down. "If I may ask, sir...exactly what are we doing?"

Matsura told him.

Then the others piled into the turbolift with them, and the captain programmed in a destination—the transporter room. As luck would have it, it was only a deck below them.

The ride down took only a few seconds. Jimenez was the first one to bolt into the corridor with his armful of containment suits. Matsura was last—but not by much.

As they spilled into the room, McDonald was waiting for them at the control console. He looked confused when he saw what the captain and his helpers were bringing in.

"Sir...?" said the transporter operator, staring at Matsura as if he was afraid the man had lost his mind.

"Don't ask," the captain told him, dumping his suits on the raised transporter platform. "Just drop what's left of our shields and beam these out into space—say, a hundred meters from the ship."

McDonald hesitated for a fraction of a second, as if he thought he might have been the butt of a very bizarre joke. Then he activated the transporter system, overrode shield control, and did as Matsura had ordered.

The captain pointed to Jezzelis. "Yours next."

His first officer deposited his load on the platform. At a nod from Matsura, McDonald beamed that into space as well.

It seemed to take forever, but the captain saw every one of their two dozen Earth Command–issue containment garments dispatched to the void. Only when the last one was gone did he take a deep breath, wipe the sweat from his forehead with the back of his hand, and start back in the direction of the turbolift.

He had to get back to the bridge. It was there that he would find out if his idea had been as crazy as it seemed.

CHAPTER
23

CONNOR DANE DIDN'T LIKE THE IDEA OF BEING PROTECTED by Aaron Stiles. For that matter, he didn't like the idea of being protected by *anybody*.

Unfortunately, he wasn't in much of a position to complain about it. It wasn't just *his* life on the line—it was his crew's lives as well. And he had no one to blame but himself.

If he hadn't risked the *Maverick* to keep the aliens from destroying the *Gibraltar,* his ship wouldn't be a useless piece of junk now. He would still be trading punches with the enemy instead of cringing every time a dark triangle veered his way.

Of course, the enemy had all but ignored him since the moment his ship was disabled. Obviously, they had more viable fish to fry. But eventually, they would finish frying them—and then Dane's ship would be slagged with a few good energy bursts.

Not a pleasant thought, he mused. He looked around his bridge at his officers, whose expressions told him they were thinking the same thing.

They deserved a lot better than the fate he had obtained for them. But then, so did everyone else in the fleet. There were brave, dedicated people serving under every one of Dane's colleagues.

And it looked like their only legacy would be a few odd scraps of charred space debris.

"Sir," said his navigator, "something seems to be happening in the vicinity of the *Yellowjacket.*"

Dane turned to her. "Are they being attacked?"

Ideko shook her black-and-white-striped head from side to side. "No, sir. It's something else. I—"

"Yes?" said the captain.

Ideko frowned and called up additional information. Then she frowned even more. "Scanners say they're *containment suits,* sir."

Dane looked at her. Then he turned to his screen, daring it to show him what his navigator had described. "Give me a view of the *Yellowjacket,* Lieutenant. I'd like to see this for myself."

A moment later, an image of Matsura's ship filled the screen. And just as Ideko had reported, there was a swarm of black-and-gold containment suits floating outside the vessel.

"I'll be deep fried," the captain muttered. He leaned forward in his chair and studied the *Yellowjacket* more closely. "There's no sign of a hull breach," he concluded.

"None," agreed Nasir, who had taken up a position on Dane's flank.

"So what are they doing out there?" Dane wondered.

No one answered him.

The captain was still trying to figure it out when one of the triangles separated itself from the thick of the battle and headed in the direction of the *Yellow-jacket*.

Like the *Maverick*, the *Yellowjacket* was defenseless. It had no weapons, no shields...no threat to keep the enemy at bay.

Damn, thought Dane, feeling a pang of sympathy for his colleague. *This is it for Matsura.*

Of course, he expected Matsura to give the aliens a run for their money—to buy as much time as possible for his crew, or maybe even try to maneuver the enemy into the sights of another Christopher.

But the captain of the *Yellowjacket* didn't do a thing. He just sat there, as if resigned to the fact of his doom.

Dane was surprised. Matsura had seemed like the type to fight to the end, no matter how small the chances of his succeeding. *Apparently,* he thought, *I was wrong about him.*

As the alien ship bore down on the *Yellowjacket,* Dane grimaced in anticipation. But the deadly energy burst never came. Instead, the triangle slowed down, came to a stop in front of the toothless Christopher...

And just sat there.

Nasir muttered a curse.

"You can say that again," Dane told him.

The triangle reminded him of a dog sniffing something new in the neighborhood. But what was new about the *Yellowjacket?* Hadn't the aliens run into Starfleet vessels twice before?

Then it came to him. But before the captain could make mention of it, his comm grate came alive with Matsura's voice.

"Don't ask questions," said the captain of the *Yellowjacket.* "Just transport all your containment suits into space. I'll explain later."

Dane looked at his first officer. "You heard the man, Mr. Nasir. We've got work to do."

Before Nasir could utter a protest, Dane swung out of his chair and headed for the turbolift.

Alonis Cobaryn was stunned.

A scant few minutes earlier, he had been entangled in the fight of his life, battered by an implacable enemy at every turn. Now he was watching that same enemy withdraw peacefully from the field of battle, its weapons obligingly powered down.

Except for one triangle-shaped ship...and that one was hanging nose to nose with the *Yellowjacket* in the midst of nearly a hundred and fifty black-and-gold containment suits, looking as patient and deliberate as a Vulcan.

Clearly, it wanted something. Cobaryn just wished he knew *what.*

Tapping the stud on his intercom, he opened a channel to the *Yellowjacket.* "Captain Matsura," he said, "you offered to provide an explanation. This might be a propitious time."

"Damned right," said Dane, joining their conversation. "Exactly what did we just do?"

"And," added Cobaryn, "how did you know it would work?"

"Believe me," said Matsura. "I didn't. I was wishing I could speak to the aliens, tell them somehow that we weren't trying to dishonor their burial mounds...and it occurred to me that what we needed was some kind of peace offering. But it had to be an offering they understood—something they would immediately recognize as precious."

"Something like . . . a year's supply of containment suits?" Dane asked, clearly still in the dark.

"Remember," said Matsura, "the aliens had never seen a human being—or, for that matter, a member of any other Federation species. I was hoping they would identify the suits as our *shells*—or at least what passes for shells in our society."

Cobaryn was beginning to understand. "And if we were anything like them, these so-called shells would have great spiritual value."

"Exactly," said Matsura. "And anyone who's generous enough to present offerings of great spiritual value can't be all bad."

Dane grunted in appreciation. "Nice one."

"Indeed," remarked Cobaryn. "However, now that we have achieved a stalemate, we must capitalize on it. We must build a basis for mutual understanding with the aliens."

"As I understand it," said Matsura, "a couple of our colleagues are gearing up to do just that."

"Hagedorn here," said a voice, as if on cue. "Stand by. Captain Shumar and I are going to attempt to make first contact."

"Who died and left *him* boss?" asked Dane.

But Cobaryn could tell from the Cochrane jockey's tone that he didn't really have any objection. It was simply impossible for Dane to cope with authority without making a fuss.

As the Rigelian watched, a pod escaped from the belly of the *Horatio* and made its way toward the waiting triangle ship. No doubt, both Shumar and Hagedorn were aboard.

"Good luck," Cobaryn told them.

A hundred meters shy of the alien vessel, Daniel Hagedorn grazed the last of the Christophers' seemingly ubiquitous containment suits.

The protective garment seemed to want to latch onto the escape pod, desiring rescue, but Hagedorn urged his vehicle past it. Then there was nothing but empty space between him and the triangle ship.

Twenty meters from it, Hagedorn applied the pod's braking thrusters. Then he sat back and waited.

"What do you think they're going to do?" wondered Shumar, who was ensconced next to him in the copilot's seat.

Hagedorn shook his head. "You're the scientist. You tell me."

"I'm not an ambassador," said Shumar. "I'm a surveyor. I've never made contact with anything smarter than a snail."

"And the only contact I've made has been with a laser cannon. Apparently, we're at something of a disadvantage."

For a moment, silence reigned in the pod's tiny cabin. Hagedorn took advantage of it to study the alien ship.

For all its speed and power, it didn't appear to be based on a very efficient design.

"It must be gratifying," he said, using the part of his mind that wasn't focused on the triangle.

Shumar looked at him. "What do you mean?"

"Your work on Oreias Eight...it gave us this opportunity. You can be proud of that."

"You mean...if we don't make it?"

Even Hagedorn had to smile at that. "Yes."

Shumar looked at him. "Either way, Captain, it's been a pleasure working with you."

"You don't have to say that," Hagedorn told him.

His colleague nodded. "I know."

Suddenly, something began to move underneath the triangle ship. Hagedorn could feel his pulse begin to race. He willed it to slow down, knowing they would need to be sharp to pull this off.

"Is that a door opening?" asked Shumar, craning his neck to get a view of the alien's underside.

It certainly looked like a door. Hagedorn said so.

"Then let's accept their invitation," Shumar suggested.

It was why they had come, after all—in the hope that they might obtain face-to-face contact with the aliens. Carefully, Hagedorn eased the pod down and under the triangle, all the while gaining a better view of what awaited them within.

The first thing Hagedorn saw was a smaller version of the alien vessel, sitting alongside the open bay door. Then he spotted some of the aliens themselves, standing back from the opening behind what must have been a transparent force field.

They were tall, angular, and dark-skinned, with minimal, vividly colored clothing, and white hair drawn back into thick, elaborate braids. Their pale, wideset eyes followed the pod as it came up through the open doorway into an unexpectedly large chamber.

Hagedorn landed his vehicle and the door closed behind him. He took a moment to scan the aliens more closely. He noticed that all four of them had hand weapons hanging at their hips.

"They're armed," he observed.

"Wouldn't you be?" asked Shumar.

It was a good point.

Of course, neither of them had figured out yet how they were going to communicate with their hosts. But then, it wouldn't be the first time Hagedorn had been forced to improvise.

He flipped the visor of his containment suit down over his face, grateful that he had had the foresight to hold a couple of the garments back when he received Matsura's instructions.

Then, his fingers crawling across his control console, he cracked the pod's hatch and went out to meet the aliens.

Lydia Littlejohn paced the carpeted floor of her office, remembering with crystal clarity the last time she had felt compelled to do so.

It was during the last push of the war, when Dan Hagedorn led the assault on the Romulan supply depot at Cheron. The president of Earth had paced well into the night, unable to lie down, unable even to sit...until she finally received a message from her communications specialist that the enemy's depot had been destroyed.

And even then, she had been incapable of sleep. She had remained awake thinking about the courageous Earth Command officers who had given their lives to see the Romulans defeated.

At the time, some people had predicted that Earth had seen the last of war. Littlejohn hadn't been one of them. However, she had hoped for a respite, at least—a couple of years without an armed conflict.

Surely, her people had earned it.

But mere months after the creation of the Romulan Neutral Zone, Earth colonies were again being attacked by an unknown aggressor, and the Federation had been forced to send its fleet out to address the situation.

Officially, it wasn't Earth's problem. But the endangered colonies were Earth colonies, and the ships they sent out were Earth ships, and the largest part of their crews were Earth men and women...and Littlejohn couldn't help feeling as if her world were at war all over again.

"President Littlejohn?" came a voice.

She looked up. "Yes, Mr. Stuckey?"

"We've received a communication from Starfleet Headquarters. Apparently, the mission to the Oreias system was a success. The fleet has made contact with the raiders and achieved a peaceful resolution."

Littlejohn felt a wave of relief wash over her. Thank God, she thought. "Were there many casualties?" she asked.

"None, ma'am."

She couldn't believe it. "None at all?"

"I made sure of it, ma'am. I knew you would want to know."

Littlejohn smiled. "Thank you, Mr. Stuckey."

"Have a pleasant evening, ma'am."

She glanced out her window, where she could see the first stars emerging in a darkening and more serene-looking sky. *I'll do that,* she answered silently. *I most definitely will do that.*

Aaron Stiles was feeling pretty good about himself as he felt his ship go to warp speed and saw the stars on his viewscreen go from points of light to long streaks.

After all, Hagedorn and Shumar had patched things up with the aliens—a species who called themselves the Nisaaren—and engineered an agreement under which Earth's colonists could remain in the system without fear of attack. It was a far better outcome than any Stiles would have predicted.

And he and his colleagues had secured it by working together—as a unified fleet, instead of two irreconcilable factions. Sure, they'd had their differences. No doubt, they always would. But they had made compromises on both sides, and found a way to construct a whole that was a little more than the sum of its parts.

Dane had surprised Stiles most of all. The Cochrane jockey had struck him as a misfit, a waste of time. But when push came to shove, he had shoved as hard as any of them. And though Stiles would never have admitted it in public, Dane had risked his life to save the *Gibraltar.*

That was the kind of action he would have expected from a wingmate in Earth Command, not a man whom he had shown nothing but hostility and disdain. Clearly, he had misjudged Connor Dane.

In fact, he conceded, he had misjudged all *three* of the butterfly catchers. It was a mistake he wouldn't make again.

"Captain Stiles?" said his navigator, interrupting his thoughts.

He turned to Rosten. "Yes, Lieutenant?"

"There's a message coming in from Earth, sir. Eyes only."

The captain smiled, believing he knew what the message was about. It was high time Abute had called to offer congratulations. But why had the man declined to address the crew as a whole?

"I'll take it in my quarters," said Stiles, and pushed himself up out of his center seat.

It wasn't until he reached his anteroom and activated his terminal that he realized why Abute had chosen to be secretive. According to the director, the board of review had made its decision...and selected the captain of the spanking-new *Daedalus*.

CHAPTER
24

ABUTE HAD SPENT A LOT OF TIME OVERSEEING, DISCUSSING, and inspecting the construction of the Federation starship *Daedalus*. In fact, he probably knew the vessel as well as the men and women who had assembled her.

So it was a special thrill for the fleet director to be the first to beam aboard the new ship, bypassing her transporter room and appearing instead on her handsome, well-appointed bridge.

He took a look around, enjoying every last detail—down to the subtle hum of the *Daedalus*'s impulse engines and the smell of her newly installed blue carpeting. He even ran his hand over the silver rail that enclosed her spacious command center.

However, Abute wasn't alone there for very long. He was soon joined by a host of dignitaries, human and otherwise, including Admiral Walker of Earth Command, Clarisse Dumont, and the highly regarded Sammak of Vulcan.

Both Walker and Dumont looked a little fidgety. But then, they had been campaigning for a long time to secure the *Daedalus* for their respective political factions—and to that very moment, neither of them knew who had been given command of the ship.

Of course, Abute knew. And for that matter, so did the fleet's six captains. But they had been ordered not to tell anyone else, so as to minimize the potential for injunctive protests and debates.

Even so, the director had expected at least a little feedback...if only from the captains themselves. At least half of them couldn't have been thrilled with the board's decision, and Abute had expected them to tell him so.

But they hadn't. They hadn't uttered a word. In fact, in view of what had gone before, their silence had begun to seem a little eerie to him.

The director wished all six of them could have been given command of the *Daedalus*. Certainly, they deserved it. The job they did in the Oreias system, both collectively and as individuals, had exceeded everyone's expectations—including his own.

It was unfortunate that only one of them could win the prize.

Just then, he heard the beep of his communicator. Withdrawing the device from its place inside his uniform, he said, "Abute here."

"Director," said the transporter technician on a nearby Christopher, "we're ready to begin transport."

"Do so," the administrator told him. "Abute out."

He turned to the bridge's sleek silver captain's chair and waited. A moment later, Abute saw a vertical gleam of light grace the air in front of the center seat. As the gleam lengthened, the outline of a man in a blue Starfleet uniform began to form around it.

After a few seconds, many people there would have a good idea of who the officer was. Nonetheless, they would have to wait until the fellow had completely solidified before any of them could be certain. Finally, the materialization process was complete....

And Hiro Matsura took a step forward.

The man cut a gallant figure in his freshly laundered uniform, his bearing confident, his gaze steady and alert. If appearance meant anything, he was precisely what Starfleet had been looking for.

But it wasn't just Matsura's appearance that had won him the *Daedalus*. It was the uncanny resourcefulness he had displayed in the encounter with the Nisaaren, which had saved the Oreias colonies from destruction and invited the possibility of peace.

Of all the qualities the review board had considered, ingenuity was the one they had valued most—the one they believed would prove most critical to the fleet's success as the Federation moved into the future.

And Hiro Matsura had demonstrated that he had this quality in spades.

The assembled officials exchanged glances and even a few muffled remarks—some of them tinged with disapproval. But then, the director mused, it was an understandable reaction. The research faction had been made to swallow a rather bitter pill.

The military, on the other hand, had won a great victory. If anyone doubted that, he had but to observe the ear-to-ear grin of Admiral Walker, who was gazing at Matsura with unabashed pride.

Of course, neither the admiral nor anyone else had any inkling how narrow Matsura's victory had been. Right to the end, Abute had learned, the board had been vacillating between two and even three of the candidates—though no one had revealed to him the identity of the other choices.

But that was all water under the bridge, the director told himself. Captain Matsura would sit in the *Daedalus*'s center seat. The decision had been made and no one could change it.

"Ladies and gentlemen," said Abute, "I give you the commanding officer of the *U.S.S. Daedalus*... Captain Hiro Matsura."

The announcement was met with applause from all present—with varying degrees of enthusiasm, naturally. In the director's estimate, it was to the credit of the research people that they applauded at all.

"Congratulations," Walker told his protégé, stepping forward to offer the younger man his hand.

Matsura shook it, a bit of a smile on his face. "Thank you, sir," he responded in crisp military fashion.

Clarisse Dumont came forward as well, albeit with a good deal more reluctance. She too extended her hand to the captain of the *Daedalus*.

"I wish you all the luck in the world," she told Matsura. "And despite the disdain *some* have displayed toward the advancement of science, I hope you will see fit to—"

Dumont never got to finish her statement. Before she

could accomplish that, another gleam of light appeared in front of the center seat. Abute looked wonderingly at the admiral and then at Dumont, but neither of them seemed to know what was going on.

As the newcomer gained definition, the director could see that it was Captain Hagedorn. When he had finished coming together, the fellow moved forward to stand alongside Matsura.

Abute shook his head. "I don't understand," he said.

Neither Matsura nor Hagedorn provided an answer. However, another glint of light appeared in front of the captain's chair.

This time, it was Aaron Stiles who appeared there. Without looking at Admiral Walker or anyone else, he came forward and joined his colleagues.

Walker's eyes narrowed warily beneath thick gray brows. "What's the meaning of this?" he demanded of his former officers.

They didn't respond. But the director noticed that there was yet another gleam of light in front of the center seat, and someone else taking shape around it.

To his surprise, that someone turned out to be Bryce Shumar. And to his further surprise, Shumar took his place beside the others.

Now Abute *really* didn't get it. What did Shumar have to do with the military contingent? Hadn't he been at odds with Matsura and the others right from the start?

But Shumar wasn't the last surprise. Thirty seconds later, Cobaryn appeared as well. And after him came Dane, completing the set.

Starfleet's captains stood shoulder to shoulder, enduring the stares of everyone present. And for the first time, the director reflected, the six of them looked as if they might be able to stand one another's company.

The admiral glowered at them. "Blast it," he said, "exactly what are you men trying to pull?"

"I'd like to know myself," Dumont chimed in.

Matsura turned to her. "It's simple, really. You tried to make us your pawns. You tried to pit us against one another."

"But we had a little talk after Oreias," Shumar continued, "and we realized this isn't about individual agendas. It's too important."

"Damned right," said Stiles. "My fellow captains and I have come too far to let bureaucrats of *any* stripe tell us what to do."

Dane glanced at Walker. "Or whom we should respect. After all, we're not just a bunch of space jockeys anymore."

"We're a fleet," Hagedorn noted. "A *Star*fleet."

"And in spirit, at least," Cobaryn told them, "we are here to assume command of the *Daedalus together.*"

The admiral went red in the face. "The *hell* you are! I'll see the lot of you stripped of your ranks!"

"Perhaps you would," Abute told him, "if you were in charge of this fleet. But at the risk of being rude, I must remind you that *I* am the one in charge." He glanced at the six captains. "And frankly, I am quite impressed by what I see in front of me."

Walker's eyes looked as if they were going to pop out of their sockets. "Are you out of your mind?" he growled. "This is rank insubordination!"

The director shrugged. "One might call it that, I suppose. But I prefer to think of it as courage, Admiral—

and even you must admit that courage is a trait greatly to be admired."

Dumont sighed. "This *is* unexpected. But if that's the way these men feel, I certainly won't stand in their way."

Abute chuckled. "Spoken like someone who has nothing to lose and everything to gain, Ms. Dumont. I wonder...had it been Captain Shumar or Captain Cobaryn who was granted command of the *Daedalus,* would your reaction have been quite so forgiving?"

Dumont stiffened, but didn't seem to have an answer. The director nodded. "I thought not."

He glanced at his fleet captains, who remained unmoved by the onlookers' reactions to their decision. He had hoped the six of them might work together efficiently someday, maybe even learn to tolerate one another as people. But this...

This was something Abute had never imagined in his wildest dreams.

Turning to the officials who had been invited to this occasion, he assumed a more military posture—for the sake of those who cared about such things. "I hereby turn over command of this proud new vessel, the *U.S.S. Daedalus* . . . to the brave and capable *captains* of Starfleet. May they always bring glory to their ships and to their crews."

Everyone present nodded to show their approval. That is, with the notable exception of Big Ed Walker. But that, Abute reflected, was a battle they would fight another day.

Look for STAR TREK fiction from Pocket Books

Star Trek®: The Original Series

Star Trek: Deep Space Nine®

Star Trek®: New Frontier

Star Trek®: Section 31

Rogue • Andy Mangels & Michael A. Martin
Shadow • Dean Wesley Smith & Kristine Kathryn Rusch
Cloak • S. D. Perry
Abyss • Dean Weddle & Jeffrey Lang

Star Trek®: Gateways

#1 • *One Small Step* • Susan Wright
#2 • *Chainmail* • Diane Carey
#3 • *Doors Into Chaos* • Robert Greenberger
#4 • *Demons of Air and Darkness* • Keith R.A. DeCandido

Star Trek®: The Badlands

#1 • Susan Wright
#2 • Susan Wright

Star Trek®: Dark Passions

#1 • Susan Wright
#2 • Susan Wright

Star Trek® Omnibus Editions

Invasion! Omnibus • various
Day of Honor Omnibus • various
The Captain's Table Omnibus • various
Star Trek: Odyssey • William Shatner with Judith and Garfield Reeves-Stevens

Other Star Trek® Fiction

Legends of the Ferengi • Ira Steven Behr & Robert Hewitt Wolfe
Strange New Worlds, vols. I, II, III, and IV • Dean Wesley Smith, ed.
Adventures in Time and Space • Mary P. Taylor
Captain Proton: Defender of the Earth • D.W. "Prof" Smith
New Worlds, New Civilizations • Michael Jan Friedman
The Lives of Dax • Marco Palmieri, ed.
The Klingon Hamlet • Wil'yam Shex'pir
Enterprise Logs • Carol Greenburg, ed.